THE QUEEN'S PROMISE

THE QUEEN'S PROMISE

Broken Kingdom Volume I

Brenda Rickman Vantrease

This first world edition published 2018
in Great Britain and the USA by
SEVERN HOUSE PUBLISHERS LTD of
Eardley House, 4 Uxbridge Street, London W8 7SY
Trade paperback edition first published
in Great Britain and the USA 2018 by
SEVERN HOUSE PUBLISHERS LTD

British Library Cataloguing in Publication Data
A CIP catalogue record for this title is available from the British Library.

ISBN-13: 978-0-7278-8793-1 (cased)
ISBN-13: 978-1-84751-915-3 (trade paper)
ISBN-13: 978-1-78010-971-8 (e-book)

All Severn House titles are printed on acid-free paper.

Severn House Publishers support the Forest Stewardship Council™ [FSC™],
the leading international forest certification organisation.
All our titles that are printed on FSC certified paper carry the FSC logo.

Typeset by Palimpsest Book Production Ltd.,
Falkirk, Stirlingshire, Scotland.
Printed and bound in Great Britain by
TJ International, Padstow, Cornwall.

In loving Memory
of
Don Wayne Vantrease
(1939–2011)

Kings are justly called gods for they exercise a manner or resemblance of divine power on earth. God hath power to create or destroy; make or unmake at his pleasure; to give life or to send death; to judge all and to be judged (by) nor accountable to none; to raise low things and to make high things low at his pleasure. And the like power have kings.

—James I in a speech to Parliament,
21 March 1610

May it please your majesty, I have neither eyes to see, nor tongue to speak in this place, but as the House is pleased to direct me, whose servant I am here, and I humbly beg your majesty's pardon and I cannot give any other answer than this to what your majesty is pleased to demand me.

—The Speaker of the House of Commons,
William Lenthall, in answer to King Charles I,
who came to Parliament in 1642 demanding
the arrest of five members for treason

PROLOGUE

I know how to look death in the face and the people too.

—Thomas Wentworth upon being told a sizeable
force had gathered to witness his execution

12 May 1641
London, England

Thomas Wentworth, Earl of Strafford, hesitated at the
last threshold he would ever cross, swallowed the fear
clotting in his throat, and stepped across. The cool air
of a May morning stiffened his resolve. His eyes scanned
the crowd. In Wentworth's last days, Charles Stuart had been
remarkably absent among the friends who had come to
mumble outrage and whisper awkward farewells. He was
absent now. *Do not worry, Lord Strafford. You have the word
of your king. No harm will come to your person or your
property.* This sincere assurance had been offered when
Parliament first summoned the Lord Deputy of Ireland to
answer for the Crown's actions in Ireland. Thomas closed
his eyes, banishing the harsh reality of that empty promise,
but he could not banish the sounds as two Tower Guards led
him to the scaffold.

Amongst the jostling and jeering, other voices echoed in
his brain. *My lord Strafford, you advised the King to recruit
an army of Irish rebels. Catholic rebels. Did you not? Speak,
my lord, did you not?* His accuser had pounded the table
before him in such fury his full wig, slanted askew and leaned
precariously over one eye, forcing the grim-faced prosecutor
to stop in his tirade and adjust it. A few brave souls who
appreciated farce when they saw it sniggered. Thomas,
buoyed by the King's promises, had answered with wry

laughter. The prosecutor's face was the color of cheap wine. He had growled, *You find this charge amusing, my lord?* A pause as he considered his manicure before looking up again. *This is no laughing matter. Have you an answer?*

How does one prove one's innocence, Mr. Prosecutor, except to affirm it? I am the King's loyal servant. I am England's loyal servant. The charge is unfounded. Summon the King. Ask his Majesty.

The trial had not lasted long. The indictment when it was read aloud by the crier was a thunderclap in a clear sky. Treason. But as Charles had predicted, the prosecution came to naught. Yet Wentworth's relief had been short-lived. The bill of attainder calling for his execution outside the para-meter of English jurisprudence was stunning. Then, even then, Charles had repeated his promise with the same assurance, *No harm will come to your person or property, Thomas. Trust your king. A bill of attainder without the royal signature is worthless.*

A mustard seed of doubt had sprouted in the Lord Deputy of Ireland when Parliament stripped him of his title and property. *Be assured you will be restored. Their action is powerless.* Reason was on the King's side. Pym and Essex and their henchmen were bold, but they were not fools to overplay a risky hand. That was precisely the time when he should have heeded that doubt and fled to the Continent like so many others. But that would have been treason and Thomas Wentworth was not a traitor. And he was not a coward.

After a farcical attempt to rescue him from the Tower, finally, abruptly, his sovereign had grown silent. The bill of attainder did now in fact bear the King's signature and Thomas Wentworth's destiny was to play out here on this crude wooden stage with one swift—*pray God let it be swift*—blow of the headsman's axe. As he approached the wooden steps of the platform, he noticed the ragged laundry basket beneath the block, a profane receptacle placed to catch a nobleman's bloody head. Outrage bubbled into his throat. It was an insult to England, an insult to the King, a deliberate slur upon the honor of a loyal servant who had served king and country nobly.

During the endless hours of the night, amidst the clanging

and the hammering outside his Tower window, Thomas had disciplined his darting thoughts, preparing himself for this moment, rehearsing in his mind so that his body would not betray him. He had prayed for strength to end his life as he had lived it, in full possession of his manhood and his dignity. But in this pearly dawn, this fickle promise of a fine May morning, as he stepped onto the platform his skin grew clammy. His bones felt as if they were melting. He forgot to breathe.

Just one more battle, Thomas. Survey the field.

He took two deep open-mouthed breaths and looked out across the crowds, cheek to jowl as far as he could see all the way to the river's edge. What field marshal could prepare for this? He'd seen men lined up to battle to the death, Irish Catholics and English Protestants, in great numbers on countless fields, listening for the trumpet sound that would begin the carnage. But this. Oh God, this was different. Surrounding the scaffold, below him on the streets, above him on rooftops, hanging over balconies, a bobbing current of angry faces howled and stamped—all screeching for the same thing: the bloody head of the King's man in Catholic Ireland.

The heat of their wrath struck him like a blast.

What had he done to incur the hatred of such a multitude? Except to serve his king.

In the predawn the onlookers had gathered, cursing, laughing, their drunken jokes and bawdy songs drifting through his high Tower window. What were they celebrating? Spectacle seekers, he'd thought with dread. Such events always drew a crowd of the curious, the worthless, the idle. But this? He blinked to clear the image before him. Thousands of souls spread out before him, their voices growing louder with each second. Why had so many left their beds early, delayed opening their shops and harnessing their plows? Not just the idle and the curious, but ordinary Englishmen, common laborers, carters, farmers, even merchants. He swallowed hard. Made the sign of the cross. An angry roar exploded. The godly ones were well represented, their plain clothes pocking the crowd like raisins in an overstuffed pudding. John Pym was surely among them, gloating.

He closed his eyes and breathed deeply, trying to remember his confessor's reassurances of the blessed afterlife. Though treason was not one of his sins, Thomas had much he needed to confess—not the least of which was his adulterous liaison with the lovely Lady Carlisle. Of all the earthly delights he'd known, Thomas thought, he would miss Lucy Hay the most.

Last night after he had drunk the heavy wine provided, she had come to him in a dream, comforting, soothing, an opiate to his fevered brain. He tried to summon her image now: her hair smelling of rosewater, the silken smoothness of her skin. His mind clung to it, to shut out the sights below. She had come to him in the Tower—what guard could resist her pretty pleas—urging him not to abandon hope. She had kissed him, telling him to take heart, she would plead directly with John Pym for a stay of execution. But on her last visit he had seen hopelessness in her eyes and felt more tenderness than passion in her embrace. She had known it would be the last time she saw him. He had known it too. Though neither could bear to say it. Wentworth's only real regret with Lucy Hay was that he'd not had more to confess. He wished they'd become friends and lovers sooner. So much wasted time. He could no more repent his adultery with her than he could repent breathing. And how did one repent lack of repentance?

Archbishop Laud, a convenient though requested confessor who was also housed in the Tower awaiting trial by Parliament, had sighed in understanding. Wentworth figured he was dealing with his own regrets. Laud's hands shook when he administered the Eucharist to the condemned man—because he was losing a friend or because the penitent's fate presaged his own? In the hushed heart of the night, Wentworth had thanked him for his blessing and said, his voice deep with emotion, 'Your grace, it will give me comfort if I know you are watching from your window when the headsman lifts the axe. I will know there is a prayer on your lips for my soul. Will you keep watch?'

'I will keep watch, old friend. I will watch, and I will pray for you as your soul takes flight.'

Wentworth glanced up at that window now, but the scaffolding was too far away to make out a figure there. No matter.

He had learned hard not to trust in the promises of princes—
even princes of the Church.

*What is to be done, must now be done. Quickly. Cleanly.
As planned. Expedite. Don't dawdle to buy one more pitiful
breath and dishonor.* Thomas strode forward, assumed the
soldier's stance, threw out his chest, feet firmly planted, and
lifted his hands in a sign that he would speak. The crowd
shushed itself in waves of silence, eager to hear this mighty
King's man plead for his life.

But Thomas would not plead.

He drew himself up tall and thrust out his chin, so his voice
would carry. The unwavering strength of it surprised even him.
He'd rehearsed the prophetic warning. It was to be a dying
man's invocation to reason.

'I do freely forgive all the world,' he proclaimed. He waited
for the jeers to die down as the Constable of the Tower admon-
ished the watchers to let the condemned man speak. He cleared
his throat, took a powerful breath, drawing in courage with
the air as if making a battlefield declaration. 'I wish that every
man would lay his hand on his heart,' here he paused and
sucked in another breath to gather volume with resolve: the
crowd too seemed to be holding its breath, 'lay his hand on
his heart and consider seriously,' another breath, this one
stronger than the last, so that he virtually trumpeted the words,
'consider seriously whether the beginnings of the people's
happiness should be writ in letters of blood.'

The last words hung in silence until a roar from the crowd,
the bellow of a great enraged beast, erased them. But as he
knelt to place his head in position, his mind conjured other
sounds, other images: Lucy laughing, high silver tones . . .
Lucy dancing at the Queen's masque, invitation in her eyes
. . . the rose-scented garden of that first stolen kiss—and more.
How he would miss her generosity of spirit. And she would
miss him. He was sure of it.

His young wife, his third, would miss him too, but she
would find other comfort soon. And if the Archbishop's
theology was right, Thomas would find his first wife waiting
to welcome him with the angels. He had loved her most,
more even than Lucy. But it was not his first wife's face that

appeared before him now. He closed his eyes, fastening hard in his brain, the image of the Queen's fountain, the fragrance of the roses, the touch of Lucy's lips against his. That's what he would take with him to the grave.

With one swift motion of his arm, he ordered the headsman's stroke.

THE QUEEN'S QUEST

When I consider the caprice and arrogance of Buckingham,
I pity the young king, who, through false council, is need-
lessly showing himself and his kingdom in such extremity.
For anyone can start a war when he wishes, but he cannot
so easily end it.

—from a letter written by Peter Paul Rubens to a
friend upon the occasion of Charles I and Henrietta's
marriage negotiated by the Duke of Buckingham

Dover, England
February 1642

I t was a rare English day, a day to ride to the hunt with
Charles beside her, a day to play blind man's buff in the
gardens with the children. Not a day for parting. Sky and
water should be gray on such a day as this, that hated, dreary
English gray her soul despised. From the ship's deck Queen
Henrietta Maria shouted into the wind, 'God save you, *mon
amour, mon cher ami,*' then louder, blowing kisses with her
free hand, *'mon cher cœur.'* Flying fingers sent sparks of color
from her rings to light like jeweled butterflies in the sun-
sparked harbor. With the other hand she clutched her favorite
sad-eyed spaniel to her breast. The thrum, thrum, thrumming
of his heart answered the frenzy of her own.

Mon amour, mon cher cœur. Words for whispering in the
King's ear, two beating hearts, one body, in the curtained bed
of state at Whitehall or in the lodge at Richmond, or the tented
pavilion in the forest glade where two of their children had been
conceived. Her French endearments always pleased him.

In everything she strove to please him, save one. Once he
had said to her, 'You must remember, madame, that your son

will someday be king. Do not fill his head with popery. It will only cause him great trouble.' Afterwards she had taken pains to see that the children's religious instruction took place outside his hearing.

This parting, this voluntary exile was Henrietta's plan to help with Charles' 'great trouble.' By the tall window, whilst Edward Hyde and the lords plotted with the King how best to put down the Scottish rebellion, Henrietta had hovered over her embroidery. She listened and watched. In their cocked eyebrows and conspiratorial glances, she had read an unfathomable circumstance: Charles needed money desperately. The royal treasury had been depleted by the uprisings in Ireland— and other things—and only Parliament could levy new taxes. Parliament refused. And yet, although Charles would not face the truth, Henrietta had gleaned enough to know that this Parliament would never fund another army for Charles Stuart— not as long as he had a Catholic queen. Nor would London's militia, the Trained Bands under the control of the Puritan Commons, likely take up arms against the enraged Presbyterian barbarians gathering on the border. Not even for their king.

On the shore the Master of the King's Guard muttered something in the King's ear. Charles continued waving, not turning to leave. She leaned against the rail, throwing kisses with both hands now, remembering her own part in beggaring the treasury: The beautiful palace at Somerset House, the gilded chapel with Master Rubens' grand painting, her retinue of Capuchins in their gold-threaded hoods. And Inigo Jones' elaborate masques at the Banqueting House—oh what fun it all was. Her enemies said she was too extravagant, but she had given England a court of glory to rival any in Christendom and she would not repent it. The last scrape from the treasury had gone to support her mother's extravagance when Cardinal Richelieu and Louis banned her from France and dear, kind Charles took her in.

Charles had been as pleased and proud as she at all the beauty and music and art until the day came that he shook his head and declared, 'Edward Hyde says the treasury is diminished, dear heart. We must not seem to be quite so extravagant,' and added he was going to have to recall Parliament, reminding her that in England only Parliament could raise taxes. He had few peerages left to sell and no more fees to levy. Some of the Lords had even gone to the Tower to keep from paying the ship-money levy, which they claimed was an illegal tax. That was more than a year ago. Shortly after he'd packed her mother and her extravagant household off to whatever duchy on the Continent was willing to harbor Maria de' Medici.

A strong-backed seaman shouldered the last chest as a royal footman handed it off. 'Lift the plank. This is the last of the lot,' he called as the chest tilted forward.

'*Fais attention!* It is the property of the crown.'

The captain cast a baleful eye on the seaman. She should not have said that. Parliament's spies were everywhere. He might request the chest be opened for inspection.

Henrietta smiling sweetly said, 'It is a gift from the King for the Dutch court. I promised his Majesty I would see to it personally. I wish it carried to my quarters.'

'As you wish, your majesty.' The captain nodded to the seaman, who took a firmer grip and moved on.

Her gaze turned once again to the shore. He was still here. Watching, waiting to see the ship safely out of harbor. In the months since Wentworth's execution, he'd been more melancholy than usual. It took much persuasion to make him see the necessity of her journey. He needed his wife by his side more than ever, he'd said wearily. But with years of practice she had learned how to bend him to her will and therein, according to her detractors, lay much of the problem. 'The King, he is pecked by a French hen.' She suspected that was not the worst they said in their gossipy broadsheets.

The ship rocked gently. The little spaniel yipped and squirmed. Henrietta handed it off to her maid. The sails filled. She leaned into the wind, willing it to cease, her eyes seeking to store up the sight of him on the shore. His mount snorted and pranced, impatient to be off. The same stiff breeze that teased her hair from out its ermine hood brushed the King's great hat, whipping its feathered plume. With her left hand she touched the pendant at her throat as though the touch of it could harden her resolve, strengthen her courage as much as any saint's medal.

Non. Restore the plank. Unload it all. Take everything back to Whitehall. Who will see that James reads his Vulgate cate-chism and Elizabeth remembers to take her medicine and Prince Charles learns all the things a king needs to know? Who will kiss Baby Henry's bald little pate and tuck him into his cradle? What if something happens and I never see any of them again? What if my ship sinks . . . what if, God forbid, the King's enemies. . . . She made the sign of the cross and mouthed a prayer to the Holy Virgin.

The captain shouted some words Henrietta didn't under-stand. The men on board coiled the cables in readiness for casting off.

Non. S'il vous plaît. Non.

As the ship inched its way out of the harbor, Charles waved from the shore. Closing in around him, the mounted guard prepared to depart.

She had not been separated from Charles these sixteen years, not since Lord Buckingham's death when Lucy Hay had taught a frightened, lonely girl how to replace the ill-fated George Villiers, Duke of Buckingham, in her husband's affections and confidence. And now she was faced with the consequences of the unpleasant truth that, like Buckingham, she had not always given wise counsel.

Act the man, my lord, she had goaded Charles when Parliament spoke against him in a way no sovereign should ever tolerate. He did nothing—until they plotted to impeach her, saying she was a malignant influence on the King and should be sent back to France. *Act the man, my lord.* So, in a gallant, but futile and ill-timed gesture, her Dearest Heart had ridden to Westminster with five hundred men at arms to arrest John Pym and five of the plotters—only to return a failure. 'The birds have flown,' he'd mumbled dejectedly. 'They were warned.'

Warned. A traitor in their midst. Some said Lucy Hay had warned her cousin, Lord Essex, one of the five conspirators. But Lady Carlisle would never betray her for a cousin. Of all the English ladies-in-waiting assigned to her, Lucy Hay had remained her friend and the only one she trusted. Now, Sir Edward Hyde on the other hand—Henrietta had never trusted

Sir Edward Hyde. He played the middle. But Charles trusted him, so she had held her tongue. These same flown birds waited in the bushes, emboldened by their King's humiliation, and she was abandoning her Dearest Heart to calumny such as this?

The wind grew more biting. Lord Denbigh, Charles' friend and her noble escort, bowed before her. 'Your majesty,' he said, 'your apartments are in readiness. The Princess Royal and your ladies have already gone below.'

'*Un moment*, my lord,' she whispered, unable to divert her gaze from the riders on the shore. Lord Denbigh removed himself to a respectful distance.

The King's black stallion pulled up short and turned again. Her husband's eyes would be searching for her. She leaned over the rail and waved both hands. '*Je t'aime*,' she whispered knowing he could not hear her now. '*Je t'aime, mon amour*.' She watched until the riders were out of sight and then, feeling as lost and alone as when she had first set foot on England's shore, she followed her servants below.

'Put the carved chest at the foot of my bed,' she said to the French footman who, like Genevieve, her Lady of the Bedchamber, Buckingham had allowed her to bring from Paris eighteen years ago. Although Genevieve was no lady, not in any real sense, she was the best dresser the Queen had ever had and the only woman she trusted completely. Henrietta had learned no sooner than she'd set foot on English soil that the high-born English ladies with their vipers' tongues and averted gazes would never do her any good service.

Except for Lucy Hay.

Lady Carlisle had been her only true friend from the beginning. Henrietta had overlooked her Presbyterian attachment until it became apparent Lucy would never convert, not even for her Queen, and Henrietta knew to whom her allegiance was pledged. When she'd left the court of France as a bride of fifteen, Buckingham had obtained papal consent by promising King Louis and the Queen Regent of France—as well as the Holy Father—that her marriage would improve the lot of all Catholics in England. She had the documents to prove it. But what did Puritans care for papal documents? Or even for the Church of England? They had shut Archbishop Laud in the Tower, and in a breathtaking act of arrogance, rivaling the fallen angels of Heaven's insurrection, Parliament had dared to threaten their Queen because she worshipped at the altar of the one true Church. No. She could no longer suffer a Presbyterian in her chamber. Not when her other ladies would attend her at mass.

Taking the little yapping dog from Genevieve, she crooned. 'Mitte, *n'ayez pas peur, mon petit ami*. I am not afraid.'

Not afraid. But suddenly very lonely. At the very least she should have brought Jeffrey Hudson with her. The dwarf always cheered her. When they got to Den Haag, she would ask Lord Denbigh to send for him.

Surveying the cramped quarters, her first gaze sighted her favorite gilded mirror and silver backed brushes gleaming on a cloth of gold. A sting of tears threatened behind her eyelids as she lifted her favorite memento, one of Van Dyke's miniatures of Charles, and raised it to her lips. The tears spilled when she saw the circle of stones arranged on her bedside table—each inscribed by a childish hand, except for the smallest stone inscribed in the King's flowing hand. Charles must have supervised the accoutrements. She could envision him, helping to collect the stones, instructing the children, then guiding Henry's tiny fingers to scrawl his name.

She turned quickly away, saying brusquely to hide the tears in her voice, 'No. Henri, don't put it there. At the foot of the bed. Strap the chest to the bedpost so it will not slide.'

'As you wish, your majesty,' he said, his long-suffering expression never changing. The two servants exchange pitying glances. She wasn't fooling anybody. Of course he would have bolted it well. Both he and Genevieve knew what the chest contained.

'I wish to be alone now,' she said, dismissing the pair. She lay down on the bed, her little brown and white spaniel curling into a ball beside her, closed her eyes and tried not to think of the task that lay ahead of her. She tried not the think of the children she had left behind. After a while the rocking of the ship lulled her into a troubled sleep.

*   *   *

Had Henrietta Maria remained on deck for just a little longer, she would have seen the silhouette of a lone rider in a large plumed hat, riding the high cliffs above Dover. He shielded his eyes as he scanned the sea until the ship that carried his wife away became only a speck on the horizon.

At the Queen's feet, secured in a hidden compartment beneath her silk chemises, the glory of the crown jewels slept in darkness.

LADY HAY'S ELEGANT SALON

In spite of masks and hoods descry
the parts denied unto the eye
I was undoing all she wore,
and had she walked but one turn more,
Eve in her first state had not been
more naked or more plainly seen.

—From the seventeenth-century poet
John Suckling's 'Upon My Lady Carlisle's
Walking in Hampton Court Garden'

L ucy Hay née Percy, Countess of Carlisle, and England's most celebrated *salonnière*, cast a critical eye over the elegant little banqueting room at Syon House. It was not the standard to which she had become accustomed when she was lady to the Queen, but considering the growing scarcity of servants and the food shortages, it was a good enough show. Dozens of candles glowed in their crystal chandelier lighting a buffet table piled with sweetmeats and savories and spiced wines. A couple of ladies and a few silk-stockinged gentlemen perched on elegantly carved chairs, silk skirts and brocade doublets sighing against damask upholstery. The salon was gradually filling up, albeit with her second-tier guests, some of whom had endured the three-hour trek from London by boat.

Lucy's favorite poets and musicians had gone to join the King. Robert Herrick was still in town and a decent fellow she had sometimes seen at court, but clerics—even Church of England clerics—didn't really fit her little soirees. Her favorites of all the King's poets, William Davenant and Sir John Suckling, had been exiled by Parliament for treason—good Lord how she missed them. Thomas Carew had frequented her salon once or twice, but as a favorite of the Queen's he would not likely still be in London.

Soon after leaving court, she had established her own salon in Westminster and a reputation as a hostess whose entertainments were coveted. Once when she had given a masked event, Henrietta had even shown up. But this night the Queen was not likely to grace Lucy's salon with her presence; she had escorted Mary, the Princess Royal to the Netherlands to meet her new husband. Whitehall was deserted, the King having first decamped to Hampton Court before fleeing to York. Most of the courtiers had likewise scattered with them, including the Queen's favorites, Henry Jermyn and Lucy's youngest brother, Henry Percy.

But literary and artistic repartee were not high on her agenda this night. This occasion marked a very personal anniversary for Lucy. Thomas Wentworth, the Earl of Strafford had met his death one year ago today thanks to the calumny of Parliament and a cowardly monarch. She did not wish to be alone. She could never forget, neither could she forgive, though she knew why Charles had signed the death warrant. It was an act of appeasement, an act that he hoped would save his Catholic wife from a Puritan Parliament's condemnation. But it had not; nor was it like to, and Lucy's dearest friend—and England's wisest counselor—had died for nothing.

When Thomas Wentworth lost his head, Lucy lost a lover and protector. When Henrietta Maria fled London, Lucy lost a friend—from looking around this assembly a lot of friends, she thought. She blamed the King for those losses. He was a weak sovereign and growing weaker by the day whilst Parliament was going stronger. With the court failing, her protector gone, the country hurling headlong into war, Lucy Hay, Countess of Carlisle had to see to her own self-preservation. But tonight, there was still music in her salon and a few lingering courtiers, a resplendent remnant who failed to notice the royal tide had receded, depositing them like so much driftwood on a bleak shore.

The smell of exotic fragrance perfumed the air. The few ladies present were resplendent in shades of the King's favorite blue satin, their royal allegiance proudly on display. One of them stood up from the harpsichord now and bowed. The jack-o-dandies applauded politely, then turned to talk of court politics, flattery and flummery.

Lucy Hay whispered behind her fan to another Lucy gathered at her intimate little soirée, the only other woman who was not dressed in blue satin. Lucy Hay was bedecked in a gown of burgundy brocade—let those present conclude what they would from her choice. Lucy Hutchinson, wife of Parliamentarian Colonel John Hutchinson, was dressed in a sober brown velvet, with a wide collar of exquisite white Flemish lace. When Inigo Jones mocked Lucy Hutchinson's plain dress as the uniform of the enemy and thus a viper in their midst, Lucy Hay retorted that she had it on the highest authority that the young woman was a brilliant scientist and a Latin scholar and besides the Earl of Anglesey spoke highly of her.

'And the Earl of Anglesey's recommendation matters because?'

'The Earl of Anglesey is one of the more moderate voices in Parliament. I respect his opinion greatly. He is in Ireland negotiating with the Duke of Ormonde, who, you probably don't know, was a *true* friend to Thomas Wentworth.'

Thomas Wentworth. The name fell like stone amidst the chatter. Inigo did not take the bait. He sipped his wine, and said, 'That whole Irish thing is so boring. Though probably not to an Irish countess,' a snide reference to her Irish title gained through her marriage to the Earl of Carlisle. He might as well have said that whole 'barbarian' thing. But she let it go. She needed to keep him in her circle. He was close to the Queen, and he was a gossip with a careless tongue. He sat to her left, ears perked. Lucy seized her chance to be rid of him. Nodding toward Inigo, she said, 'The man talking to Henry Lawes. I don't believe I know him. Go and fetch him and present him to us, please, dear Inigo.'

He answered with the same petulant expression the Queen had inexplicably found amusing. 'You invited him. I saw his name on the list. He is Dr. Thomas Browne. His new work has made him the talk of London.'

'His new work?'

'*Religio Medici.*'

'I do not know it.'

'It is a medical book and a book of sage advice, Countess. Not a book of love poems.'

Lucy ignored his sarcasm. 'Present him,' she said. 'I would like to know one who is the talk of London.

The court architect bowed curtly and left to perform his errand.

'Inigo is a boor—and a bore, albeit a very talented one. He is an artist,' she said to Lady Hutchinson. 'They must sometimes be forgiven their personal shortcomings for the sake of the sublime things they create. I must confess I am curious—' She lowered her voice. 'What does the wife of a reputed stalwart Puritan, such as Sir John Hutchinson, do for entertainment? This is the first time I have seen you at one of my gatherings.'

The girl blushed. 'Yes, it is, and I am very grateful for the invitation. I must confess I was quite taken aback when I received it. Please don't think me a spy. I am here because you have a reputation for gathering learned society as well as courtiers. I have little opportunity to speak with scientists and academics and others who share my interests.'

'You are most welcome, my dear. As to politics, I try to steer clear of it. I am ill-suited to it, but I do have a passing acquaintance with John Pym. He, among others, recommended your name. His exact words were, 'Invite Lucy Hutchinson. She'll introduce a little *gravitas* to your frivolous little affair.'

In all honesty, '*gravitas*' was not the sauce Lucy Hay was stirring, but how could she turn John down? 'I am very glad you accepted my invitation,' she said. 'You are acquiring a bit of a reputation as a learned Latin scholar. Maybe it's just because you dare to go where others of our sex do not. But John Pym says you have a brilliant mind. That is high praise.'

It was as though this shy Lucy suddenly sprang to life like one of those new dolls with gears and a wind-up engine. 'John Pym also recommended to me that I accept your invitation. He spoke of you and your entertainments very highly. He said that there would be poets and music and he especially mentioned that you had invited Dr. Browne. I am very anxious to meet him.'

'You know his work?'

'I know it well.'

'That does not surprise me. You share your love of learned tomes with my own father. They called him the Old Wizard.'

'The Duke of Northumberland was your father. I would love to have met him.'

Lucy laughed. 'Among his dusty old volumes, housed with him in the Tower you mean? I spent many forced hours there as a green girl, my only company his Latin books and Italian scientific theories.'

The other Lucy sat up, eyes wide, hands extended as though reaching for the Holy Grail. 'What a joy that must have been to be surrounded by the original works of the greatest minds in history.'

Lucy Hay was a little taken aback at this other Lucy's interpretation of her childhood home. 'Well, yes, I suppose, but I had joys of another kind on my mind. My late husband, my dear Jamie—James Hay, the Earl of Carlisle—was paying me court, and I was too busy scheming ways to escape my father's clutches and elope with a *hated Scotsman* to care about scientific theory and dusty Latin.' She sighed and added, 'That was a long time ago. But you are about to meet Dr. Browne. He will be better company than 'the old wizard' would have been.'

Suddenly weary of trying to engage with this scholarly young woman, Lady Carlisle looked around the room expectantly. 'Inigo probably made a side trip to the wine bar, which necessitated another side trip. But I see a poet whom you might enjoy meeting is just coming in—a rare pleasure this night since so many have deserted our fair city.' She motioned to Edmund Waller, who was already making his way toward them. Approaching, he thrust a rose in Lucy's face, appearing not to notice Lucy's attempt at stifling a sneeze or her companion.

'Go, lovely rose,' he intoned, 'tell my Lady Carlisle that when I resemble her to thee how sweet and fair she seems to me.' Then bowing deeply, even as she shoved the hand holding the rose aside, he continued in his flowery address, 'Bid her come forth, suffer herself to be desired and not blush so to be admired.'

It was a delight to see him, but she feigned displeasure and scolded, 'You may keep your rose and your fulsome lyrics. You are truly a man without shame. I know you wrote those lines for another. Your newest lady has fled to the country and you are merely seeking a diversion.'

The poet pulled a face of mock shame. God alone knew how she missed this: the carefree flirting, the fun, the lightness of it all.

She patted his shoulder and added, 'Don't be sad, Edmund. Handsome poets, no matter how fickle, are always welcome in my salon. Have you met Lucy Hutchinson? She is also a writer.' The poet clicked his heels together and turned to take the other Lucy's hand, who just stared at him with a curious gaze. But suddenly Lucy had an urgent thought and interjected, 'By the by, Edmund, have you heard aught of John Suckling? They say he is in exile in France and very ill.'

'Alas, Countess. I'm afraid it is worse than that, Suckling has died,' he lowered his voice, 'and it is rumored by his own hand.'

'Oh dear,' she said. 'Such sad news.' No posturing here. She felt a sudden stinging behind her eyelids. 'He was a good and steadfast friend and I loved his poetry well.'

John Suckling had been a friend of Wentworth's too and loyal to the last. Now he too was gone. And by his own hand? The ranks of her admirers were thinning at an alarming rate.

Inigo Jones returned with the doctor in tow. The newcomer bowed stiffly. 'My lady Carlisle, I am delighted. The hospitality of your salon quite surpasses its high reputation as the most admired in London. As does your beauty.' He took her offered hand clumsily.

Here's a new face and a pretty speech to cheer the mood. 'You flatter me, Doctor, but it is a flattery much to be coveted because it comes from a celebrated author who surely has been entertained in many grand houses.'

'Not really.' The young man blushed. 'I'm afraid I have little with which to compare your ladyship's hospitality . . . but I'm sure you set a standard to which other hostesses only aspire.'

'That is a very diplomatic answer. You are well spoken. I shall have to read your work.' She flicked her fan with practiced skill. 'Tell me, have you an opinion about the conflict between Parliament and the King? Who is most at fault? Mr. Pym or the King?'

'Mr. Pym?'

Was he really that ignorant or just stalling for time? Lucy suspected the latter.

'Why, man, the leading voice in the Commons,' Waller said injecting himself back into the conversation. With nervous fingers he bruised the petals of the rose, releasing the sweet fragrance into the intimate space.

Browne smiled and acknowledged the poet's comment with more grace than his tone deserved. 'Ah yes, of course. My head has been too long in my medical books.' Then, turning his back to the poet, he answered Lucy. 'My lady, regarding the . . . ah . . . disagreement between King and Parliament, here among my betters, I shall listen so that my opinion might be instructed in order to be better formed—when it is formed.'

A man's familiar laughter soared above their quiet conversation. Lucy's fan stilled as she looked around for its source then turned back to her companions. 'It is a rare but happy circumstance,' she said, 'to encounter one who is not overly eager to share his opinions, informed or otherwise. London is awash in uninformed opinion. Every fool with access to a printing press thinks himself wise and peddles his ordure on the street like rotting fish. It quite fouls the air.' The fan snapped shut. 'By the way, Dr. Browne, I wish to introduce you to one who has not only read your work but has endured the tedium of my salon to meet you.' She turned to the other Lucy and drawing her new friend forward, said, 'Lucy Hutchinson, meet Dr. Browne. He is a scientist whose discourse I am sure you will find pleasing.'

Mistress Hutchinson favored the young Dr. Browne with a shy smile. Almost a reverent smile, Lucy Hay thought. She only half-listened as the younger Lucy began to explain to her new companion about her latest work '. . . stumbled upon the most beautiful poem . . . Latin poet Lucretius. *De rerum natura* . . . particles in all material substances.'

'Yes, atomism. I have heard a little about it. But the Latin is laborious.'

Lucy Hutchinson's voice seemed to have risen an octave. 'One day perhaps you can read it in English. I have already begun to attempt to translate *On the Nature of Things* into English. The poetry is exquisite; it is quite a labor of love.'

What a lot of bother over some ancient, dull books. Scanning the room for a means of escape Lucy saw the source of the laughter. James Whittier. Close enough to overhear the conversation. Her fan flicked open and fluttered again. 'Please excuse me, Dr. Browne, Mistress Hutchinson. I must greet another guest. I shall leave you to your learned discussions.'

The two appeared not to notice the departure of their celebrated hostess.

'My lord Whittier, how kind of you to favor us with your presence.' She held out her hand to be kissed. Smiling, he pressed his lips against it. A small shiver quivered at the base of her spine. *Silly woman. He is younger than you by a—well what was a few years.* She could always read a man's face and she read appreciation in his eyes. Here was a language she understood. A long, slow breath and then she added, 'It has been too long, my lord.'

'Yes, indeed, Countess,' he said, his gaze never wavering, but he offered no excuse for his absence from her circle.

'Your laughter, Lord Whittier, would indicate you do not agree about the importance of keeping one's opinions private. I don't think I've heard your thinking on the current contretemps between Parliament and his Majesty.'

He paused, a gentle mockery in his half-smile. 'Oh, my dear Lady Carlisle, I quite agree with your assessment of Dr. Browne's opinion. I shall follow his wise example so that I may likewise bask in my lady's praise.' He grinned. 'I too desire to be taught and not to teach.'

Cheeky fellow and a practiced flirt. It was so tempting, but if Lucy Hay knew men—and she did know men—she didn't think he was a man to be played.

He tossed his head so lightly as to be scarcely discernible, but her glance followed his to the door where the King's Counselor, Sir Edward Hyde, filled the doorway. 'Well here is a surprise,' she said, noticing the rumpled clothing, the unkempt hair—*why could the man not at least pretend to a*

little bit of courtly fashion? 'He usually spurns such entertainments, too frivolous for his taste, I suppose,' she murmured,
but her voice carried clear as she hailed the King's advisor,
'Counselor, welcome, have you news of our beloved sovereign?
We are all eager to hear.'

Conversation ceased. All eyes turned toward Edward Hyde,
who looked so out of place and ill at ease that she felt a
moment's sympathy.

Hyde cleared his throat. 'His Majesty is in York gathering
arms and men to answer those arms and men being gathered
by Parliament. I fear war is inevitable,' he added picking at a
dried spot of gravy on his tunic.

But the pronouncement, though matter-of-factly delivered,
was answered with gasps and raised eyebrows. Were they
unaware? So totally ignorant of what went on around them?

'The treasury cannot sustain another war,' Inigo Jones said,
indignation pursing his priggish mouth into a pout. 'I've barely
enough funds to finish the new Banqueting House at White
Hall as it is.'

Hyde gave him a long-suffering smile, 'My dear Mr. Jones,
this is not just another war. There is more at stake here than
perhaps you are aware. If the King cannot raise an army, there
may be no one to feast in your Banqueting House and
Parliament will use it to stable its horses.'

The look of outrage on the architect's face was laughable.
The man was a genius, but his self-importance and perfec-
tionism were hard to bear, as though the world depended
on the graceful drape of a curtain fabric or the placement
of a tree in one of the Queen's elaborate masques. As though
the loss of his latest project was the be all and end all of war's
horrors.

Appearing not to notice the architect's apoplectic expression,
Hyde accepted a plate of cheese and a Banbury cake but
refused a glass of the French wine which Lucy had purloined
from her brother's cellars. He took a bite of the cake, brushed
a crumb from his double chin, and cleared his throat. The
murmuring ceased.

'There are many within the kingdom who are already sacri-
ficing for the royal cause,' he said. 'Masters at both Cambridge

and Oxford have sent this day a goodly supply of plate to be melted down, which I am on my way to deliver.' He paused, took another bite then put down the plate and, pushing a swath of his fly-away hair from his forehead, looked around at the silk-clad courtiers. 'Indeed, if any in this august company should decide to part with an expensive bauble or two or some gold coins in that good cause, I shall deliver your contributions and solicitations, which will be gratefully received by his Majesty.'

This was answered with nervous laughter, as though the King's chief advisor was making a joke when any fool could see that he was not. This was followed by an awkward silence and then a rush of chatter. From the corner of her eye, Lucy watched her new young friend being led by Dr. Browne through the garden door, an easy escape from an awkward moment. Lucy put down her fan and picked up the last biscuit from a silver plate on the table. Handing the biscuit to Edmund Waller, she said matter-of-factly but loud enough to quiet the whispers in the room, 'Here, fair poet, pray you make a lyrical metaphor out of this. Or eat it—whichever suits. I have need of the plate.'

Slowly, deliberately, she removed the diamond and emerald 'baubles' that dangled from her ears and held them up. The flickering glow of the candle flames enhanced the sparkle. 'These were given to me as a token of affection from a dear and departed friend,' she said, placing them in the plate with a clink. Struggling to keep her face a mask of equanimity she paused before adding, 'Consider them a gift to Charles I of England from Thomas Wentworth, Lord Strafford, who served his King admirably and his country faithfully—to the very end.'

A collective gasp was followed by a lone 'bravo.' This from the handsome Lord Whittier, though she wondered exactly what it was this sentiment applauded since he had so lately refused to offer even verbal support for the King.

Sir Edward Hyde's gaze met hers as he gave a nod of understanding. 'That is a very generous gesture, Lady Carlisle. Thomas Wentworth was likewise a friend of mine. I shall inform his Majesty of your unparalleled generosity.'

'Inform him or not as you wish, sir. It matters not to me. These 'baubles' evoke a painful and very personal loss. I only wore them this one last time as a tribute to his Majesty's most loyal servant who died . . . needlessly.' The words of accusation and royal blame hung unspoken in the air as though they were written there.

She handed the plate with its glittering burden to Lord James. 'Please pass this around so that others of the King's loyal subjects who wish to contribute to the royal cause may do so. It will cost them much less than it did Thomas Wentworth to prove their loyalty.'

Lord Whittier with an inscrutable smile on his face, took the silver plate and moved with it around the room. Reluctantly, her guests fumbled with rings and gold chains in awkward silence. When he had paused suggestively in front of every single person in the room, she rose.

'Now,' she said, 'let us have no more talk of things political. Lady Hamilton, please return to the harpsichord and sing for us. We shall eat and drink and be merry, whilst we still can.'

But a pall had been cast over the little assembly. After a few half-hearted attempts at merriment, Lucy wearied of their company. Sir Edward Hyde left with his loot; Lord James Whittier shortly thereafter. When these two worthies had departed, Inigo Jones, emboldened by another flagon of Algernon Percy's finest, grumbled about a waste of good gold on toys of war. Lucy had noticed that he made a very slight contribution, less than a handful of coins, which he thumbed out one by one like the Pharisee in the temple. Her guests made excuses and drifted away in search of the watermen who would convey them back to their own uneasy beds. Finally only the brilliant artist was left dozing in a corner, a half-filled wine glass tipping red stains onto his blue satin doublet. Lucy summoned a hired footman to rouse Inigo and see him home.

Sir Edward Hyde leaned back against the hard leather of the carriage seat and belched loudly. He should have known better. Court society always interfered with his digestion. A sober and honest man had no place among such vanities. He rummaged in his voluminous pockets for the leather pouch, extracted Lucy's earrings, and held them up to the single candle in the lantern above his head. Poor Strafford must be turning in his grave. Wentworth probably gave them to her so they would not go into the crown's coffers with the rest of his estate. Who could ever know the mind of a woman? One thing was sure—with this gesture the dead man's paramour had lined up solidly behind the King who had signed his death warrant. Charles would be singularly pleased by her gift. He'd been burdened by Wentworth's death and a man of his morose nature could only stand so much guilt. The Queen's departure had wounded the King deeply, and he'd been in agony at being forced to abandon his motherless children.

The youngest children were still at St. James's Palace, but his spies said their household was about to be dismissed and they were now under the 'protection' of Parliament. Edward felt tremendous pride to have been entrusted with the care and safety of the two older boys, but the heavy burden of it robbed him of sleep. He had the Prince of Wales and his brother James in a safe house for now until their father could send for them, but he would need to devise a better strategy. No one place was safe for very long. He as well as anyone knew to what depths the Commons would seek to gain control. If they could get Prince Charles, the war would be over before it began.

He was contemplating his strategy for young Charles when the coach pulled up sharply. Probably making way for another to pass on the rutted lane. The horse neighed. He heard the crack of a whip and a loud curse. Still the coach did not move. Bother! An axle stuck in the mud—where was the crown to get enough money to fix these roads? But at least his driver was a skilled and burly man. He should be able to extricate the wheel.

Edward leaned his head out and shouted into the darkness, 'Tom, you want me to get out to relieve the weight?'

A small laugh and then a voice answered. ''Twould would make my job easier.'

Though the man's voice had a familiar tenor, it was not the coachman's voice for all the affected country brogue. Edward could not quite match that voice with anyone of his acquaintance. But he had no trouble discerning the silhouette of a

black-clad horseman waiting beside the coach door, his face
well hidden in shadow. But in the light of a suddenly breaking
three-quarter moon scudding though the clouds the pistol
pointed at Hyde was unmistakable.

After her guests had departed Lady Carlisle did not go to her
bed. Heart pounding with anticipation, her spirit light as though
it had been removed of a great burden, she went instead to
the back garden, where she waited under an overhanging eave
in a drizzling rain.

It was too early. He would not risk being seen. She breathed
deeply, drawing in the damp, cool air. It was good to be alive
on such a night as this. Her head felt light from the spiced
wine and the absence of the heavy earrings—and her heart
lighter than it had been since Wentworth's execution. In
giving the earrings to the King's cause, she had achieved a
kind of absolution. Take these, your majesties. Now let me
go in peace.

The minutes passed. The clop-clopping of a carriage—she
arched her neck to peer though the gloom—then the sound
faded.

What if she had made the wrong choice? Cast her lot on
the wrong side? But nothing could be proven, she was sure.
Had she not this very night shown herself a loyal supporter
of the King? Edward Hyde would report her gift. If he reported
her words, Charles—fool that he was—would think them a
sign of her forgiveness, and she fervently hoped those same
words would sting his conscience with sharp remorse.

The rain ceased, and the clouds parted for a three-quarter
moon.

The mist clung to her skin, now more stifling than refreshing.
She thought of the Queen separated from her children—say
what you will, Henrietta was a devoted mother. Why did the
news books not print that? The tiniest tinge of remorse threatened when she thought of the royal children, but their fates
were beyond her influence. Then her mind caught on a more
immediate need.

What if he didn't come? It would not be the first time he
had missed an assignation. But as she watched the moon hide

again in a cave of clouds, he emerged from the shadows of the yew-lined garden.

'I was afraid you had been detained, my love,' she said rushing to meet him. But when she saw what he held in his arms, she stopped short. 'John Pym, is this what it looks like—?'

'My lady, allow me to introduce you to young Henry Stuart,' he whispered, so as not to wake the King's youngest son.

Breathless, he sat down beside her, the child's head resting on his shoulder—the same shoulder she'd cried on that first time they had met, when she'd approached John Pym to beg him to intercede with Parliament for Wentworth's life. She'd waited for three days outside of Parliament House. When she'd called out to him, he had granted her an audience in his private office, *lest such a beautiful woman amongst so many angry men cause a riot,* he'd said.

He had listened patiently to her impassioned plea, but to no avail, saying his hands were tied and the Commons had already decided. The argument against him was too strong. The evidence showed that Wentworth was not an innocent man. He had suborned treason even if he had not directly committed the act. The evil counsel he'd given the King was enough to earn him the death penalty.

'Whose argument, Mr. Pym, if I may ask?' she had said quietly.

'Mine was the loudest'—then he'd added with the ghost of a smile—'and perhaps the best delivered.'

She had not appreciated the flippancy of the callous remark, but she had admired his honesty. It was a rare quality among the sycophants of her acquaintance. The smile had vanished, and his tone turned somber. 'Thomas Wentworth is an arrogant counselor. As long as he has the King's ear, there will be no sharing of power with Parliament. Despite your tempting pleas, I will not intercede on his behalf because'—he paused and fixed his level gaze on her so she could not doubt the import of his next statement—'it is less damaging to the kingdom to remove a counselor than a king.'

That was when she had started to cry, real tears, not the easy tears summoned on a whim—real eye-reddening, nose-dripping tears—and after a few awkward attempts to calm her, he had taken her in his arms and let her cry on his shoulder. She had darkened the brown velvet of his doublet. And when he had called on her after Wentworth's execution to convey his sympathy, she had done it once again.

The sleeping child stirred now against that same shoulder. John Pym winced, his face growing paler in the light of the emerging moon.

'Here, give him to me,' she said. 'Your arms must be weary.'

He gently transferred the child to Lucy's shoulder. 'It's not my arms. My stomach. Probably an excess of choler.'

'Let's get him inside. It's damp out here. I'll see if I can find a tincture for your stomachache.'

The two-year-old child was a solid chunk of boyish slumber, heavy against her breast, his breath forming wetly on her neck. She supported his back with her free hand as they slipped in quietly through the back stairs and up to her chamber. The baby smell of him broke her heart.

'Why ever have you brought him *here?*'

'You are the Queen's friend; he's the Queen's child. Do you want Parliament to decide who holds him when he cries out in the night?'

Or who helps him say his prayers. 'John, I am in no way prepared—is he still nursing?'

He opened his eyes wide and blinked hard as though that thought had not occurred to him. She laid the child in the window seat overlooking the carriage house and dragged a chair against it so he would not roll off. John sat down on the bed.

'I didn't know what else to do,' he said as if suddenly too exhausted to stand. 'I've just come from a meeting at Westminster. They have decided to dismiss all of the children's Papist guardians, the entire household.'

'You just marched right up to St. James's Palace and snatched a royal child from his cradle in the middle of the night. That is a treasonous offense.'

'Treason? Parliament decides what is treason now. I just thought—he is very young to be in the care of strangers. I can talk them into letting you keep him here.' He smiled weakly. 'After all, even though you're a friend of the King's Catholic wife, you are a good Presbyterian. You are Algernon Percy's sister and Essex's cousin. They and at least three others in Parliament have reason to be grateful to you.'

She sighed looking at the sleeping child and reached out to smooth back a damp curl clinging to his temple.

'I am a stranger to him, too, John. I haven't been at court since before he was born.'

'Yes, but I know your heart. I'll not worry that we're wounding the innocent if he's with you.'

Worry about wounding the innocent? The man was a study in contradiction. Both naive and cunning, both sensitive and cold. 'John Pym, you are a fool to think you can protect the innocent. This thing you and your compatriots have prodded awake will devour many innocents before it bleeds out.'

He looked at her directly with that open, honest gaze that had first attracted her to him. 'But this one we can save, Lucy. You and I.'

'And what about the other children?'

'The two oldest boys have gone with their father—I think. They're not at St. James's Palace. Rumor says that Princess Mary may have gone with her mother. She is betrothed to Elector Frederick's son.'

'Mary is ten years old. Things must be bad if the Queen is willing to let the House of Orange get their clutches on the girl so soon. What about Princess Elizabeth?' It hurt to think about the little girl with her quick mind and wise ways being punished by some stern Puritan because she chanted the Latin prayers her mother taught her.

'She's still at St. James's Palace. I was hoping you would agree to accept both.'

She shook her head wearily. 'Syon House is not even my house, John. It is my brother's house. Algernon is not here. I cannot ask him—'

'All the more reason they will be safe here. The Earl of Northumberland will not object. King's High Admiral or not, when he obeyed Parliament's order to send ships and arms to Ireland to put down the Catholic rebellion, he showed where his loyalty lies. Besides, he's in Suffolk with the Royal Navy. The children will be with a friend of their mother's

and Parliament will not object—with a little persuasion.' He
paused and looked directly in her eyes. 'Lucy, consider this.
There is some talk of giving them to the guardianship of Lord
Pembroke.'

'Phillip Herbert!' The thought of the Earl of Pembroke with
little Elizabeth made a queasy spot in Lucy's stomach. The
Queen had hated Philip Herbert. And the feeling was recip-
rocated. Henrietta would be enraged to think he had her
children, and as for Lucy, well Herbert was another who had
vigorously argued for Thomas Wentworth's death, but unlike
John Pym, he held no charm for Lucy. She would not so easily
forgive the self-righteous man, and it would be a pleasure to
thwart him now.

'I think Lord Pembroke is not above seeking revenge upon
the Queen's children to feed his resentment at being passed
over at court.' This was John Pym's last and best argument,
and from the look on his face he knew it.

She just looked at him and nodded, thinking how her
midnight rendezvous was not turning out at all as she had
hoped. The child whimpered in his sleep and worked his mouth
in a sucking motion. 'Go get his nurse,' she said with resignation, 'and hurry. And bring back his clothes and nursery things.
See if there is a poppet in his crib.'

'Poppet?'

'A soft plaything, rag doll. If not, bring his blanket. It will
be familiar to him.'

He nodded gratefully and kissed her, just a quick kiss on
the lips, not at all the passionate embrace she'd anticipated as
she waited in the rain.

'Bring Elizabeth, too,' she said. 'It will be a comfort for
them to be together.'

Hours later, Lucy Hay wondered as she lay beside the sleeping
John Pym just what it was about powerful men that she found
irresistible. In the light of a faintly breaking dawn, she considered her lover's round face, tipped with a little pointy beard
so sparse she could see the pink knob of his chin shining
through. The soft hairs of his mustache feathered with each
even breath, and besides being neither young nor handsome,

he had a wife—a fact which seemed to trouble his Puritan
conscience more than it did her Presbyterian one. Yet there
was that unnamable something that drew her to him.

How surprised and touchingly grateful he had been when
she'd warned him about the King's plans for arresting the
Parliament leaders, though later, after they had become lovers,
he had teased her about trying to have a foot in both camps
and had then said soberly he admired a man or a woman with
mind enough to discern which way the wind was blowing.

When he had returned with the nurse and Princess Elizabeth,
he had helped her set up the makeshift nursery and then,
kissing her lightly on the lips, had said he thought he'd rest
a bit while she finished settling the children. She touched him
gently now, hoping he would wake to fulfill the long-delayed
expectation of their lovemaking. He did not waken. She lay
back upon her pillow. I'll write to Henrietta in the morning,
she thought. I'll tell her I'll see Henry and Elizabeth will have
every comfort. She owed her that much.

THE HIGHWAYMAN

*Some eminent governors in the universities gave him
[King Charles I] notice that all the colleges were plenti-
fully supplied with plate . . . wheresoever his Majesty
should think fit to require that treasure, it would all be
sent to him.*

—Edward Hyde in *The History of the Rebellion* (1648)

Sir William Pendleton's newly minted knighthood had
given him no satisfaction, his wife Caroline thought as
they headed home to Oxfordshire. He was more preoccupied than usual, brooding in silence as the driver picked
his way through the narrow London streets. She was glad the
ceremony at Whitehall was over. It had seemed to Caroline
a perfunctory affair.

'The King must have been scraping the bottom of the barrel
to make a wool merchant knight bachelor,' William had said
when they received the news. Just another of the King's
schemes for replenishing the royal treasury—even this lowest
rank of knighthood carried heavy fees paid to the treasury
annually—but neither had complained. William, a king's man,
had held his tongue and she, not wishing to cause him more
distress, had made a mighty effort to curb hers.

In a rare gesture of affection, he reached for her hand. His
palm was moist, almost clammy. She gave it a gentle squeeze.
Her reward was a frail smile and a nod. He was not the kind
of man to share his problems. A quiet, gentle man. A good
man. Solid. Dependable. No longer young. Old enough to
be her father and truly she had once thought of him as a
kindly uncle.

Young Carrie had never had uncles—kindly or otherwise—
or even a father or brother. William had been the first man of

memory to enter her life. As a girl she had delivered pies to his London house in Gresham Street, the house they had just left, where he had lived with his first wife. Letty was her name, the mother of the son Caroline loved like a younger brother. That same son had thundered off in a shower of hoof beats and angry words three months ago, leaving his father choking on resentment. William had not even spoken Arthur's name since the storm that broke on that golden fall day, and he had not been the same man.

The road roughened as the hired coach passed into the countryside. Caroline, still holding William's hand, shifted her position. He did not stir. His eyes were closed. He might have been asleep, but Caroline doubted it. Probably running sums in his head, profit and loss. He never discussed business with her, telling her not to worry her pretty head. Despite the King's fees and the threat of war, they would be fine.

Caroline knew from a dropped word here, a muttered epithet there, that the Guild meeting he had attended after the ceremony had not gone well. Wool prices had fallen. Weavers were opting for the new cotton fibers being imported from the colonies. Not good news for a sheep-breeder and wool-merchant.

Beside her William stirred. Opened his eyes. 'It has started to rain,' he said. ''Twill make good pasture.' He removed his hand. 'Are you chilly?' he asked, spreading the coach blanket over her lap. 'We can stop in Rickmansworth for refreshment, if you wish it.'

'No. I've no need, if you do not.'

'Very well, then.' He settled his head against the seat back and closed his eyes again.

Caroline watched through the rain-streaked windows and thought of Arthur, hoping wherever he was, he was warm and dry. She would gladly swap her new title to see her husband and stepson restored to their happy relationship, cocooned in the quiet contentment of the farm and its secure seasonal routines, surrounded by their friends, Squire Powell and his family—the only real family she had ever known. Except Auntie of course, Auntie who had died suddenly. Caroline had found her body in front of the oven, a lump of

pastry still in her hands. Terrified and alone, Carrie had fled
to the Pendletons, who had been kind to her.

Beside her, William's head tilted, his chin resting on his
chest. That was good. He had scarcely slept at all last night.
Only Caroline was awake to see the mounted, black-clad
stranger waiting at the North Road cross.

The horseman paused in the bend of the crossroads to rest
his horse. He leaned forward, hand on the pommel of his
saddle, and waited, watching as orange and mauve painted a
backdrop in the western sky. The road east out of London
would have been better, but at the last minute, he'd remembered that before he left for the Continent he needed to place
an order from a papermaker in Rickmansworth. He could
order the paper to be delivered to the print shop in Fleet Street
and with any luck still make port at Harwich in time to catch
the dawn packet day after tomorrow. A jeweler in Paris would
relieve him of the jewels and a metalworker in Ghent would
take the Oxford plate and candlesticks off his hands no questions asked. Surely this could fetch enough to purchase a
decent press from a printer closing out inventory, but there
was little margin for negotiation. His wooden press was too
small for serious printing.

His conscience pricked but little. The gold and silver would
only have gone to buy weapons, whichever side got hold of
it. The donors had been as reluctant in their contributions as
if they were being robbed—all except Lady Carlisle, and he
was pretty sure she was buying insurance. Buying satisfaction
too. Her little speech accompanying her offering was pure wit,
pure Lucy Hay. The diamonds were not sacrificed to honor
the King but to prick his conscience, reminding him of his
betrayal. Yet the gesture was oddly touching.

The horse snorted and tossed his head, drawing attention to
a coach approaching at a decent clip. Even in the dying light
and from the distance of a couple of furlongs James Whittier
could see it bore no crest. More and more, like Edward Hyde,
the rich and noble traveled anonymously, not wanting to
encounter hostile soldiers. Brave souls, whoever they were,
to be abroad this time of day when brigands and outlaws came

out to play. But a well-off merchant would have something to add to the bundle strapped to the saddle. When the recognition of that opportunity struck him, he almost laughed out loud. Reason, fellow to conscience, pricked in tandem. Highwayman. A career that carried a noose at the end. But hadn't he, after all, already crossed that Rubicon? Later he would ponder how one simple impulsive action might spur another until a path was chosen, but not tonight. Tonight, he was merely raising capital to fund a legitimate endeavor.

He could see the coach clearly now. A hired conveyance. The driver would be easy. He'd run like a flushed hare in a hedgerow. In for a penny, in for a pound. He searched inside the pocket of his cloak and found the Venetian mask, the one he'd worn at the Queen's last ball, and smiling at the irony, pulled down the wide brim of his hat and spurred his horse.

One glance at the pistol and the driver reined in the already tired team. When the horses came to a full stop, he raised his hands without having to be told.

It was as though he slipped into a brigand's skin when he donned his mask. 'I see you are a wise man,' Whittier said, affecting the same low country brogue he had used with Edward Hyde. He eyed the driver. 'You know the procedure well enough I'm thinking.'

Grunting in disgust, the coachman slumped in his seat but kept his hands still, holding the reigns in the air. 'Aye, I've encountered your kind twice already within the last fortnight.'

Whittier laughed. 'You look a sensible sort. I'm thinking if your purse has been robbed so recently, it will be light. I'll let you keep it—as long as you cooperate.' He pushed the pistol in the coachman's face. 'Get down. Very slowly. Take the reins and wrap them around that crossroad sign. Then go stand over there by the tree.'

The coachman did as he was told.

Easy enough, he thought, until a woman stuck her head out of the window and screamed. The door flew open. The horses neighed and for one moment, he thought they would bolt. He waved the pistol in the face of the man who was stepping down from inside the carriage.

'Best calm your woman, if you don't want her killed in a runaway coach,' he said loud enough for whoever was in the coach to hear. 'I'll not hurt you—or her—if you do as I say. Now go stand over there by the coachman.'

'Please, I'll do whatever you say. I'm a wool merchant just coming from London. I have a little money. Just take it and leave us in peace.'

'Pitch your purse over here.'

The merchant nodded. He seemed a calm enough sort, but his hand shook as he threw the small leather pouch in the dirt.

The robber waved the pistol slightly in the direction of the coachman. 'Pick it up and bring it here.'

The driver, each movement deliberate, did as he was told.

He took the pouch and, weighing it in his hand, whistled softly. 'The price of wool must be down.'

Contemplating letting the merchant go—so small a sum would scarcely make the difference to his enterprise and he felt almost sorry for the fellow—he let his guard slip. He did not even hear the coach door open, so quick was the woman who hurtled toward them.

'William, are you all right? Don't you dare hurt him.' The word *dare* carried a fierceness, given the circumstances, that was almost laughable.

With a firm but weary tone, her husband said, 'Caroline, get back in the coach.'

'I'll not, William. There's two of us and only one of him. Three counting the coachman,' whom she looked at pleadingly.

'The man has a pistol, Caroline. That evens out the odds. Get back in the coach, please. Now.'

The woman looked at her husband, wanting to challenge further, he could see it in the flash of her eyes, in the brief hesitation. She shook her head fiercely, her jaw firmly set. He pointed the pistol closer to her husband's head.

'Do you really think that wise, madame?'

To his great relief, the woman hiked up her skirts, showing a shapely ankle, and climbed back inside.

'We pose no threat to you. You have what you came for, now for the love of God, as you are a gentleman, leave us in peace.'

Gentleman? What gave him away? Or was the 'gentleman' a ploy, a plea to his better nature?

'Driver, you may resume your position, but I have my pistol pointed at this man's head. If you should try to drive off before I give you the order, you'll find yourself atop a runaway carriage with a hysterical woman.'

The driver, slow and deliberate in movement, hands in the air, mounted the coach bench. Then Whittier motioned with the pistol for the merchant to climb back in the coach. He should have ridden away then, he would think later, they had only seen him in silhouette against a dying sun. But he had a curiosity about the woman. His mask would protect him. And their jewelry might make up for the lightness of the merchant's purse.

'There is no need to frighten my wife. I assure you I have nothing else of value on my person.'

'I believe you, merchant. I just want to pay my respects to your lady and perhaps receive some token from her in return.' Still holding the cocked pistol to the man's left temple, he whispered, 'Better a live husband than a dead hero.'

The merchant, holding his hands in the air, shook his head at his wife as he climbed in and sat down across from her.

'Madame, I am sorry to trouble you. You need not be afraid,' he said, lowering the pistol only slightly. The merchant's wife stared at him with a tight expression, her eyes wide. She was a very comely woman, young enough to be the merchant's daughter.

'Don't worry, my dear. He is just a common thief, more to be pitied than despised.'

But it was not pity he saw in the eyes glaring back at him. Her shapely mouth twitched with anger, each word a hiss. 'The penalty for highway robbery is hanging.'

'Hush, Caroline. This will all be over soon.'

'But, William—'

'Sooner, if you keep quiet.'

His eye rested on the forefinger of her left hand, a gold ring, studded with pearls. Her wedding ring was of respectable worth also, but he could not bring himself to take that.

'Your pearl ring, madame. It is lovely. May I have a closer look?'

The woman hid her hands in the folds of her cloak and shook her head.

'Let him have it, Caroline,' her husband said. 'I'll get you another.'

She lifted her hand and withdrawing the ring leaned forward. He had a sudden vision of her pulling down his mask and raking her nails against his face. Pointing the pistol more directly again, he said, 'Just give it to your good husband. He'll pass it over.'

Her gaze still locked on his face, she handed the ring to her husband.

Suddenly anxious to be away—he'd tarried here much too long—without another glance at the purloined ring, he slid it into his cloak pocket along with the merchant's pouch. 'Coachman, do not ride on until I'm out of sight,' he called, then without a backward glance, spurred his horse toward Rickmansworth.

Just after dark, he pulled up outside the papermaker's shop and took a few coins from the pouch to pay the vendor. The balance he secured inside the saddle bag with the candlesticks and trinkets and the King's plate. He fingered the pearl ring and then put it back inside his cloak pocket. He would not sell it with the rest. Probably wouldn't bring enough to make a difference anyway so he would keep it, a token to remind him of an encounter with a very unusual woman—with uncommon eyes, eyes that reminded him of another's. But the owner of those eyes had married his brother.

She had been trouble, too.

THE QUEEN'S BARGAIN

Nor is that a limit to me which is a boundary of the world.

—translation of the Latin inscription on a gold medal cast by Nicholas Briot for Charles's coronation in celebration of his divine right. (British Museum)

The Netherlands—The Hague

While Genevieve threaded a string of pearls in her hair, Henrietta gazed into the mirror of her dressing table. It was mid-afternoon and after a sleepless night she had finally allowed herself to be dressed. Her body ached from the hour spent kneeling at her altar and she longed for a nap, but one did not keep the Prince of the Netherlands and the King of Denmark waiting. Not when one was seeking favors.

'Your majesty is displeased?' Genevieve asked.

'*Non, tu me coiffe toujours trés bien,*' Henrietta was quick to reassure her, but the image staring back at her did not please.

The eyes were red and shadowed where she had cried into her pillow until the early hours. In the coded messages that passed between them, Charles had said when he left Hampton Court he'd taken James and Charles with him, but had left the young ones, Elizabeth and Henry, behind at St. James's Palace. They had nurses, of course, and godparents and were sometimes separated from their parents for weeks during a royal progress, but her mother's intuition told her this time was different. Thank the Virgin that at least Princess Mary was securely ensconced in her own royal apartment as the bride of William of Orange.

Genevieve held out to her a small mirror, so she could

inspect the back, but she shook her head, not caring enough to look. 'Bring me the King's necklace,' she said. Having already surmised her lady's needs, she withdrew it from its velvet sheath and fastened it about Henrietta's neck.

Henrietta touched it, feeling the tightness in her forehead release. Charles had given it to her more than a decade ago in her beautiful new garden at Somerset House. Young Charles had just been christened, and his father was very happy. There, among the roses and the elegant statuary, she had basked in her husband's approval. It had been the first time she'd seen the love-light in his eyes, and she had resolved then that she would be the one to replace the dead Duke of Buckingham as the King's companion.

She was still at the dressing table, her hand on the reassuring stone resting in the hollow of her throat, when the gentleman of the chamber knocked. 'Your majesty, Frederick, Prince of Orange, and his Majesty, Christian IV, King of Denmark, desire to wait upon you.'

'Il est temps,' she said, standing up and smoothing her skirts. 'S'il vous plaît, admit them maintenant.'

After the appropriate homage and exchange of pleasantries—much bowing and hand kissing: was everything to her liking, how did she like Den Haag; and then much thanking of the Prince for his hospitality—she bade her visitors sit on the two brocade chairs beneath the chamber window. She sat on the bench at the foot of her bed facing them, careful to spread her blue satin skirts. It was her best gown. She might feel like a beggar, but she would not look like one.

Christian IV of Denmark looked at her as though he were appraising goods. He was reputed to be a great womanizer and said to have a score of children amongst his wives and mistresses. He was a hulk of a man, which might appeal to some, but not at all as elegant as her Charles, despite the bow-tied white-lace sash that only accentuated his girth. 'How does, our nephew, Charles I of England?' he asked.

'Très bien. My husband sends greetings to your majesties.'

Her salutation included Mary's father-in-law Prince Frederick, though technically he was not a crowned head but an elected Stadtholder of Holland, Zeeland, and Utrecht, a fact which to Henrietta made him unworthy of her daughter's hand. But because the House of Orange was Protestant, a powerful trading ally, and a strategic defense partner against England's old enemy Catholic Spain, Parliament had been quick to put its stamp of approval on the marriage. Wise strategy or another one of Charles' acts of appeasements? Who could know? Their response to her request could be the first test of the wisdom of Mary's sacrifice.

Frederick looked around uncertainly as if expecting someone else, then after a moment's hesitation asked, 'The Princess Royal, is she pleased with her apartments?'

'She is pleased, your grace. And your William? Is he pleased she has come?'

'Very pleased.'

'They are becoming fast friends, already, I hear,' the King of Denmark interjected. She ignored the smirking smile that accompanied the remark, addressing her comment to the father of her son-in-law.

'As her mother, I am grateful for your understanding that Mary is much too young to assume the responsibilities of wife and princess of a foreign court. We agreed when they were married last year, *oui*?'

'Indeed, your majesty. We did agree. All in good time, now that the marriage has been finalized by proxy. Your decision to accompany her was wise. You are welcome to stay as long as you wish and assist in her tutelage. It is our hope whenever you do return to your country, we will have earned sufficient trust that you are comfortable leaving her in our care.'

'*Merci beaucoup.*'

'We are pleased to have been of service to your husband's widowed sister and her household as well.' He smiled. 'It is a rather large household. Have you seen her majesty the Queen of Bohemia? All of the children are here except the oldest son, who is now Elector of the Palatinate, of course and still in Heidelberg.'

'I saw Elizabeth and her daughter Sophia briefly. Mary and I brought them greetings and good wishes from Charles.' Then she added, a self-conscious elevated pitch in her voice—she was never a good liar—'I brought her assurances of our love.'

'We pray the conflicts that have driven that decades-long war will be resolved. Of course we are in sympathy with the Protestant Union, but it would seem a little more tolerance could be shown on both sides don't you think, your majesty? The Protestant Union can be very aggressive in spreading the faith and Rome is so . . . intransigent and political.'

Henrietta swallowed the answer she wanted to give, realizing that he was probably baiting her deliberately to throw her off her guard. She said instead, 'Prince Frederick, the King, and I are very grateful for your support for his sister and her family.'

How quickly he had turned his own son's marriage to a king's daughter into an act of Dutch charity and managed to lecture the Queen of England about religion and politics.

His face a mask of feigned sympathy, he said, 'It must be difficult to be forced into exile after so short a time. And then to have lost her husband. I understand theirs was more than a political union. I am sure she is heartened by the welcome company of your majesty, whose devotion to her own husband is often remarked upon.'

As is my devotion to the Holy Father, but you knew that already, probably also knew I was not in favor of your son's marriage to my daughter. But she could not say that. Instead she said, 'Poor Elizabeth. Heidelberg has been her home since she left England as a young bride many years ago. I hear her time in Prague was as brief as her reign. I am sure she misses her eldest son and the beautiful gardens of her palace in Heidelberg. She never tires of talking about them. As do you, I hope her sojourn here will be short.'

In this sentiment Henrietta was sincere. Henrietta liked having Elizabeth as far away as possible. They were hardly kindred spirits.

'She is welcome to stay as long as she needs to, as are you, your majesty. Perhaps you can find comfort in your shared circumstances.'

She longed to slap the smugness from his face.

An awkward silence developed in the room. The Prince seemed reluctant to broach the next item to be settled between them. His posture was one of expectancy. Beside him Christian

IV also remained silent. She wondered if there was some protocol peculiar to his court that she had neglected. Finally, Frederick cleared his throat and spoke. 'We are prepared to discuss the matter of your offer: the other purpose for your majesty's honoring us with your presence.'

'*Oui*, yes,' she nodded.

He looked puzzled, then frowning slightly blurted out, 'Have we come untimely?'

'Untimely?'

'I see your negotiator is not yet here.'

'Negotiator? I am sorry. I do not understand.' She could feel the little bunch forming between her eyebrows, the little wrinkles Charles always kissed away. She tried to relax them.

'Someone to speak on your behalf. Lord Denbigh perhaps.' He pulled on his little pointed beard. The Dane nodded in agreement.

She smiled at them, a smile calculated to charm, but a smile not wide enough to show the space from the missing molar she had lost after giving birth to little Henry. The doctor had said it had gone to help the infant's bones, so she did not begrudge it, but she'd smiled more carefully since.

'Lord Denbigh has returned to England with a message for King Charles. I speak for myself—and for my husband Charles I, King of England, of course.' She raised her chin and gazed directly at her visitors, first the Prince of Orange then the Danish king. You have seen the—' she groped for the right word—'merchandise. Have you an offer?'

The King of Denmark cleared his throat and glanced at his companion, his face flushing brightly. 'Your majesty, the rubies and the pearls are exquisite . . .'

'*Oui*,' she nodded in encouragement. He seemed ill at ease, as if he did not know what to say next. 'They were part of my dowry. From the Medici family. They are the finest stones in *le monde*.'

The high starched collar at his throat wiggled a bit as he cleared his throat. 'I am prepared to make an offer for some of them,' he said. 'But I fear—' He glanced at the Prince of Orange for support.

Frederick responded. 'The King of Denmark is afraid, your

majesty, that since you are not held in the highest regard—
please forgive me for speaking plainly—among your subjects,
and since England appears on the brink of civil unrest—'

All the words were jumbling in her head. Were they refusing
to buy because she was not popular with Parliament?

'*Mais oui*, the crown jewels of England carry their own
value, *non*?'

'Yes, your majesty, but because they are the crown jewels
of England, if the conflict should go in Parliament's favor,
Parliament might demand their return.'

She looked at them as though she didn't understand, because
she didn't.

'They will say you had no right to sell them,' he said.

His embarrassed tone added humiliation to the words. Her head
began to throb with the recurring headache she'd had for the
past week. This was simply beyond her comprehension. If
the jewels belonged to England, then they belonged to its king
to do with as he pleased—at least in the world she inhabited.

'We will buy your dower jewels outright,' Christian of
Denmark offered. 'They are truly extraordinary. The crown
jewels and the crown plate are another matter. But we are
prepared, because of the kinship between our families and the
friendship between our sovereign nations, to lend you a
substantial sum with the crown jewels as surety, though it will
be much less than the desired sum, because . . . forgive me,
your majesty, but should your husband not be successful in
squelching this rebellion by the English Parliament—

'Charles I, sovereign ruler by divine right of England,
Ireland, and Scotland, will be successful. He will be successful
because God wills it.'

'With all due respect, your majesty, do you not suppose the
Puritans and the Scottish Presbyterians feel that God also
wishes their cause victorious?'

Her mind leapt to where else she could go for aid. She had
already been to her Catholic friends in France begging for
money to assist the Irish Catholics against whom Parliament
warred. And they had been generous. But they had their limits.
This time she would go directly to the Pope. But the papal
considerations were very deliberate. It had taken months for

her mother and Louis to get permission for her to marry a Protestant.

The two men watched her expectantly, waiting for her response. She wanted to scream at them to get out of her sight.

She looked directly at the Dutch prince. 'Mary, the Princess Royal, will be gratified to learn, when she is old enough to understand such things, of the high regard in which her new father-in-law holds her father's kingdom.'

The looks they exchanged showed that her sarcasm had hit its mark.

'But I am grateful for your offer of assistance. I will refer it to his Majesty, Charles I of England. *S'il vous plaît*, be so kind as to put the specific offer and the sum you are offering in writing.'

'Of course, your majesty.'

Her visitors rose to take their leave, again with much bowing and hand-kissing, obviously relieved that their delicate errand was almost finished.

She was thinking how glad she would be to see the back of them, when the Dane spoke as if in afterthought. 'Your necklace, your majesty, is exquisite. Is that part of the dower jewels as well?'

'*Non, ce nes't pas,*' she shook her head vigorously. Her hand flew to the necklace, as if to shield it from his greedy gaze. 'For the necklace I will not negotiate.'

After her visitors departed, Henrietta had sent Genevieve for a soothing tonic. Every part of her body hurt, and her heart still beat too rapidly, but as the night sounds of the castle settled into silence, her fatigue, along with the honeyed wine, soothed her to a troubled slumber. She dreamed again of the old familiar torment.

She is a girl again, walking through the narrow streets of London. It is her first pilgrimage, a penance to Tyburn Hill with its horrid hanging tree where the Catholic martyrs died at the hands of the Protestant English.

Sharp stones cut her bare feet. Filth and slime squish between her toes. She tries to think only of the martyrs as her Jesuit confessor instructed. She clutches a statue of the Virgin in her hands, reciting as she goes, lips barely moving, frozen in fear: Obsecro te O intemerato . . .

Her mind conjures distorted images of the hanged martyrs, even the smell of rotting corpses.

Ave Maria, gratia plena, Dominus tecum.

Her naked skin shivers underneath the rough pilgrim's smock.

Benedicta tu in mulieribus, et benedictus fructus ventris tui, Jesu.

Her fingers are numb and white from cold,

Sancta Maria, Mater Dei . . . *But the Holy Mother sends no blessing and the statue does not warm beneath her touch. The girl's progress to the holy site outside the city gates is excruciatingly slow. Ugly Londoners line the uglier streets, cheek to jowl, fine linen brushing homespun rags. Pope's whore, they shout, their faces twisted with rage. She does not understand their English slurs, but she understands enough to know they do not want her here. They despise her for her devotion to the Virgin. They despise her for the tears she cries for the Catholic martyrs.*

The foul and fetid smell that chokes her breath is not the conjured smell of the martyrs. It is the smell of hatred. Or is it the smell of her own fear? She struggles to break free of the dream so oft repeated that in her dream she knows it is a dream. And yet she cannot move.

This time the dream is different in one horror.

'Wake up, up my lady, it is only a bad dream.'

Ora pro nobis peccatoribus nunc . . .

She tries to cry out and has no tongue. A woman's low moan, sad and anguished, calls to her. She ceases her murmured prayer, stares into the crowd. Her own visage, a queen's visage, is painted on every mournful face, keening like a choir of angels at the crucifixion. The face of the girl carrying the Virgin is changing too. Beneath the pilgrim's plain white hood is the face of her eldest daughter. And on her girlish cheeks, tears as big and bright as the King's diamonds glisten. . . . et in hora mortis nostrae.

The statue crumbles in her hands.

GILDED VANITIES

*. . . [S]he [The Church of England] shall spoil and havoc
your estates, disturb your ease, diminish your honor,
enthral your liberty under the swelling mood of a proud
clergy who will not serve or feed your souls with spiritual
food . . . it is not in their purpose . . . undress them of
all their gilded vanities.*

—Excerpted from John Milton's Conclusion in
The Reason of Church Government, 1642

I n Tower Prison, Archbishop William Laud knelt before his
makeshift altar and tried to pray for the soul of his friend,
one year gone. The image of Wentworth's bloodied head
intruded, chasing the words from his brain, words so oft
repeated they should require no concentration, and yet the
Latin hovered just out of reach. It was no image birthed of
memory, but a devil's conjuring trick, since he had not
actually seen Wentworth's head when it was separated from
his body and lifted high. But in his torment, it was a distinction
that mattered little.

The red velvet cushion, golden tassels gleaming against the
grime-encrusted floor, did nothing to mitigate the cold
stone grinding against worn-out knees. He scratched through
the rubble of his besieged mind for the words and mumbled
incline domine aurem like any ordinary Papist chantry priest.
Surely the Latin prayers of an archbishop counted for more
than an ordinary priest's. But the startling images had flushed
the Latin from his memory, so he finished the Office of the
Dead in English. *Grant Lord Strafford an entrance into
the land of light and joy and the fellowship of saints. In the
name of the Father, Son, and the Holy Ghost.* How his Puritan
enemies would chortle to hear their hated archbishop falter so.

He struggled to stand and considered for a long moment the crucifix before which he genuflected. No glorious image of a suffering Christ chiseled in marble like the one that hung in the Queen's Chapel at Somerset House, yet even this small wooden crucifix and the pewter candlesticks that flanked it would be enough to enrage the Scottish Protestant rabble and the Puritans in Parliament. They knew nothing of beauty. The mystery of the mass, the blood, the body, all lost to their plebian minds. Pearls before swine. The Brownists, the Baptists, the Separatists, and the Calvinist Presbyterians, the whole sorry lot, had screeched like stuck pigs when he'd moved their plain pulpits from the center to the east end of the church and replaced their rough-hewn communion tables with beautiful stone altars. But the screeching had not bothered him over much. In the beginning. If the Puritans had the strident voices of the dissident pamphleteers, Archbishop Laud had the Star Chamber and royal enforcement of Church rules.

Like Thomas Wentworth, he'd thought it no contest.

But in the end, the pamphleteers' pens had proved mightier even than the King's heavy-handed courts. Parliament destroyed the Star Chamber and seized its power. Now who was left to defend the Church of England? Not Charles, its titular head, Defender of the Faith, a title first given to old King Henry. This Stuart king had not the lion heart of a Tudor, and no skill for timely confrontation.

Archbishop Laud sat down on the bed the Queen had provided him and leaned his back against the wall. They had an uneasy truce—the Queen and he. She did not appreciate the many warnings he'd given her about publicly flaunting her Roman worship, or his admonition to abandon her allegiance to Rome and accept the King she loved so much as the true head of the Church.

'Charles is my cherished husband, your grace, but he is not the Holy Father,' and she had frowned and flounced away in a rustle of French silk. But for all their differences, Laud and the Queen had many common elements in their worship—and a common enemy in Parliament. It made for a fragile bond, a threadbare alliance.

Hands crossed in his lap, he contemplated his dingy cuffs

with distaste and picked a nit from his sleeve. It was impossible to keep one's self, let alone one's garments clean, no matter how much one bribed the gaolers. A dusty slit of light from a late afternoon sun pierced the archer's window high overhead. The personal servant he was allowed would bring his supper soon. At least he did not have to eat the slop the warders ladled out. At the creaking of the cell door, he bent to pull his small writing table forward, another of the Queen's token gifts.

But it was not his servant who entered. Sir Edward Hyde greeted him.

Laud grunted in the counselor's direction. 'An unexpected pleasure. Please forgive me for not standing. I plead old bones. I would offer you a chair but as you see, my furnishings are spare. Have you any news? How fares his Majesty?'

Sir Edward plopped uninvited onto the narrow bed beside him, his black cloak puddling around him, his dress almost as austere as a Puritan's, though he wore no high crowned hat. His bushy hair looked as if it had not seen a comb in a fortnight. 'You've not heard then, your grace?'

'Heard what? How can I hear? My visitors grow scarcer each day.'

'The King has quit Whitehall for York. There was a disastrous attempt to bring an armed force against some leaders in Parliament—a course against which I advised.' He shook his head and frowned. 'Would that he had listened. Now his enemies grow bolder with each day.'

This was a surprise. The state of affairs was worse than he had expected. But then he reminded himself in a world where an archbishop could be held like a common criminal, anything could happen. 'As a friend of the Church and the King's advisor, can you tell me what that means for my bleak circumstances?'

Hyde was studying him, a wary look on his face.

'Nothing good, I am afraid, your grace. They—John Pym and William Prynne in particular—want to charge you with subverting the true religion and for causing the present war with Scotland by forcing a common prayer book on the Scottish Kirk.'

'Prynne? Isn't he that seditionist whose ears the King ordered cropped off for preaching falsely?' *Ordered at his, Laud's, request. The Church condemns, the King disposes.* 'That didn't quiet him? What about the King, surely—'

'His Majesty has lost all power over Parliament. And the people of London have been further inflamed against him by unlawful publications and dissidents who preach against you— and his Majesty's support of you—in their pulpits. Parliament's chaplain Steven Marshall is most eloquent and the poet Milton has been especially persuasive with his reasoned argument against the Episcopacy.'

'You call it reasoned. I read the thing. Some dissident-sympathizing, smirking turd of a guard brought it to my cell. I call it the ravings of a heretic. Mr. Milton is no friend of the Church of England. It was a vicious attack. And Steven Marshall is hardly a worthy adversary.'

Hyde answered with a shrug.

How Laud resented that shrug and the shoulders that carried it. Hard to force that resentment down. 'I am at their mercy, then. Of Prynne and Pym, the insidious ink mongers and their ignorant ilk? What says the Queen?'

His visitor sighed, his visage a mask of long-suffering exasperation. 'Your enemies may be a lot of things, but they are not ignorant. You underestimate them at your peril. As for the Queen, don't look for much help there. Indeed, I fear for her position, even her safety if she returns. England has a long history of disposing of unpopular queens. I think the King feared for her safety, too. That's why he suffered her leaving.'

'So. It is to be all-out war, then? Between King Charles and Parliament? I knew it would come to this. Jackals always gather after a kill. When his Majesty signed the order for the Earl of Strafford's execution, the dissidents smelled the royal weakness.' He did not add *Thanks to your duplicity, as advisor to the King, you could have influenced him against signing an unlawful bill of attainder against a loyal subject.*

Get the beam out of your own eye. Wentworth's last vision on earth must have been the empty window where his arch-bishop and friend had promised he would be keeping watch, praying for his soul at the moment it took flight. He and Hyde were both in the club for cowards. When Thomas Wentworth, Lord Strafford, mounted the scaffold, the archbishop had been watching the execution from this very same Tower window. When he'd seen the headsman lift the axe, he had fainted dead away. The memory of that betrayal had tormented him every night since.

He considered his visitor now, hoping his disdain for the man did not show. Hyde thought himself a negotiator, but he was just a craven conniver trying to have a foot in both worlds. When he had stood as MP for Wootton Basset, he was sometimes on the side of King Charles, sometimes on Parliament's. Well a pox on his compromising perfidy. One did not make an alliance with the devil. Parliament and King Charles could never govern together; they both wanted absolute power. One had to be vanquished. But Laud kept that opinion to himself. He needed Edward Hyde to throw the Roundhead jackals off his scent lest he share Wentworth's fate.

Hyde's scanty, ill-kept beard bobbed against his double chin. 'The Scots have taken up arms to protect their Presbyterian rights against the Church of England's forced liturgy. And they have named you as the villain of the piece. It was unwise, your eminence, to force the prayer book on them.'

The book! How could something as glorious as Cranmer's Book of Common Prayer provoke a call to arms among Christians? It wasn't even a Latin text, for God's sake. Their outrage was a ruse, nothing more—an excuse to exercise their beastly, rebellious natures.

'Scots were ever a stubborn and troublesome lot,' he said. 'I merely wanted to bring some uniformity, some sense of the sacred to their scandalous worship.' The dingy lace on his cuffs trembled. 'For Christ's sake! What is wrong with everybody saying the same prayer? Don't we all share the same fallen state? Don't we all need to confess and be forgiven?'

But, though he would not admit as much to Edward Hyde, his months in the Tower had taught him that he'd over-reached. At least tactically. He'd thought it of no matter if a few Presbyterians got upset. It was the King's law, what recourse would they have? But it appeared he'd underestimated the

Calvinists—and his enemies in Parliament. He should have been more vigilant.

'I fear, your eminence, in making martyrs of your enemies, you hand the printers a weapon with which to bludgeon you. William Prynne—who suffered full measure of your *spiritual* discipline—wears his disfigurement like a badge of holiness. Huge crowds follow him everywhere, hanging on his every word, hailing him the saintliest of the *saints.*'

Laud pondered this accusation. Tactically he could not have disagreed more. The mistake was in being too merciful. He wished he'd done more than have the man pilloried, his nose slit, and his ears cropped. He should have silenced him forever. His vile rhetoric had been as responsible for the Puritan rebellion as anyone's, setting the tone for the pamphleteers who poured their venom daily into the minds of an ignorant populace.

'Harumphh! You call them martyrs. I call them heretics, enemies of the Church of England, enemies of Christ. Their preaching is unlicensed and seditious. Prynne practically called the Queen a whore for her court entertainments.'

Hyde held up an open palm and shook his head, impatience marking his clipped words. 'Whatever you call them makes little difference now, as they have gained a lawful advantage. The Star Chamber is gone. The courts reside now under Parliament's power. Wentworth's death was proof of that. Parliament decides what is criminal, not the King's Bench. You should have been less zealous in the imposition of your ecclesiastical authority. But I shall do what I can to see that any official action against you is deferred. The English are a compassionate people. I will put out the word that you are in ill health. You might thereby procure some sympathy from your enemies who have least against you.'

'If I have to spend much more time locked up in here, my ill health will not be a false report,' the archbishop said.

Hyde stood up to leave.

'I would consider it a great favor if for friendship's sake you would send me some candles to lighten this purgatory,' he called to Edward's Hyde's retreating back.

The counselor gave no indication that he heard.

If I must beg favors from my inferiors, my humiliation is now complete, he thought.

Lady Carlisle watched from their picnic spot as Elizabeth, arms akimbo, holding the ball in her small-fingered grip, scolded her little brother, 'Now, Henry, watch me. HOLD IT LIKE THIS,' she commanded, pausing for emphasis before each syllable as though the words came down on stone tablets with Moses. A little like her mother.

How much had changed for England and for Lucy in the last three years since, unable to suffer Henrietta's extravagant whims and idolatrous worship one more day, Lucy had asked the Queen's permission to withdraw from court. Permission granted. Fairly quickly. She suspected that, friendship aside, her refusal to attend her majesty in the Royal Chapel was beginning to wear on the Queen's nerves. Henrietta, for all her diminutive person, could be formidable when crossed. So after the Queen's distant and majestically formal goodbye, Lucy, having packed up her gowns and satin slippers in layers of rosemary and lavender, distributed a few mementoes—along with a few discreet kisses—to her admirers, begged prettily that they not forget her, and made her exit with relief. It was like fleeing a house with smoldering timbers and tiny flames already licking at the roof. But she felt a heavy sadness, too, as though she were abandoning Charles and Henrietta and their little brood to the destruction to come.

Wentworth had supported Lucy, setting her up in a townhouse not too far from Whitehall. She had gathered a smaller, but no less distinguished circle about her, gaining a reputation for her entertainments of subdued elegance in her London salon. Even the Queen had come to her—eventually, saying it was like a little rustic retreat from court. Faint praise. But still she came. All appeared to be well.

And then the great betrayal had come: the King had signed the bill of attainder against Lord Strafford. With Wentworth's execution where was she to go? Syon House had been her only real choice, of course. Knowing her brother could hardly banish his celebrated sister to Alnwick, that ancient pile in dreary Northumberland, she had petitioned him. He'd pointed out to her, rather ungraciously she thought, that she could go to her Carlisle estates in Ireland. Lucy had answered Lord Percy that she could hardly bear the place. She had only visited once during Wentworth's Irish campaign. In the end her brother had relented, saying he'd just wanted a bit of sport, payback for her teasing.

You see, Elizabeth, brothers have their uses, and they have long memories, she thought watching the child interact with her younger sibling.

The little princess stamped her foot, for all the world like a miniature Henrietta remonstrating with the King that he was too lenient with Parliament. 'Stand up and do it right, Henry. You are as stupid as Papa's fool.'

Henry just looked at his sister and put down the ball.

'Play nice, Elizabeth. You'll get your way much faster.'

The widower James Hay had taught Lucy that. He had been her first lover. Not the most handsome man she'd ever seen—she'd heard the sobriquet camel-face whispered behind his back. But how he made her heart dance; before or since, no man had ever courted her with such exquisite generosity and grandeur. A favorite of the old King James, and wielding almost as much power as Buckingham, James Hay wore the King's grace and favor like a mantle, but lightly, as though he'd been born of noble blood. He was a man who knew the art of pleasing.

Old Northumberland hated him for his common birth. Bad enough James Hay was the son of a gentleman farmer—but her father vowed he would never give a daughter of the house of Percy to a cursed Scot. In the end, Lucy had gotten her way. When her tears, tantrums, and cajoling had failed with her father, she had changed targets, done a little pleasing of her own, and acquired James Hay's promise of marriage. She had sneaked out of the Tower and flown straight to the hated Scotsman, who even though he was away had left money and instructions that she should be given protection until his return. The wily Scot promised the old man he would work to gain his release from Tower Prison in return for his daughter's hand. James Hay might not have been every young girl's dream, but Lucy had eagerly swapped one stern old lord for a kinder, generous, and much more exciting one.

She had also exchanged Tower Prison for a royal palace, and at her husband's side, Lucy Hay learned the power of influence: how to get it, how to keep it, and how to wield it. By the time she realized that there were many others to whom her generous husband gave his 'protection,' she no longer cared or needed him.

And now what advice, dear Jamie, would you give me? she wondered, feeling a little self-pity at her current situation. But she knew what he would say. She could still hear his good-humored laughter, the Scottish lilt in his voice, which he never troubled to hide—why bother, with a Scotsman on the throne of England? *My darling Lucy, look around you*, he would say. *Is this such a bad place to land? Of course, Algernon has gained the title and the lands, but he would have done anyway. He was the heir. Use your beauty—yes, you've still some currency left; use your brains, and what I've taught you. You'll do just fine, lass.*

'Henreee!' The high little-girl whine soared over Hay's imagined voice, penetrating her pleasant reverie.

The toddler, too young to understand the innate power of his gender, just gazed at the female who outranked him in age. His wide blue eyes considered her as though she were some great curiosity before giving an abrupt toss of his blond curls and uttering with ducal authority. 'No.'

Maybe he did understand after all, Lucy thought; maybe that understanding was imbued to him along with his male appendage. Then again, maybe it was just the only word in his vocabulary.

She had brought the children outside, thinking they and she might enjoy the warm sunshine, and it would provide a diversion from Elizabeth's endless questioning. *Is Maman coming home today? Not today, I don't think. When then? Soon, my lady, soon. She misses you as much as you miss her.* And from the wide gardens sloping down to the river, Lucy could see the traffic on the river and watch for Pym. He had not come yesterday; surely, he would come today. She had laid out a picnic of bread and cheese and jam and some strips of cold roast chicken on a blanket.

Still he had not come.

After they ate, she showed Elizabeth how to pick wild flowers in the meadow and make daisy chains, an occupation to which the child applied herself with intense concentration, her little mouth pursed, as the flower chain coiled in her lap and spilled over the edge of the coverlet. 'I shall make a chain long enough to reach Maman in Holland. She can follow it back to us.'

The skirts of Lucy's gown—pale cream satin, proud for a picnic, but she was hoping to be surprised in this pastoral landscape—flowed out prettily on the ground beneath a large oak that provided her with a backrest and occasionally dropped a lazy leaf into her frothy lace bodice. It was a scene worthy of Inigo Jones, she'd thought as she hummed to the child, who for a while snuggled in her lap content to watch his sister weave the flowers. (Indeed, he had grown quite clingy in the weeks since John had brought him to Syon House.) But his contentment was short-lived. Torn between the seductive comfort of being lulled by a female bosom and the call of adventure he'd elected the latter and waddled forth to finally engage his sister.

Elizabeth stamped her royal foot. 'Throw it, Henry. Now, I say! Throw the ball to me.' Whereupon Henry dropped the ball and plopped awkwardly on his bottom, then looking back with regret at his deserted lap of luxury, he let out a wail. Flouncing over to him with righteous indulgence, his sister said. 'Here, you little baby, let me show you.' She picked up the ball and declared, 'Watch. I'm going to throw the ball to Lady Carlisle, and she will catch it.'

The afternoon warmth was becoming oppressive and Lucy felt its heaviness pressing. Tears and tantrums were about to erupt between the children and John Pym was not coming today

'No, your grace. Lady Carlisle is not going to catch it,' Lucy said, getting up and gathering the picnic things into a pile. 'I think it is time for us to go in. Henry needs his nap. I'm sure he will be more cooperative when he wakes refreshed. Your nurse is wondering where we got to.'

The little girl's brow drew up in a frown and her mouth set into a pout. 'But I do not wish to go in.'

'Oh, but we must. You see those gray clouds on the other side of the river? Those are thunderheads. You don't want to be caught out in a storm, do you?' Lucy had picked up the wailing Henry, who cuddled against her again for comfort, his eyes growing wide with fright. *You know that word don't you, poor little mite. You know what a storm is.* But his sister just glanced at the horizon and then back at Lucy, and shaking her head said, 'Lady Carlisle, that doesn't look like a storm to me. Those are just fluffy clouds.'

Lucy could have beaten her. But one didn't beat a king's child—or even threaten to. Henry was wailing. Lucy sighed and said in her most reasonable voice, 'You are right, Princess Elizabeth. The storm might go around. But we have been gone for hours. A messenger might have come to bring us news from their majesties.'

The little princess drew in a quick breath, her mouth bunching in consideration. Lucy felt a great wash of sympathy and a little twinge of guilt. There would be no royal message, of course, but maybe there would be a note from Pym. She gave one last longing glance at the river, winding like a gray rope, in the distance and, not seeing any boat heading toward their water stairs, bent to pick up the picnic blanket. She longed to see him. And more, she needed information. Parliament was considering what to do with these two youngest of the Queen's children. He thought he could convince them to let Northumberland have custody—which of course might mean Syon House and Lucy. He would do what he could. 'I'll tell you as soon as I know,' he'd said.

That had been two weeks ago.

Elizabeth slipped her hand into Lucy's and said, 'Stop all the blathering, Henry. There might be a message from Papa or Maman waiting for us. They may be coming home.'

The child's hand slipped into hers and she gave a little skip, her words of hope only adding to the weight of Lucy's disappointment. There would be no happy message for either of them this day.

John Pym came that night, after she had seen the children were fed and comforted and put to bed. When she saw the drawn look on his face, she was almost afraid to ask. She drew him into her sitting room, tried to give him refreshment, but he shook his head, saying he'd no time. He had to return tonight. Her heart sank. She needed the weight of his body next to hers in the darkness, the comfort of his embrace, the reassurance of his passion. Instead he gave her a quick kiss. His lips felt cracked, almost fevered, his breath sour. He slumped on the bench beneath the window where he'd first deposited the sleeping child. Seizing power from a king was hard work.

'Are you well, John?'

His smile was a thin little line that didn't reach his eyes. 'Just tired. So many diverse and strong opinions. We are working on a final document to present to the King. Nineteen Propositions. If he agrees, we can avoid war. If not—' He shrugged.

'What sort of propositions? Anything about the fate of the children?'

'It is laid out in Proposition Four. How fares the King's children?' he asked. Then before she could answer, 'I assured Parliament they were secure here and looked after—in a godly fashion. You haven't given the Capuchins access, I hope?' he asked referring to the French cadre of monks who had shadowed the Queen's every move.

'No, John. You may assure the ministers they are well and safe, bodies and souls. Princess Elizabeth misses her mother keenly, but I doubt the members care. Some are so hard-hearted, they might even be glad of it. It breaks my heart to listen to her praying so earnestly every night for her mother's return. She is just a little girl, an innocent who has done nothing wrong to have to suffer so.'

She waited for him to comment. When he did not she said, 'Does Proposition Four say I am to be allowed to keep them until the Queen returns? They are safe and happy here.'

'I have suggested placing them under the care of Algernon Percy and this is Percy's house. I think the council will agree, even if the Queen does return. That is being written into the proposition we will present to the King.'

'What about the Queen's rights?'

'As their mother she will have visitation rights of course.

And of course, the King can see them whenever he wants—if he signs the document.' He looked down, picked at a leaf clinging to his boot, then asked, his tone as casual as if he were making idle talk, 'Have you heard from Henrietta Maria?'

'I have not. I've written to her, but I've received no answer.' It suddenly occurred to her to wonder if she would have told him if she had heard.

'Where did you write to her?'

Yes, my love, I'm certain of it. You are pumping me for information. 'Why would they give the children to Algernon, John? Algernon is Lord High Admiral. And besides that, he's never here, and there's talk that he's to marry soon.'

'It looks as though if there is a declaration of war, the navy will side with Parliament. As a member of his household and his sister, the children may remain here for a time. The committee will be in no hurry to move them, I think. Unless something untoward happens. Can you keep them out of sight? Limit your visitors for a while? At least, until the Nineteen Propositions is law. I know that's a lot to ask for a woman of your talents and sensibility.'

'If you mean my salon, you need not worry. There's hardly anyone left in London, anyway. And even if there were, yours is the only company I crave, John.' She gently touched his face. 'I wish that you could stay.'

But he rose to leave. 'I wish I could stay too, Lucy. More than anything. But with so much at stake . . . if you want to protect the children we must be discreet.' He looked down and picked a thread from his sleeve, not meeting her eyes. 'At least until custody is official. Parliament should not think my recommendation influenced by personal alliances. Where did you say you wrote to the Queen?'

'I didn't say. But I gave the letter to Counselor Hyde, if you must know. He said that he would put it with the King's letters. Did you come by the river?'

'No, my horse is just outside, in the kitchen garden. I need to get back before I'm missed. I knew that you would want to hear. I'll come to you when I can.'

'When will that be?'

'Soon, my love, soon.' He ran his finger down the line

of her chin, lingering on the pulse point at her throat before kissing her lightly.

Then he was gone. As she watched him ride away, a great sense of loneliness descended. She wondered, and not for the first time, just who was using who in this 'alliance.' But one thing she believed: John Pym was an honorable man, and both England and Lucy Hay were very much in need of an honorable man just now.

NO CAKE

*To all subjects north of the Trent or within 20 miles
southward: We intend to erect our Standard Royal in our
just and necessary defense, and whence we resolve to
advance forward for the suppression of the said Rebellion,
and the protection of our good subjects among them,
from the burthen of the slavery and insolence under which
they cannot but groan until they be relieved by us.*

—Charles I in his proclamation of war

12 August 1642

The King's second son was summoned from sleep by his
older brother of three years. James was dreaming of
his mother—half dream, half memory—how she had
lifted his chin when she left and with tears in her eyes
had told him to be brave. He should look after his father, she
said, and try to cheer him up when he was sad. *Maman,
please don't go.* Fighting unmanly tears, even in his dream,
for he was not yet nine years old, too young not to miss his
mother, his beautiful mother who danced and sang and even
prayed with such *joie de vivre*, his mother who still cradled
him in her arms when he cried.

With one shake of his shoulders from Charles, the princely
brother who never cried, his mother vanished. 'Leave off,
Charles,' the boy mumbled squeezing his eyes tight, trying
to bring the vision back. 'Go away.'

Another shake, this time rougher and accompanied by a slap
across his shoulders, 'Get up, lie-abed.'

'It is barely light outside,' he whined, blinking against an
encroaching dawn, all hope gone with the departed vision.
He rubbed the sleep from his eyes. The golden-haired prince

grinned down at him. He has our mother's smile, James thought, heaping irritation onto injury.

'It is already an hour past dawn. Father says we are to be dressed and in the courtyard within the hour. Wear your silk tunic and breeches. Stockings too. It is to be a ceremonial occasion.'

'It's early still. I don't want to get up,' he whined. 'It was a hard ride from Warwick and late when we got in. My valet isn't here to help me dress.'

'Dress yourself.' Charles pitched him the shiny blue satin suit of the House of Stuart. 'Grooms are scarce for warriors in the field,' he said disdainfully.

James just sat, holding the satin crumpled in his hands, and watched a beetle struggling, trapped on its back within the seam of two flagstones. This room was not a pleasant place in which to wake, he thought, bare stone walls, dank and sweating even in the early morning. No tapestries, no rugs, not even an indoor privy—just another of the dreary string of castles in which he'd awakened since their mother left. He was in no mood for Charles's silly games, just grandiose notions of heroes and battles and 'noble deeds of valor.' James wanted to scream at England's fair prince to bugger off, but with the vision of his mother still lingering and because he was in the habit of obeying his brother who one day would be king, he only pantomimed the words to Charles' back.

The beetle gained its legs, climbed out of its grave, and scuttled across the floor. The boy pondered whether God's lesser creatures were capable of valor. But what did it matter? The beetle survived to fight another day. Survival was what mattered.

'What ceremonial occasion? Where are we anyway?'

'Nottingham Castle. And the occasion is the raising of the Royal Standard. All sorts of dignitaries will be present.'

Here was some good news at last. If there were dignitaries, there might be cake.

'What dignitaries?' he asked, struggling with his hose.

'Well, Lord Digby and his regiment of horse, William Cavendish, the Earl of Newcastle, Philip Stanhope, Earl of Chesterfield and—' Charles paused to help him fasten the wide collar of Flemish lace around his little brother's neck. 'There. You look presentable enough for the second son of the King of England.'

'And who else, Charles?'

'Who? Oh. Our cousin Rupert.'

'Rupert's here?' He wasn't as fond of his Bohemian cousins as Charles. Rupert played the dashing warrior prince with too much bravado for all his reputation in the Germanic wars. But still, he was never boring, always up for merry sport in which he was sometimes willing to tolerate them. 'Did he bring Boye with him?'

'Yes, Rupert's here and yes, he brought his dog. He was here when we arrived.'

'Why didn't you tell me?'

'You were asleep. The footman had to carry you in like some big baby.'

'I am not—'

'I know. Almost nine. Soon to be a man at arms,' he said a little too mockingly for James's comfort. But it was hard to be mad at Charlie for overlong. He was always so good spirited. 'You should have seen Boye yapping at Nottingham's curs. You'd have thought the little wad of white fur as fierce as a wolfhound—held behind the ramparts of Rupert's arms, of course.'

'You should have woken me when he came,' James grumbled. 'What is the ceremony for? It is to welcome our cousin?'

'More important than that, little brother.' His eyes widened as though propped open with some great secret. 'Our father has finally decided to stand his ground. It is to be war.'

James exhaled a weary sigh. 'Another war?' Father was always so preoccupied when he was at war. 'Is it France this time? Or Spain?' Then he paused thinking of Rupert's sudden appearance. 'Father is not going to enter the German wars?'

'No. Father is too smart to be drawn into that. No. This time it's different. This time it's Parliament.'

'Oh that. You are exaggerating again, Charles. You mean a war with words.'

'No, little brother. A real fighting war. Or at the very least a skirmish.'

'Just pretend, right. Another of your games.'

'No game. For real this time.'

'I don't believe you. You are smiling? You'd be scared if it was for real.'

'It's real, I tell you. I am smiling because I am glad. The King of England cannot allow himself to be pushed around by a bunch of Roundhead Puritans and a craven gabble of Scottish rebels. That's what Maman would say if she were here.' His expression changed then from excitement to contempt, eyes flashing with anger. 'The cur of a man in charge of the arms depository at Kingston upon Hull refused Father entry under order of Parliament.'

James, fighting back tears, was about to say that he was too young to be a soldier. Charles would mock him if he saw him cry. But Charles was not looking at James. He was looking out the window, where a commotion had begun in the courtyard.

'Digby's men are already here. They are assembling. Hurry,' he threw the words over his shoulder as he ran out the door and headed for the stairwell. James followed, hopping on one booted foot as he pulled a boot on the other. Maybe it would be all right after all. Charlie seemed to think so. And then he had another thought that made him feel better. War or not. With his royal cousin here there was sure to be cake.

But there was no cake.

The crowd was small. Some among the nobles muttered about burning down the town to show the King's disfavor at his subjects' lack of support. Even the sun refused to show its face. James heard a distant rumble of thunder, but Digby's men sat bravely on their mounts whilst the horses nibbled the sparse dry grass or stamped the dusty ground, snorting their impatience.

Finally, the Royal Standard—St. George's Cross and the emblem of the Royal Arms, emblazoned above a Latin motto saying something about *Giving Caesar his Due*—was presented. But the Earls of Newcastle and Kingston, who had acquired the honor to plant the standard by a throw of the dice, could not force the pole into the baked earth. As the small crowd whispered behind their hands, the earls pecked around in the dust until finally with a hastily retrieved spade from the kitchen garden they achieved a hole.

When the drums and trumpets sounded at last and the herald read the Declaration of War, a thin shout went up, 'God save the King.' But like the bedraggled feather adorning the King's broad hat, the red standard's cloven tip hung limply in the humid air. Father looked displeased, but it was hard to know for sure. Of late he wore a general air of melancholy.

How can I be expected to carry out Mother's command to cheer Father when he no longer has the time for a game of bowls or even cribbage? And now he is at war again.

About midway through the King's speech, the gray sky squeezed out a few reluctant tears so the speech was shorter than it might have been. The lords knelt in the rain-pocked dust to kiss his father's ring and offer him their swords. The cavalrymen dismounted and, swords raised, formed two lines, shouting with wilted enthusiasm *God save King Charles*. When the heavens answered with one more rumble of thunder and a downpour, the King returned to the shelter of the castle attended by two of his advisors.

One by one the courtiers, the soldiers, and the few towns-people who had come out in support drifted away. When James did not see Charles, he trudged up the steps to his room alone, banging the tip of his ceremonial side-arm against the sweating stones in disgust. A few minutes later his brother returned, carrying Boye in his arms. He placed the wriggling poodle in James's arms and, peeling off his damp satins, reached for leggings and jerkin as he said, 'Rupert and I and some of the lords are going into town for a drink. To size up the locals. We aim to show the King's disfavor in a manner to emphasize the need for loyalty.'

His brother, putting on airs as if he were so much older and wiser and braver, quoted Rupert's words, no doubt. Their cousin was probably only letting him tag along out of charity—and because Charles might be king someday. But James said nothing, just held the small white dog, stroking its long hair. He wished he had a dog like Boye, he thought, suddenly wondering about the little spaniels left behind at Whitehall.

Who was seeing to them? His mother had taken one when she left, her favorite, his favorite too.

'You can keep company with Boye for a while, little brother. I think Rupert would like that. And, you'll be glad to know that I passed a page on the stair bringing you something to eat.' As if the small age gap between them had suddenly yawned into a great gulf.

'Aren't you hungry?'

'Rupert and I will get something at the tavern.'

The careless, cocky way he said it really irritated James, but he didn't know how to put words to it. Charles pirouetted, slashing at the air with a dagger, then pushing the dagger into a sleeve in his boot, strapped on his short sword. James scarcely heard the knock as the page entered with a covered tray and placed it on the table. Then suddenly the room was empty except for James and the little white furry dog yapping at his feet.

He removed the greasy cloth covering the tray.

No cake there, either.

Just a bowl of soup and a hunk of bread and a pear. He put the soup on the floor for the dog, who didn't seem to mind that it was cold, and bit into the pear. From the archer's window, he watched as Rupert's party thundered out of the courtyard, hoots and hollers testifying their spirits were undaunted by the now steady rain. Fools, thought James. Let them go. He didn't care.

After they had gone, he continued to watch at the window, wondering if he should go and see his father, wondering where his mother was, wondering if she missed him. He did not notice that the Royal Standard lay in the dirt, its cloven flame extinguished by the mud. Picking up the little dog, he lay down on the bed, and, curling into his loneliness, wondered what this day would mean for him.

The evening star had just made its appearance as Caroline Pendleton drove her little cart and pony into the stable yard. Something about the house, hiding itself in the purple shadows, stabbed her with foreboding. After giving the reins to the stable groom, she entered, calling William's name. She found him seated beside his desk, head thrown back against the high back of his chair, legs outstretched, eyes closed, a half-full bottle of the brew the Scots called *aqua vitae* at his elbow. The hand that held the beaker's companion cup was strangely stilled. Caroline had noticed this phenomenon before: William's occasional tremors seemed to end at the place where another's might begin. It was as though the liquor lessened some pain hard within him, freeing his mind for the work of the body.

'William,' she said softly, 'I'm home.'

He opened his eyes and smiled up at her. 'Ah, my beautiful wife returns. Is the room brighter or is it my imagination?'

'Your imagination most likely,' she said, bending to light a taper from the banked embers in the fireplace. She was aware of his eyes fastened on each movement of her body as she shared the flame with the other tapers in their sconces. 'You are in a strange mood. Shall I tell cook to serve supper. She was plucking a chicken for stewing with dumplings when I left.' She brushed her lips lightly, affectionately against his forehead.

'Not just yet,' he said pulling her forward to kiss her full on the mouth, a long lingering kiss, a kiss that tasted of the *aqua vitae*. When he finally released her, he motioned to the settee opposite, his voice a little ragged around the edges, yet sharp with purpose, 'Sit down, I have something to tell you,' he said. 'And some instructions.'

He drew himself up straight, filling the chair. He was a tall man, a strong man, the kind of man a woman could depend on, Caroline thought, reminding herself how grateful she should be. She noticed among the neat arrangement on his desk, a new addition, its seal freshly broken but still affixed. The waxen image of a warrior king, mounted and taller in the saddle than in real life, brandished his sword for battle. She could just make out the salutation, 'To our trusty and well-beloved knight, Sir William Pendleton.'

A beloved knight whom he has never met, Caroline thought. She asked, 'Is that—?'

His fingers flicked at the letter, the silver mount of his lapis ring scraping against the parchment. 'It is a—' he paused, draining the glass before continuing, 'a request from his Majesty.'

She paused, gathering breath. 'What request?'

'A request for support from a sovereign unjustly under siege.'

The shadows in the room closed in around her, choking her voice to a whisper. 'What kind of support?'

'The usual: Provisions, saddles, pistols, muskets, pikes. Justice Powell and I have pooled our resources and will comply as best we can.' Shaking his head like a man shaking off a dream, he added, 'Parliament is mustering forces in East Anglia and Kent. The King must defend himself against that kind of unholy insurrection. And, we might as well face the sure knowledge that as a knight of the realm, I will be called to join the fight.' He cleared his throat, prelude to the importance of his next pronouncement. 'That eventuality is what I want to talk to you about.'

'Oh, William. Must we?'

'We must,' he said, his voice strong and sure. 'Now listen carefully. Pay attention to what I'm telling you.'

And then he began to talk about how he'd taken in no new wool inventory in preparation—the barns were empty—and he'd entered into no new contracts that she would have to fill. There were some accounts owing, and the receipts should be enough to keep her in ready money to run the household and pay the servants on the next quarter day He showed her the ledger where she should enter the receipts, and if she should run short he'd arranged for the local grocer and butcher to honor her custom until his return. She need not worry about the livestock. He'd sold it all, except his prize breeding pair of Merino sheep from Spain. These he had relocated to the barn and its fenced pasture. Parliament was already scavenging the countryside south and east, butchering any livestock in open pasture. If soldiers should show up demanding money or provisions, she should plead that this holding was a lease-hold of his worship Squire Richard Powell of Forest Hill and therefore under the King's protection.

She just stared at him, her mind spinning. *This was real. How soon would his summons come?*

'Caroline, are you listening?'

She nodded, trying to concentrate on his words, trying to remember everything he was saying as he explained that he had ordered extra provisions to be laid in the back room of the cellar and hidden a cache of coin in a secret drawer in his desk. Twisting around in his chair, he showed her how to press down on the facing, while lifting up simultaneously with his thumbs.

He was just being scrupulously careful as always. Always an abundance of caution.

'Now you try it,' he said, motioning for her, his tone intense.

Her hands trembled. He waited patiently. The panel sprang open on the third attempt. 'Again,' he said, and 'again,' and again and again, until she performed the function with ease.

He had dismissed the livestock handlers and wool packers, he continued, but she could trust the steward. He would not leave a musket with him. Who knew where a man's loyalties lay in these times? Instead, he was going to leave with her one of the pair of his Spanish pistols and tomorrow he would teach her how to use it.

He paused and poured himself another swallow of the liquid. The candlelight glowed bravely against the encroaching darkness. A servant shuffled in quietly and stirred the embers to counter the slight chill that came at night, even in August, then lit the remaining tapers.

When the servant had gone she said, endeavoring to keep the tremor from her voice though she scarcely had breath enough for the words, 'You were only recently knighted. Surely you will not be among the first to be called. His majesty may be satisfied with the provisions you are sending.'

He waved the letter in a gesture of dismissal. A residue of hard wax, the color of dried blood, dropped on the fine gray worsted of his tunic. Silly to read it as an omen, she thought as he brushed it away. Foolish fancy. Don't be alarmed, Caroline. There is no real news here after all.

'If it is to be war, Caroline, every man who is not bearing arms with Parliament will be called to show his loyalty.'

'And you are loyal.' The words echoed harshly, more accusation than tribute.

'I am a man of honor, Caroline. I am loyal to my wife—and to my king.'

Thinking of Arthur, she bit back a rejoinder about a seeming reversal of priorities, then dropped her head, so that he could not see the water pooling in her eyes. *No news here. Not really.*

Tilting her chin up gently, he tried to smile. 'But it may not be tomorrow. Or even next week. I am a man who likes to be prepared. You know that.'

He studied her with a mixture of regret and longing and affection, giving the lie to his reassuring words. He did not expect the war to last long, he said. In any event he would not likely be more than a couple of days' ride away and would come home when he could get leave. Then he added, but if she should not hear from him, if she was afraid or distressed, she was to lock up the house and return to Forest Hill. The squire would not be called since he was a magistrate and would be needed to keep order in Oxfordshire. They had spoken and Caroline was to be reassured the squire would welcome and protect her as before.

'Now, then, wife,' he said, 'enough talk of unpleasant things. Let's see if we can lay waste to cook's stewed chicken.' The hand that refilled his cup did not tremble.

That night, after he had eaten a hearty supper though she had scarcely touched her own, after the doors were secured, the tapers extinguished, and they lay in the large four-poster bed, he did not turn his back to her with a cursory good-night but made love to her with a lack of restraint he seldom showed. And when he had finished, allowing, as he never did, his seed to spill inside her, he rolled onto his back and fell fast asleep.

For a long time, Caroline lay awake, staring at the darkness above her head, seeing nothing but the moving images her imagination conjured: images of blood and flashing swords, the air around filled with smoke and screams of the fighting and the dying. She lay very still, not wanting to awaken the gentle man beside her, thinking soon, too soon, he would not be sleeping beside her. Aware of her chest rising and falling with each careful breath, she wanted to move onto her side to spoon against him. But she shut her eyes and lay as still as any corpse, not wanting to disturb his seed inside her.

DEFENSELESS DOORS

Captain or Colonel, or Knight in Arms,
Whose chance on these defenceless dores may sease,
If ever deed of honour did thee please,
Guard them, and him within protect from harms,
He can requite thee, for he knows the charms
That call Fame on such gentle acts as these
And he can spred thy Name o'er Lands and Seas . . .

—From a sonnet by John Milton, posted upon his door

November 1642

Isolated with the children at Syon House outside of London, Lucy Hay didn't get much of a warning. She was otherwise occupied when the message came. A misty rain had fallen for the last two days. The children were restless from staying inside the salon and when the rain stopped Elizabeth had pressed to go outside.

'It is too muddy and damp,' Lucy answered. 'Henry has a runny nose. We cannot do it now. Maybe later.'

'When later? You promised to take us up on the hill, so we could see across the river to Richmond Park, but every time you have some excuse.' Elizabeth's lips formed an accusing pout. 'We lived there once. It is a grand palace. Not like this. Father used to take me riding in the deer park.' She gazed out the window at the shrouded lawn and sighed, 'I miss my father.' She looked as though she would burst into tears at any minute, this little girl who prided herself on her bravery.

'But, Princess Elizabeth, we could not see it anyway. We would need a clear day.' Lucy dredged through her mind for some distraction. 'But I think I know a place where maybe, just maybe, if the mists lighten—no promises, mind you—we can see across the river. And we don't have to get all wet and nasty trying.'

The child's face visibly brightened. 'Henry will come too. I wish him to see where I lived before he was born. He probably only remembers St. James's Palace. We shall go now.'

The little boy, playing with wooden blocks on the floor, stood up suddenly and held up his arms to Lucy. 'Henry go.'

She picked him up and wiped his nose with her already damp handkerchief, then balancing him on her hip, they carefully ascended the narrow stairs the servants used.

'I have never seen a place like this before. Why are all these rooms so tiny and this passage between so narrow?'

'This is where cook and the housemaids live.'

'It is not very grand, and it smells funny. Do Carter and Tom live here too?'

'No. Carter and Tom live on the ground floor.'

'Why did the other footmen leave? And your lady of the chamber, did she leave also? I don't know why you ever left the Queen's House for such a place as this. Nurse said that Syon House is just an old abbey ruin.'

'She did, did she?' Lucy shifted Henry to her other hip and pointed to an arch of light on the floor beneath the vaulted window. 'Look, Princess. If we are going to see Richmond Palace we should try now.'

Elizabeth rushed to the window. She stood on tiptoe, craning her neck. 'But I am not tall enough. I cannot see,' she wailed.

Lucy set Henry down, but he still clung to her skirts, the only familiar thing in this place. 'Help me drag this stool, Henry.' The child transferred his chubby hand to the edge of the wooden stool and then sat on it. Lucy pulled both stool and boy beneath the window, then stooped and picked up the child. She pointed out the window. As if on cue the grayed-out sun shed its light on the great palace. It was a distant view, but clearly visible like a misty painting in the distance.

'I can see the turrets. Aren't they beautiful? They go all the way to the clouds. See, Henry.' Elizabeth's voice was breathless with excitement. 'The side with the fourteen turrets—that was Charles'—our brother's rooms. They were grand. And see those tiny little dots on the great lawn. That is probably the red deer.'

Ignoring his sister as usual, Henry wriggled down to explore the corridor, with Lucy following behind to keep him out of mischief.

'They were not like the forest deer,' the girl continued, not caring that he was no longer listening. 'They were so tame, Father would let me feed them from my hand.'

The wistfulness in her voice brought tears to Lucy eyes. She let the girl stand there, on tiptoe, looking out that window, until the sunlight thinned.

As they were picking their way down a darkening stairway— Lucy had to carry a lamp in one hand and hold on to Henry with the other—they encountered old Carter coming up. He looked startled to see them, but said with his characteristic quiet dignity, 'I have looked everywhere for you, my lady.' He reached into his pocket and withdrew an envelope. 'This message came for you some time ago. The courier said that it is urgent.'

Lucy's heart jumped when he put it in her hand. The Great Seal of Parliament. 'Carter, take the children to the salon. See that they are fed before nurse puts them down for the night.'

He nodded gravely. As Lucy rushed down the narrow stairs, she was only half aware of the princess talking to him animatedly about Richmond Palace. 'The countess said that we could come again. Every day, if we wanted to.'

'Did she now?'

'Maybe we can even take a boat to the park and feed the deer.'

Not until she reached the privacy of her bedchamber did Lucy break the seal.

John was warning her that her cousin Robert Devereux, Earl of Essex, was on his way to Brentford with two regiments to turn back the King's forces assembled on Hounslow Heath. It looked to be a battle with many casualties, but it was necessary to prevent the King's army progressing into London. He did not think the fighting would get as far as Syon House, but if she should come under pressure from Rupert of the Rhine and his forces she should use her former loyalty to the Queen as leverage.

'Under no circumstances mention the children and keep them out of sight. You and they are safer if their whereabouts are not broadcast. My darling, I wish I could bring you to Westminster and keep you safe in my arms. But should the King's forces prevail, you might fare better there than here as I suspect you have not burnt all your bridges and your friends would treat you kindly for the sake of your former loyalty.' It ended with his instruction to burn the letter, which she promptly did.

It wasn't long after she retired for the night that she heard, or imagined she heard, the sound of cannon fire in the distance. She lay awake, dozing infrequently. Just after dawn she heard the thundering of horses beating their way up Syon Road, a great company of them. She rang urgently for Carter, who came quickly.

'I fear we are about to have unwelcome visitors, Carter. Wake the children's nurse, and you and she take them up to the servants' quarters. Stay with them and see to their needs. Do your best to keep them quiet. Just tell them you are taking them up for another look at Richmond Palace.'

'But what about milady? Who will protect you?'

'Just go quickly, Carter. Do as I say and don't let them come down until I come to fetch them. I have my wits to protect me and friends in both camps.'

Lucy watched anxiously as the old man shuffled off doing his best with his waffling gait. *Please God, protect this house and all who are in it, protect these children. They have nothing to do with this hideous war*, she breathed as she dressed.

She heard Elizabeth's thin little-girl voice as they headed for the stairs. 'But it is very early, Carter. What about morning prayers and breakfast?'

'We can get a better look early, your grace, and the nurse has gone to the kitchen to get us some breakfast. We can picnic in the attic.'

'But is the countess not coming with us?'

'She will be along later. Now we need to hurry so we catch

the early eastern light. And go quietly. We don't want to disturb any of the maids who might still be abed.'

Poor Carter. If she could not get rid of the soldiers, he had a task before him. He could be stuck with them for hours. Peeking behind the drapery on the west window, she saw two lines of cavalry riding up Syon Road. At least fifty horses followed by two wagons carrying cannon. As they drew closer, she let the drapery fall back in place. King's scarlet or Parliament's buff? She couldn't tell until they got closer. Maybe they were headed toward Turnham Green and would not stop. As she hurried to be near the door she was remembering that she should have removed the children's toys from the salon. She stood in the hall, waiting for a pounding on the door to see whose soldiers she would have to cajole.

It came quickly. 'Open in the name of the King.'

She stepped out onto the porch, trying to look surprised.

Two men with red sashes and muskets already on the ground. King's men. And the King's nephew was dismounting. In his arms he carried a familiar small white dog.

She dropped him an attenuated curtsy. 'Your royal highness, welcome to Syon House.'

He looked at her quizzically then grinned in recognition.

'I remember you,' he said. 'You were at court. One of the Queen's ladies. Countess of Carlisle.'

'I am flattered you remembered, your grace. It has been a long time. You were hardly more than a boy.'

'How could I forget. Every man at court—and some of us boys—knew who Lucy Hay was.'

Her palm itched with wanting to slap him. He had always been cheeky. 'Your mother, Elizabeth, is she well?'

He shrugged. 'As well as a queen without a country can be.'

'Yes, an unfortunate outcome. Theirs was a holy cause.'

'Your queen did not think it holy. Probably why my uncle did not offer aid to his sister's struggle.'

'Ah, but in spite of that you have come to the King's aid. I am sure he is very grateful. What brings you to my door? I'm afraid I have already divested myself of my most prized valuables in the Royal cause. I am but a poor widow with little left to give.'

He laughed. 'But you own a great castle in Ireland.'

Even she could hear the bitterness in her laugh. 'There is not much left in Ireland undamaged by the uprisings.'

'Do not worry, Countess. Minimal damage will happen here. At least not from us. We might even afford some protection. The Roundheads are notorious for their looting.'

Lucy stifled a laugh. This from a man who was reputed to plunder without mercy.

'I am sure as a friend of the Crown you will not mind if we put a few musket men on your outside wall. And maybe a cannon or two. We are on our way to join the King's forces mustering at Turnham Green. I think the Roundheads may be planning to bring a barge or more loaded with arms and men upriver.'

She nodded in assent. 'It is my duty to serve my beloved sovereign any way I can. I hope the cannon will be positioned far enough away that the house will not be damaged if Parliament's men return fire.'

'If they do, the fire will probably be coming up from the river. Not within very close range. We will position them on the garden wall.'

Then as if remembering something, he asked if she was alone.

Is he thinking about John Pym? Does he know that Essex is my cousin? Has he heard about the children?

'Yes, I am quite alone, except for a few servants. We are not well provisioned, but cook can probably scare up something for your soldiers. How many have you?'

'You needn't bother, we broke camp before daylight and are anxious to make Turnham Green by noon.'

'Give my love to the Queen when next you see her.'

He nodded and to her great relief was turning to go when the little dog leaped from his arms and scurried through the door behind her. He bolted down the hall and in the direction of the beige door leading to the back stairs. Lucy's heart nearly stopped. But at Rupert's whistle the dog turned sharply and ran back. In his mouth he was carrying a cloth doll and ragging it back and forth as though it were a bunny he had just captured. Lucy laughed picked him up, doll and all. 'You must give it back, Boye,' she said in her most coaxing voice. 'It belongs to my chamber maid's young niece.' The dog growled lightly and let go. She handed him back to Rupert, who was looking at the doll with a questioning expression on his face. 'I can't believe you carry him into battle with you,' she said to distract him.

'I can't believe you remembered his name.' He rubbed the dog's head. 'He's my good luck charm. But he's not the original. Not the one you remember. This one is the smartest. He's learned to raise his leg whenever he hears King Pym's name.'

Such juvenile humor, Lucy thought. But the boy never was one for serious thought. It was all a game to him. The war. The bloodshed.

'That's what we call John Pym. You know the MP who is behind all the rebels in Parliament. Do you know him?'

'I was introduced to him once. Briefly,' she said, glancing over his shoulder at the open door.

Without waiting for a command, the men were already taking the wagons across her lawn, tearing wide ruts. A dozen soldiers at a nod from him led their horses and packs down to the garden wall and took up guard positions. She wondered what else they might have done, what liberties they would take with her property and her person if they knew of her alliance with John Pym.

After Rupert had mounted his horse and led his men away in the direction of Twickenham, she climbed the stairs to relieve Carter, breathing a little prayer of thanks and carrying with her a sudden and very personal sympathy for others who were less well connected. That night she slept in the children's room trying to comfort them against the sounds of musket fire and cannonballs raining down on the river below. She would not learn until weeks later how those cannons had been employed and how many lives had been lost.

WHAT CAUSE FOR CELEBRATION?

On this day a fast and feast do both jostle together and the question is which should take place in our affection . . . (the children) may be so addicted to their toys and Christmas sports that they will not be weaned from them.

—Thomas Fullerton delivering a fast day sermon on
Holy Innocents' Day, December 1642

25 December 1642

'Mistress Powell's roast goose was delicious,' Caroline said, snuggling deeper into the beaver rug that William had tucked around her.

A light Christmas snow had started to fall, frosting the little mare's harness. She put her head on her husband's shoulder, luxuriating in the strong, solid feel of him. It had been two months since she told him about the baby. She had waited until she was sure the child was growing inside her. By her count she was a little over four months. Already she was wearing her loosest garments. As they sat at board, Mistress Powell had whispered that she had some clothes that might suit Caroline for the next few months. She was welcome to them. God knew she hoped to never need them again, she'd said smiling at the gaggle of children around her table.

William had said he was pleased when she told him, but she noticed he was more preoccupied. He worked harder than ever now to get their 'affairs in order,' sitting with his books and ledgers until late in the night, often riding far afield in the day to collect accounts still owing. The new plan was that if he should be called to the King's service, she should go immediately to stay with the Powells until he returned, taking with her the contents of the secret drawer. But with each passing day her anxiety lessened. There had already been fighting at Edgehill with some heavy losses on both sides and still he had not been called.

'That's a good sign, isn't it, William?' she had asked.

He had answered with a smile and a wink, that maybe they thought he was too old, but what did they know?

'Or maybe they think you've paid enough with all the money and arms you've provided. I certainly think so,' she had answered. Then he'd gently chastised her for the resentment in her voice, saying they all had to do their part, reassuring her that he would take care of 'my wife and my son.' Sons, she'd wanted to yell at him, wanting to ask if he would someday throw away the son, or daughter, she carried in her belly, to satisfy some misplaced loyalty. But she did not.

'I was glad to see you enjoying your food for a change,' he said. 'I take that as a sign that the sickness is finally over.'

She laughed. 'Yes, I would say that is a sign. I could have eaten another helping but I didn't want to appear too greedy.'

'You should have signaled me; I would have slipped you some of mine.'

'You are a good husband. But I dare say neither the babe nor I needed it.'

The wind picked up and William put one arm around her, pulling her closer for warmth, flicking the reins with his other wrist. 'The bumping of the carriage over these frozen ruts is not good for the child. I'm going to take the shortcut road through the woods. It won't be quite so rough across a carpet of dead leaves.'

The snow was falling harder now. Grateful for the sheltering canopy over the carriage, she snuggled closer as they entered the little path through the silent winter woods. 'Look, William. How beautiful. Every branch has a wide lace collar to rival the King's.'

'This path is dangerous. Too many robbers, though less so in winter when there is scarce cover. Don't you ever take this shortcut. In any season.'

'It was good to see Mary. She seemed quite content to celebrate Christmas without her husband.'

'I can't think how that situation is going to resolve itself with a husband in London and Mary at home with her parents. I tried to ask the Squire about it, but he just brushed it off as if it were of no consequence. Quite content to have his daughter at home without the irritating Puritan he apparently despises.'

'Well, it was all his doing. Did he not tell you that he practically sold her to Mr. Milton to satisfy a debt? What's she to do now, just stay at Forest Hill, an aging,'—she looked for the right word and finally settled on—'*spinster* until her parents die from old age?'

'The squire never mentioned the debt to me. Probably too proud. Though given our long history together, I was surprised when he asked for the rent upfront. It makes some sense now that under financial pressure he might think he could stomach his daughter's marriage to a Puritan. But don't worry overmuch about Mary, Caroline. She seems content. It is not as though she will be destitute. Her brothers will inherit the estate from the Forest Hill lands and forest rights not to mention the Wheatley incomes from their mother's portion. She will always have a home and hearth to tend.'

But not her hearth. Did he not realize that a good marriage with children was the only real currency a woman would ever have? But she held her tongue.

'The squire is just going through a rough patch. An estate like Forest Hill is a money mire. That's why I'd rather rent than own.'

'There may not be anything left to inherit after this awful war, William. And even if there is, what then? Not being able to ever marry or have children? Their marriage was never consummated, you know. Mary told me that. Do you think she could get an annulment?'

'Maybe,' but William's attention had snared on something in the distance. They were emerging from the woods. She could already see the smoke of home curling from the chimney. And something else, less comforting.

'It looks like we have company,' he said, his voice tight. He flicked the little whip, spurring the horse on.

As they approached, Caroline could see two men, King's men by their Stuart livery. One held the horse's reins as the other dismounted and approached the front portal.

'Oh, William,' she said, her chest tightening.

'Don't assume the worst, Caroline. It could be just another request for money and arms.'

'Of which we have neither.'

'I'm going to take the carriage around to the side. You go in by the kitchen door.' As he helped her down, he gave her hand a squeeze. 'Go warm yourself by the hearth in the kitchen and try not to worry. It's not good for the child.'

Opening the kitchen door, he motioned for the stable-boy and cook's helper to punch up the fire, and straightening his shoulders went up the short flight of stairs where the messenger would be waiting in the hall. Caroline was huddled by the great hearth, scarcely breathing, when he returned almost immediately. One look at his ashen face and she knew.

'When?' she asked.

'I'm to report to General Fairfax in Oxford in three days.'

But William did not report in three days. In the wee hours of the morning Caroline began to bleed and William lost a second son to the war. Squire Powell sent a messenger to Oxford begging his Majesty's forbearance that Sir William Pendleton should be delayed. When he rode out a week later, Caroline's body was recovering. But her spirit? That was another matter altogether.

Lucy Hay surveyed the great hall with a critical eye. Syon House was not Hampton Court, not Whitehall or Wilton House, but its hall was impressive. The house had not suffered much in that long night of cannon and musket fire from the river—only one broken window on the second floor and some gaps in the garden wall. For her Christmas dinner she could have chosen the more intimate, more elegant setting of the salon, but Lucy had not entertained in the salon since she'd sacrificed Wentworth's diamond earrings. Not a happy memory.

And then there were the children. Now that they could no longer spend time outdoors they had quite taken over the salon. Spinning tops, whirligigs, and other youthful detritus lay scattered about. The gilded chairs, covered with plain linen to protect their damask upholstery, were stacked against the walls so that Elizabeth and Henry had room to play. Lucy had not

the energy or inclination to restore it to its pre-child state. Nor
did she have the heart to banish her young charges. They had
been banished enough for a lifetime.

It was only mid-afternoon, and the light was already fading
to gloom. 'Carter, I think we shall need to light all the tapers,'
she said as she flicked away a burnt cinder from the rosy-apple
mouth of a merely respectable boar's head.

The feast was not up to her usual standards, but given her
brother's miserliness and her lack of staff, she had acquitted
her hostess duties bravely enough. All the able-bodied male
servants had volunteered or been conscripted for military
service. The only real footman left was old Carter, limping
along, assisted by his half-wit grandson, who could not tell a
salt cellar from a silver salver. If Parliament needed musket-
fodder, would it not have been more efficient to take these
two who could not together make a whole servant? She would
have gladly bargained two for one—especially when the one
was her favorite footman. Robbie knew how to put a sparkle
on a serving spoon. Knew too how to bow with just enough
humility so as not to be considered cheeky. (Well with that
wicked wink, maybe a little cheeky, but nothing that she could
not handle with a lift of her chin and an icy glare.)

Watching old Carter grimace with pain as he stretched to
light the tallest tapers, she instantly repented that thought.
There were other measures of a man besides—well, loyalty
must surely count for something. The thought about cannon-
fodder, that was unworthy of a good Presbyterian woman.
More than unworthy. Shameful. Lucy had, on more than one
occasion, envied the Queen's convenient confessional.

A clattering sound signaled another casualty to her
cupboard—the third one in as many hours. She gave the boy
her most long-suffering smile, an act of contrition, though
she knew it was neither a real smile nor act of contrition. There
was not enough contrition in the world for some thoughts.

'Don't worry about it, Tom,' she consoled. 'Just take the ladle
to the kitchen and ask cook for another.'

Despite Carter's limitations, the chamber soon glowed with
a multitude of softly flickering lights. Perhaps Algernon would
not complain about the cost of so much beeswax—not with

his new bride coming to Syon House for the first time. Cook had done her best with her attenuated staff. Surrounding the burnt offering of boar's head was a carved loin of beef and silver dishes heaped high with puddings and tarts, both savory and sweet, even a pie of lark's tongues, though she suspected that bubbling beneath its golden crust was more leek than lark. (Who was left to tend the traps?) She hoped the food was plentiful enough; even this much was a feat given such short notice. It would be just like Algernon to spring unexpected guests.

In honor of the holy day Lucy had arrayed herself in a gown of pale green silk and scattered other touches of green about the great chamber: bunches of holly fastened below the wall sconces, a great wreath of it gracing the stone chimney, ivy twining through the candelabra. And in expectation of the most important among Algernon's notable guests—at least to Lucy—a pinch of mistletoe adorned a velvet ribbon circling her neck.

The flames in their sconces flickered and damp air entered the hall. From the antechamber Carter's nasal whine was followed by men's low voices. Her ear picked out one special voice. He had come as promised. But she had thought he would. If not for her own eager self, which had proved not enough of late to pull him away from his intrigues, there was the added incentive of the distinguished dinner guests. She greeted them, surprised to find her brother unaccompanied by any female companion. Perhaps his new wife was coming later in her own carriage.

'Here, Master Pym, let me take your cloak,' she said, flicking rain drops from his simple brown mantle.

Averting her gaze, lest it linger too long, she handed the cloak to Carter.

After the most perfunctory of greetings to his sister, Lord Percy led the two sober-faced gentlemen in, indicating with a nod and swift motion of his hand who should sit where. He seated himself at the head. Lucy took her seat at the other end of the table, feeling suddenly uncomfortable, as though she had barged in on a private council meeting. Hardly the occasion for which she had prepared. She wished she could just

flick her wrists and say *begone* to her brother and her cousin.
How lovely it would be to spend this day with John, alone
together, feasting, drinking, as though the world around them
was not falling apart. Maybe later, when the others were gone.
Her fingers touched the velvet ribbon at her throat, which now
seemed foolishly chosen.

'Algernon,' she said in a bright voice, falsely cheerful even
to her ears. 'Where is the lovely Lady Northumberland? I was
so looking forward to greeting your bride. Is she coming later?
Should we wait dinner service for her?'

Algernon raised his chin in the dismissive way he'd acquired
sometime between the death of his first wife and this
marriage to his second, an admiral's persona she supposed.
My wife begs forgiveness for her absence but pleads her
excessive duties at Northumberland House. She says she
hopes you will attend us there sometime soon. When it is safe
to travel again of course.'

A snub? Or just bad manners. The Howards had never been
known for their diplomacy—or their loyalty. Why should her
new sister-in-law be any different? 'I was looking forward to
entertaining her,' Lucy said, 'I had not noticed it was not safe
to travel. Only this morning, I had a visit from Lady Pembroke
inquiring about the children's activities.'

Pym's eyes widened in alarm, those intelligent gray eyes
whose blue-veined lids she had kissed. 'My dear Lady Carlisle,
I hope you satisfied her that the children were not celebrating
inappropriately.'

Lucy restrained a twitching smile. 'I assure you, Master
Pym, all of you,' she added, her gaze including the others, 'no
Capuchin has darkened the doors of Syon House.'

She could tell by the anxiety playing around his brow that
he was wondering whether she was lying or had smuggled in
some French Papist to recite a Latin mass. But of course, she
had not. She didn't know where to find one. Most had fled to
France when the Queen left. But she had done the next worst
thing. First, she had tried to placate the devout little princess
by promising they would celebrate their own mass. God would,
of course, understand—and Maman too. There was precedent,
Lucy had argued. At the Last Supper there had been no priest.

The girl had answered, jaw jutting upward, eyes squinting to a suspicious slant. That would not do at all. She needed to confess, and she could never confess to anybody but a priest and besides the disciples did not need a priest because Jesus was the high priest and he was there with them.

What kind of a sin could press so hard on the innocent soul of a seven-year-old? Finally, helpless before the child's pious distress—and somewhat ambushed by her theologically advanced argument—Lucy had relented. In the end she'd smuggled in a Catholic recusant priest with the help of Carter, who had whispered to Lucy that he had an uncle who still practiced the old religion of Queen Mary,' and if her ladyship thought it seemly—well, he could probably procure a priest. In the strictest secrecy. It was not seemly, of course, and dangerous. What if the priest talked? Parliament would be outraged if they should learn of it. Maybe even take the children away from Percy custody. But as instructed, Carter had brought the priest to the house unaware of his young penitent's identity. Before she let him visit the royal nursery she had secured the Papist's indignant reassurance of confidentiality. The secrets of the confessional were sacrosanct, he'd answered.

John's warning gaze lingered on hers a moment longer than necessary. Lucy looked away first, motioning for Carter and Tom to begin serving. Her cousin, Robert Devereux, third Earl of Essex, and newly appointed captain-general of Parliament's forces—one of the five 'flown birds' for whom she had betrayed her king—turned in Lucy's direction. With each word his pointed beard penetrated the lace of his old-fashioned starched ruff, the kind his father had worn to the block. 'Was Lady Pembroke satisfied, then?' he asked. Before she could answer, he asked, 'Are we to be allowed to see the children tonight?'

'Only if you insist, my lords. They are very tired after our morning prayers as you might imagine, it being a different ceremony than what they are used to, and with Lady Pembroke's unexpected visit. But yes, Lady Pembroke was quite satisfied—as far as Lady Pembroke could ever be satisfied.'

All three men nodded and smiled in acknowledgement of that lady's reputation, but Algernon raised an eyebrow and inquired, 'Ceremony, Lucy? What ceremony?' His voice was demanding, reminding her that he was master here.

'We may still celebrate our Lord's birth, I hope, gentlemen. It would be a sorry thing if we could not. It was just a simple prayer, a reading from Isaiah, then from the gospel of Luke. You cannot have forgotten, brother, the babe in the manger, the angel's announcement of his divine birth,' she said archly. 'Father used to read it to us when we were with him in Tower Prison. Oh, I forget—only baby brother Henry and I were forced to live with the old wizard, while you and sister Dorothy celebrated at Alnwick.' She glanced down at her plate then, not quite able to deliver the straightforward lie, not with John Pym present, and added, 'And the Princess did read it in English.'

This seemed to satisfy the three worthies at her table: Her brother, her cousin, and her lover, in their postures as Lord High Admiral of the Navy, General and Chief Commander of Parliament's army and the most influential man in Parliament. Or had she got it backwards and they were not posturing at all and it was their roles as brother, cousin, and lover that were subordinate. No matter. Whatever relationship was dominant at whatever moment, each of them was in her debt. But if growing up in the confines of the Tower had taught Lucy Hay anything, it was that both family loyalty and Cupid's strings could be as easily broken as a virgin's maidenhead. What a clamor would ensue if these three knew that Lady Pembroke, who had come to spy for her husband, had entered the front door of Syon House even as the Papist priest was being ushered down the servants' stairs by Carter.

'Mister Pym, I see your cup is empty.' She motioned for the boy, watching relieved that though he moved clumsily around the table refilling each cup, he did not spill the wine. Half-wit, he may be, but he was doing his best and didn't deserve abuse by her guests. He refilled her cup too, and she lifted it to her lips, content for a moment to be ignored as the men ate heartily, talking Parliament business between bites. There had really been no time 'til now to ponder her good fortune that the morning's activities had not been discovered. Lady Pembroke would have gone screaming to Parliament had she encountered any evidence of the priest. Upon entering, her gaze had not lingered on the children, but darted restlessly about the room, looking for signs of some Romish altar, or some little detail to prejudice Parliament against the Percy guardianship in favor of her husband. Lucy's heart had leapt into her throat when she saw that the Princess still clutched the Latin prayer book in her hand. But Princess Elizabeth, with a grace and understanding beyond her years, suddenly dropped to the floor as if to retrieve a doll that had fallen there, and rising pushed the offending missile under the bed with her toe. Lady Herbert was too busy gazing at the painted miniature on the table beside the girl's bed to notice.

'Do you think that appropriate, Lady Carlisle?'

'What, my lady? Is what appropriate?' But Lucy had known what she meant. Beside her the girl froze, like a fawn at the edge of the forest.

'The picture of that . . . that French woman. England is well rid of her.'

Princess Elizabeth lifted her chin.

'It is a picture of the child's mother,' Lucy said quietly, placing one arm lightly around Elizabeth's tense shoulders. 'It eases her loneliness. Would you, a Christian woman, take that small comfort from her?'

The woman paused, muttered defensively, 'Perhaps not. At least not until she gets used to the idea that her mother is not coming back.'

Lucy longed to slap the hateful harridan. 'My lady, you are quite mistaken in your characterization. The Queen has not 'deserted' her children. She has only gone to Holland to visit with the family into which the Princess Royal has recently married. A mother's natural duty, I would think. Now, may I offer you some refreshment or must you take your leave?'

Lady Pembroke pressed her lips into a thin line, then answered. 'No. I'll be going. But I shall come again. Lord Pembroke is very interested in the children's welfare. I will be frank with you, Lady Carlisle. My husband thinks the royal children would be better looked after at Wilton House. The King brought Prince James and Prince Charles there to hunt, before—'

'You may remember, my lady, though you may not, since you were seldom at court, the children are also very familiar with me. I frequently played with them in their mother's presence. Before the present unpleasantness of course. They are happy here. And well protected from all—' she paused, 'injurious influences.'

Lucy could tell by the stiffening of her guest's spine that her barb about court had hit home. John had said that the only reason Philip Herbert had sided with Parliament was because he'd been unable to find sufficient favor with the King. The woman pinched her lips together and asked with fake nonchalance. 'What of the dear older boys, Lady Carlisle, do you know of their whereabouts? Are they with their father?'

Lucy shrugged. 'I am sure you know more of that than I. You might ask your husband, I am a mere woman, hardly privy to Parliament's intelligence.'

After the snoop had left it had taken half an hour to soothe the child, to tell her that of course her mother was coming back. Hadn't they received a message from her only last week, telling them how she could not wait to be reunited with them? By the time Elizabeth had sniffled into silence, her little brother had awakened in his cradle and was wailing for Maman too. Before Lucy could rush off to array herself in the green silk, she'd had to tell the children a story about The Hague—a made-up adventure about a heroic Queen named Henrietta who missed her beloved children so much on Christmas Day that she vowed she would never spend another Christmas without them.

Carter placed a confection on her plate, star-shaped and sparingly dusted with golden flakes. Lucy returned her attention to the task at hand, whispering that he should remind the kitchen to send the children the marzipan she had ordered for them. She listened to the political chatter, trying to find her way back into the conversation. Apparently, her guests never realized her attention had wandered. They were talking war, hardly noticing as Carter removed their empty plates and placed the confections in front of them.

'Congratulations on turning back the King, Robert,' Algernon said. 'At least he and his troops were denied entrance into

London. It was a stroke of pure genius to retreat and join forces with the Trained Bands.'

'More fortune's stroke than genius, Lord Percy,' Essex admitted. 'After the casualties we suffered at Edgehill, we had no choice but to retreat. I'm afraid our troops took out some of their frustration on the way.'

'I read in the news books about the looting of Buntford.' John's tone did not sound congratulatory. 'I hope the report was exaggerated. If we are to gain the support of the surrounding towns, you need to discipline your men, my lords. And feed them well so they don't have to plunder to survive.'

Essex bristled at the blunt criticism. 'Where do you suggest I procure the stores to feed them well, or at all? Is Parliament prepared to vote the revenue?'

'Parliament is set to levy a new tax on the populace of London. It will be a hardship, but it is inevitable. If not now, soon,' John promised.

Lucy's carefully planned Christmas feast was turning into a contentious strategy session. The three most powerful men in England right here at her table and none took any more notice of her than if she were a serving maid. She would not be ignored. 'So you turned the King's forces back, cousin. What about Charles? Did he join the fight?'

'The King was there. And the young prince and his brother James as well.'

'The King took his children into battle? That seems unlikely.'

'Not unlikely at all when you think of it, Lucy. They did not, of course, actually engage. But young Charles is old enough to learn the ways of war. And I expect the King's nephew is teaching him. Rupert was right there, trying to live up to his reputation, striking a warrior's gallant pose in the saddle, shouting commands this way and that.' Essex shook his head and added, 'I must be getting old. He looks hardly more than a youth himself.'

'He's twenty-three and very fond of his uncle Charles,' Lucy said. Then added casually. 'He was here, you know.'

Now she had their attention.

'Here? At Syon House?' her brother asked in alarm. 'You saw him?'

'I spoke with him. Those were his musketeers firing on you from the garden wall.'

'My God, Lucy. Do you know that we lost two barges that night just below here? Scuttled by those brave soldiers under fire, most of whom drowned in the Thames, to keep Rupert's men from getting their slimy hands on the heavy cannon and ammunition they carried. You let them set up snipers knowing—'

'Let them? What else was I to do? This is your house, Algernon, as you are quick to remind me. Why weren't you trying to protect it? You should be thanking me. Unless you have forgotten there are children in this household for whom you are supposedly responsible. Without my cooperation they would have destroyed Syon House and put the cannon on the wall anyway.' She looked at Robert Devereux. 'And you, dear cousin? Oh yes, you were otherwise engaged. Celebrating, because you thought you had turned the King's forces back. I had no choice.'

'Quite right, Countess,' John said. 'Under the circumstances, you acted wisely and courageously. Did Prince Rupert—'

'He did not see the children and I do not believe he knows they are here.'

But his eyes still held a question, so she added. 'He remembered me from court. He behaved courteously to me.'

'He's just an upstart youth with a few nasty little tricks up his sleeve. That's all. No real substance,' Devereux sneered.

'If I were you, Lord Essex, I would not dismiss his youth too quickly,' John said quietly. 'He has more than braggadocio. He brings strategies he learned in the German war. There is rumor that he mixes foot soldiers among the horse to great effect. And imagine coming all this way just to help an uncle.' He sipped at his wine and said quietly, 'You've got to love the contest for that.'

Contest? Why was everything a competition with men? Politics, the battlefield, even love? 'How do you know the young princes did not engage?'

'I saw them all through my telescope,' he said. 'Charles and James were in their tent, well behind the lines, looking bored and restless. They appeared to be under the guardianship of William Harvey, who was largely ignoring them. With my new Kepler telescope I could even see the book he was reading. Galen. Some Greek philosopher, I think. Or maybe medical. Harvey's not one for poetry.'

Lucy couldn't help wondering if Henrietta would approve Charles taking her sons into battle. But when you come right down to it, they probably were safer where the King could see and protect them from his enemies—and theirs.

'Where are they now? Charles and his two older sons?' Lucy asked.

'Fled back to their Royalist nest in Oxford, I suppose,' Robert Devereux said.

Pushing his empty plate back, Devereux fished into his pocket and placed a coin on the table in front of Lucy.

Base metal. More token than coin. But it bore a portrait of Lord Essex on one side and a crude engraving of Parliament on the other.

'Go ahead, look at it closely.'

Around the Parliament engraving was the motto—she held it closer to the closest candle, squinting to make it out—*In the multitude of Counselors there is safety.* Well that could be debated, she thought. And on the reverse, surrounding Devereux's portrait, *The sword of the Lord and of Gydeon.* She wanted to laugh at her cousin's outrageous conceit, but she suppressed a smile and handed it back to him without comment.

John coughed behind his hand, an understanding glimmer in his eye and changed the subject from Essex's vanity. 'By the way, my lords, have you heard what Lord Whittier is up to?' Pym asked. 'He doesn't seem to have entered the fray on either side.'

Lucy's ears perked. That was a name she had not heard in a while, regrettably. She had not laid eyes on James Whittier since the night she had given away Wentworth's diamonds.

Essex frowned as though his wine had just turned bitter. 'Haven't seen him since he refused his seat in the Lords after the death of his brother. Probably gone abroad to wait out the war. Whittier wouldn't risk his little finger for either side unless he had a wager on it. Good riddance I say. The last time I saw him he beat me at that Italian card game. Can't think of its name.'

'Bassett,' said Algernon. 'He lightened my purse as well, I regret to say. He's shrewder than he pretends to be. I tried to recruit him into the navy. Even offered him an officer's command He just laughed. Said he never played a game where there couldn't be a winner.'

'Well, my lords,' Pym smiled, 'you'd best hold onto your wallets because Whittier is not abroad. He's in London. And he has, as you might expect, found a way to turn the present circumstances into profit.'

'After the scandal surrounding his brother's death, I would have thought he would have preferred remaining on the Continent. This can't be a new venture; he hasn't the resources,' Essex said. 'Last I heard he lost what was left of the family's shipping fortune in a bad venture.'

'I don't think he had a fortune to lose,' Pym said. 'By the time he inherited the title, his older brother had already squandered everything. He was the wastrel. James, being the second son, has always had to live pretty much by his wits. He even studied for the clergy but decided that was not a fit either. Clergy or military are the only ready choices for a second son.'

'What is this latest scheme, then, since he has rejected both those choices?'

John Pym toyed with his wineglass. 'Scheme or shrewd investment. Time will tell. He's become a printer and publisher of news books and broadsheets.'

Lace cuffs flopping around his wrists, Essex reached into his little enamel snuff box, and raising a bit of the nasty brown dust to his nostrils, sniffed. 'Broadsheets! You mean those scurrilous little pages that ragamuffins sell on the street!'

'More than broadsheets—pamphlets, news books. A brisk trade in Paternoster Row.'

'Surely there's no profit to be made there?' Algernon chimed in, shaking his head in response to Devereux's proffering of the snuff box.

'I don't know about profit. Time will tell, I suppose. Some of the content of the news books is ridiculous, unfounded nonsense, some mere rumor and innuendo, and of course all lurid and sensational or extremely partisan—exaggerated reports of casualties, sensationalistic reports of brutality—' Pym raised his hand and jabbed at the air as though he were making a point before Parliament, 'but do not be deceived. There is coin of another kind to be found beneath that smudge of black ink—influence. Profit always follows influence.'

'Influence, John, surely you jest,' Algernon said. 'How can there be any merit or worth in such untrustworthy sources? Who reads that bilge water anyway?'

'All of London reads it, my lord admiral. Everywhere you go, outside our lofty meeting rooms, the pamphlets are all the people talk about in the streets, the taverns, the counting houses, even in the stews.' He reached inside his tunic pocket and pulled out a pamphlet. Slapping it down on the table, he shoved it toward Devereux. 'You might be interested in this one, my lord commander, it relates in gory detail your men's recent ignoble passage through the village of Buntford.'

Pym held up his hand, stopping Essex's protest. 'My lords, the people's opinion matters to the success of Parliament's enterprise. And that opinion is fickle and easily swayed. Whittier is no fool. His effort may turn out to be as crucial to the outcome of the war as yours or mine.'

The general and the admiral looked at him as though he had just said a pile of horseshit was worth a king's ransom.

But Lucy scarcely noticed their reaction. It was influence of another kind she had in mind. 'When you next see Lord Whittier, Mister Pym, please tell him Lady Carlisle wishes him well in his new venture. He was always a favorite at my London salon.'

Pym looked at her directly. 'You may tell him so yourself, Countess. He has set up a press on Fleet Street. I'm sure he would welcome any gossipy tidbits and insights favorable to our cause that you might feed him.' He looked away from Lucy then, gazing directly at his companions. 'Indeed, my lords, I think we too should endeavor to renew his acquaintance. We may have *news* which would interest the public.' He picked up the pamphlet and waved it in the air. 'This could prove to be a valuable tool for our cause, if we have the foresight to grab hold of it. Or a bludgeon with which to beat us, if we do not.'

Shortly after, the three men left together, with scarcely a thank-you to their hostess. Apparently, they had arrived together. Perhaps that was the reason John did not stay. And for once she was almost too weary to care. Carter and Tom came in to clear the remains of the table.

'I'll take that,' she said, as Carter picked up the pamphlet.

After she had checked to see the children were sleeping peacefully, after she had undressed, removing with a sigh the green velvet ribbon with its drooping mistletoe, after her sometime maid had brushed out her hair and helped her into her nightdress and given her a perfunctory good-night curtsy, Lucy sat at her dressing table for a long time, reading by the light of her bedside candle. When the flame began to gutter, she laid the pamphlet aside and closed her eyes. She did not sleep well.

Her dreams were filled with images: Wentworth's gleaming diamonds resting in the gaping mouth of the grinning boar's head, the sound of cannon fire and the bodies of drowned men floating in the Thames, flames leaping from burning rooftops, mothers screaming, children crying. And over all the screams and blood and chaos, she heard James Whittier's easy, charming laughter.

REPORTS OF WAR

Thousands had no mind to meddle with the wars
But greatly desired to live peaceably at home, when
Rage of soldiers and drunkards would not suffer them

—retrospect of Richard Baxter, Protestant Chaplain

February 1643

'*P*ardon, monsieur,' but I can no longer sit.' With a weary
wave of her hand Henrietta dismissed Van Dyke's young
protégé, for whom she had promised to pose during her
stay in Den Haag.

Before she left London, the portrait painter had solicited
this promise. They had been standing under Peter Paul Rubens'
magnificent ceiling panels Van Dyke was installing in the
Banqueting House. He knew full well how devoted she was
to all things beautiful and those who created them. As she had
remarked upon the beautiful Baroque detail, the sumptuous
color, the use of light, noting the influences of both Tintoretto
and Caravaggio, they had mourned together the great loss of
Rubens' genius. It was the first time they had spoken since
his death. Van Dyke had been visibly shaken by the loss of his
teacher. He had persuaded her saying that she would be doing
not only a great service to a worthy young artist but to him
as well by helping him honor his dead patron—here he had
pointed to the beautiful ceiling panels—through helping other
students as Rubens had helped him. And then he'd added
that there would of course be no commission.

'You will have to finish it from memory, *monsieur*,' she
said now to the young artist. Brush frozen in mid-air, as if
being summoned from another world, the portrait painter
looked up from his palette. The bells of Jacobskerk clamored,

marking the hour. The spaniel on her lap, a veteran poser,
scarcely stirred as Henrietta shouted above the bells. Just one
of many things she would not miss in this town. The clamoring
would go on far too long to wait. 'I will be departing on the
morrow.' What sweet words she thought even as they left her
lips.

'*S'il vous plaît, un moment*, your majesty.' Hans—at least
she thought that was his name, for weren't they all named
Hans? —Hans added with a shout of his own and a pleading
smile, 'I wish to capture your majesty's elegant features as
they deserve.'

Flatterer, she thought. But despite her weariness she nodded
curtly, struggling to relax her face into a lying mask of tran-
quility. Her shoulders ached with fatigue. *Ennui* tormented
her spirit. The only doctor who had attended her, his potions
succeeding no better or worse than her English doctors, was
a Portuguese Jew.

'They are not banished?' she had asked Prince Frederick.

He had only laughed and said, 'The Jews? How can we
banish them? They are half of the merchant class. Do not be
concerned, your majesty, they are also very good doctors. I
understand that England's Queen Elizabeth even suffered the
administrations of one.'

Henrietta doubted that was true. Charles had told her the
Jews had been expelled way before the Tudor monarchs and
she'd never seen a Jew in England—at least that she knew of.
Now that she thought of it, she wasn't altogether sure she
would recognize one.

'And,' Frederick had droned on in his supercilious way, 'I
understand some Puritans are calling for tolerance in their
English pulpits.'

She had shrugged. 'The Puritans are tolerant of nothing.
If what you say is indeed true,' her tone implying that she
doubted it, 'Parliament would only let them back in to convert
them. The Puritans would convert cows and baptize sheep to
increase their tribe.'

In the near distance beyond the broad window, on one of the
many buildings of the Binnenhof, a storks' nest perched, an
ugly pile of sticks at least six feet wide. Two storks, no English

songbirds these but great ungainly birds, unable to sing or even squawk, guarded the nest. Her dreary hosts protected them, thought they brought good fortune, a silly superstition— everybody needed to believe in something, she supposed. The birds' long beaks click-clacked their anxiety, or their *amour*, or whatever else they felt like clattering about.

These Dutch were clatterers too, talking on and on about their canal building or some other prosaic, dull matter. Den Haag was no great city like Paris or even London, just a collection of government buildings, a city of bureaucrats who placed matters of business in the highest priority. No courtly entertainments, salons, delights. Little music and scant frivolity. But what could one expect from a country of Protestants?

Poor Princess Mary. Henrietta would have to give her daughter something special to lighten her days in this kingdom of excruciating boredom, though she was pleased that the girl seemed to have settled in well. Some days she was even too busy with her lessons and her various entertainments to tolerate her mother's company. Henrietta glanced at the only other occupant of the room besides herself and the artist. She would give Jeffrey Hudson to her daughter—if she could bear to part with him. He had proved himself an amusing companion even in exile.

'Summon the maids to start packing my personal belongings, Jeffrey,' she said to the exotic little creature, who had mischievously been striking poses at her whilst she sat.

The dwarf, meant as a diversion to distract a young Henrietta from the inattentions of her new bridegroom, was the only worthy bribe Buckingham had ever given her. She had grown very fond of him over the years. She had already promised Mary the pet monkey in her favorite portrait. She could not give up Jeffrey too.

The dwarf was suddenly as serious as a magistrate, strutting across the room, hands clasped behind his back like some pompous English barrister. 'My queen, do you think it wise? I too wish to return home. But the clouds are heavy, and the palace seer says they portend storms.'

'He does, does he? What a *splendide prophète* he must be to pronounce that clouds portend storms. *Mon petit ami*, we cannot wait. I care not what Prince Frederick's astronomer fool says. It is just a ruse to delay. The longer we stay the longer they have to deliver the final installment on the jewels. The arms and stores are already loaded, and the ships are waiting in the harbor. Perhaps the Dutch Vice-Admiral Tromp will arrange with his Jewish captains for their Jehovah to part the waters. Surely they are as capable as *Monsieur* Shakespeare's Prospero.'

The elegant little man shook his head in a gesture of long-suffering. 'The magician did not part the waters. He conjured a tempest. Your lowly companion thinks we should delay until the signs are more favorable. It will be a miserable day to set forth on the sea.'

What her lowly companion lacked in size he made up in boldness. Of course he didn't want to leave. The ladies of the Dutch court were quite charmed by him, flirting and spoiling him shamelessly, wondering no doubt—though much too shy to say as the French ladies did—if his manly hidden parts were as perfectly proportioned as his silk-clad calves.

'My dear Lord Minimus, do you remember the Barbary pirates who waylaid you on your journey here?' Knowing exactly which string to pull on her puppet doll, she took a perverse delight in seeing him blanch. 'It is less likely there will be Barbary pirates abroad in rough seas.'

Mitte, as if disturbed by something in Henrietta's tone, bounced from her lap to stand beside the dwarf. 'You take his side, do you? Well, the pirates would put you in a *fricassée*.' Then to the dwarf, 'My ships are sailing with the morning tide. I have already promised his Majesty. Summon my ladies before I punish you by taking away that fine gold ring I gave you on your natal day. I might even leave you here in this dull Purgatory to entertain the Princess Mary.'

'Your majesty, if I may have a word,' the painter asked as he was packing up his easel, 'I have a friend who desires an audience. You have been so gracious to me.' His face reddened in embarrassment, but his blue eyes pleaded. 'I uh told her you were leaving but she uh insisted that I ask. She is a widow, a very dear friend of my mother's. She and her son have come all the way from Amsterdam to bring you a gift.'

A flash of irritation caused a pain in Henrietta's shoulder. That was the trouble with a generous nature. It was never enough. They always wanted more. 'I'm sorry, *monsieur artiste*, there is no time,' she said crisply.

The young artist fished inside the bag in which he carried his paints. 'She bade me give you this then.'

Some dreary little token, no doubt, she thought as she reached out to receive the tribute. 'Please give my regrets to your friend and thank her for her kind—' She looked down at the necklace in her hand and gasped. It was the necklace she had reluctantly parted with to buy arms—at Charles' suggestion, which in spite of its being the only practical solution to close the deal with the Dutch, had wounded her to the quick.

'It is only a replica, your majesty,' the young artist said as, incredulous, she accepted it into her cupped hand. 'Amsterdam has many fine goldsmiths. My friend learned the trade from her late husband. She saw the original around the neck of a Portuguese lady and enquired of its provenance. The woman who was a friend of Prince Frederick said it had belonged to you. My friend felt sympathy that you had to part with something so beautiful to—' his faced turned a deeper shade of red, 'to serve England's cause.'

Did all these dreary Dutch know her business? She should return the gift, send the woman away. The necklace was exquisitely wrought. Even she could scarcely tell it from the original. She suddenly wanted to meet the woman who could do this.

'*S'il vous plaît*, tell your friend I will grant her audience if she can come within the hour. I wish to thank her for her generous gift.'

The young man grinned. 'She can come immediately.' He hurried to the door and opened it, motioning with his hand. A soft rustling and the woman, who had apparently been waiting in the anteroom came in, greeting her with a deep curtsy worthy of any courtier. She was followed by a young man of about the artist's age, who bowed stiffly. 'Your most humble subject, Johanna Cartwright, your majesty. I too am from England. You are very kind to receive us.'

'Us?'

'This is my son, Ebenezer. If we could just have a moment of your time, your majesty.' The woman's voice was low, but self-assured and dignified as she said, 'I much admire your devotion. I too have a devoted cause, if you would be so kind as to hear my petition.'

'*Un petition.*' She should have guessed. The beautiful necklace was but a bribe. But the woman had gone to much trouble and expense. The large diamond might only be cleverly polished glass, she wasn't sure though it sparkled prettily, but the gold was real. Henrietta was well acquainted with the feel and the soft luster, enough to know it was not cheap gilt. 'It would be most ungracious of me to entertain a petition from one who has made me such a generous gift,' she said.

'It is an act of kindness I am beseeching, your majesty, not for me or even my son but for a very deserving people.'

'Speak your request, Madame Cartwright. I shall consider it.'

The woman paused as if trying how best to voice her request. This was tiresome. She should already have memorized what she was going to say. The room was very quiet now. Even the bells had ceased. Both Jeffrey and the portraitist had discreetly withdrawn.

The woman inhaled deeply, as if it were of no importance that she was delaying the Queen of England, and then finally lowering her eyes said softly, 'It is about the Jews, your majesty.'

'The Jews?'

'Since you have been in the Netherlands, you may have been surprised to observe many Jews. You may have even noticed how they go about their business, creating no ill will in the community, and that they are a very productive people. You may be surprised to learn just how much they have contributed in trade and commerce to the Netherlands. The Dutch people have been well compensated for their tolerance through enhanced prosperity. Indeed, we have become like the hub on a wheel. Traders come from many ports carrying goods to and from in a great flurry of enterprise. The Jews are unhindered in their business as in their practice of religion. Their only influence on the Netherlands has been a positive one.'

There was a long pause. The room was strangely silent. This speech had indeed been delivered as though it had been

rehearsed. Henrietta was taken aback. So what exactly was
the favor this woman was seeking?

Madame Cartwright took a deep breath and then added,
'As an English woman, I wish there could be such justice
in England.'

'Justice in England.'

The woman dropped her gaze, but said nothing. And
then Henrietta realized what she was asking. 'For the Jews,
you mean?'

'Yes, your majesty, for the Jews,' she answered.

'I assure you, madame, I bear no ill will toward any people,
not even the Jews as so many do. Our Lord was a Jew. But
what has this to do with me?'

The woman smiled, nodding, clearly not wishing to give
offense, but in that same firm tone said, 'You are the Queen.
You have great influence. I was emboldened to come to you
when I heard that you had attended the synagogue in
Amsterdam to hear the great preacher, Dias Soeiro, who
speaks so eloquently on the persecution of the Jews. Your
interest gave me hope. If you could speak with the King on
the matter of the Jewish people's return from exile, you could
be a force for great good for England, both morally and
economically.'

Before she went to the synagogue Henrietta had never
heard of this Soeiro and had not listened closely to what he
said. She merely went to satisfy her curiosity and to humor
her sister-in-law who had suggested the visit as a diversion,
as if any pursuit Elizabeth Stuart proposed could ever be a
worthwhile diversion. Henrietta had spent most of her time
not listening to the sermon at all, curious about the sparse-
ness of the synagogue and the shawl-wrapped golden scroll
from which the preacher/rabbi/priest—whatever he was
called—read in what she supposed was Hebrew. Mostly she
had used her visit to Amsterdam for the greater purpose of
visiting the artists' quarter where, though she had been
tempted, she had restrained her acquisitive impulses. Proud
of her new austerity, she had reminded herself she was here
to buy arms not art.

'But I thought you said you were English. Madame,

surely you or your son have not converted to the religion of the Jews?'

She could not keep the outrageousness of such a notion from seeping into her tone. The corners of Madame Cartwright's mouth twitched as though Henrietta had said something amusing.

'No, your majesty. I am a Baptist, as is my son, and I am as devoted to my faith as you are to your Catholic faith. But I, being a Baptist, strongly believe that no man—or woman—should be persecuted for his beliefs—and that includes the Jews. With your majesty's forbearance, we have brought you the writings of others who can say it much more eloquently than we.' She motioned to her son, who withdrew a sheaf of papers from his sleeve, and bowing, held them out to Henrietta. Not wishing to be rude to the woman who had gifted her with the necklace, she accepted the three pamphlets with a nod.

'One of these tracts was given to your husband's father several years ago. It is still widely read among many Europeans. One is by a man named Wemyss and is more recent and puts forth the Christian ideal that not only should no man be persecuted for his religion but should have freedom of disputation and argument. The third is by a young man named Roger Williams. He too makes a very cogent argument for a freedom of religion that includes the Jews.'

Henrietta was taken aback, her tone sharp. 'That somewhat surprises me, madame. I have observed no such tolerance among the Puritans for the Catholic minority in England.'

'I understand, your majesty, I do. But I pray you to remember that there are many stripes among dissenters just as there are degrees of intolerance among the Catholics.'

Henrietta knew this was a veiled reference to the Inquisition. *Mon Dieu*, must they all forever suffer because of that hateful Spanish stain?

'I was very young when I came here. The Jews of Amsterdam have been very kind to me. They are a good, God-fearing people. They deserve to be able to go home—wherever home may be.'

Henrietta felt a sudden weariness. Her body ached from so

long sitting. She still had to bid her daughter farewell. She should have never offered the woman an audience. 'I would like to help you, but I'm afraid, Madame Cartwright, that you overestimate my influence. The English king has restraints that other kings do not. It is Parliament who would decide such a matter. And I am not much loved by Parliament.' Then she added with reluctance, 'I feel I should return the necklace to you. I do not wish to take it under false pretenses.'

'Oh no. It is a gift from an English woman to her Queen, and I thank you for your patience in listening to me. I will do as you suggest. I will take my petition to Parliament, when the time is right.'

After Madame Cartwright curtseyed and left the room, Henrietta stood for a long moment looking out the window, wondering . . . but no, there was simply nothing to be done, not now when Charles was at war. She started to throw the tracts away but something about the woman, her quiet courage, continued to plead her case long after she was gone. She wrapped the necklace inside the papers and put both in her jewel case, which was now almost empty. Maybe she would read them later. Maybe even give them to Charles, when the war was over. He had too much on his plate now to be bothered with such a triviality.

The next morning the Portuguese ships set sail. Jeffrey pointed out the wall of gray on the horizon, feeding her general feeling of unease. But she was determined. Charles would be waiting. His last letter was loosely stitched inside her sleeve. She was to tell Vice-Admiral Tromp their exact point of entry only when they were well at sea. In the distance, lightning—a rarity in February—snaked across the sky. But the sails filled, and the ship moved out of the harbor.

'We are going home, Mitte,' she whispered to the spaniel she held in her arms.

Wisely the dwarf did not gloat when, two days out of sight of land, they were forced to turn back. Henrietta would have braved the roughest seas to return to her dearest heart. Unfortunately, Van Tromp, who was neither Moses nor a tempest-controlling magician, would not.

*   *   *

Arthur Pendleton was on his way back to the Gloucester garrison to give his reconnaissance report. He'd seen the town of Cirencester burning, even got close enough to see the King's cavalry herding the townspeople into the church while they ransacked and looted the town. They would not burn the church—the priest was a well-known supporter of the King— though he wasn't sure what abuses the people held inside might suffer. The cannons had ceased, but now and then, he heard musket fire.

Outside of town, he came upon the officers' camp, encountering first the horses tied beside a grove of aspens. Settled behind a stand of brush, he watched a lone groom brushing their sweaty flanks whilst their riders passed a flask or took a morning piss. Once Cirencester fell, the cavalry must have pulled back, leaving the infantrymen to despoil the town. A disgrace. No discipline at all. Captain Cromwell would never have stood for such.

Plumes of smoke in the distance smeared the dawn. Most of the town's buildings were still smoldering: cottages and townhouses, merchants' shops, all belonging to the many supporters of Parliament. Not that it mattered. No such thing as neutral no matter which soldiers took the town. You were either on their side and easily identifiable—or you were fair game. But if the rumors about Rupert's men were true, he pitied the poor souls in the church. Though truth to tell he'd heard of Roundhead atrocities too. Arthur had not lost faith in Parliament's cause, but he had grown war-weary and was glad enough to be one of the dragoons assigned scout duty. Not that he was afraid to die. It was the killing he found hardest.

Raising the telescope to get a better look, he thought he identified the one they called Rupert of the Rhine. Tall, royal insignia on his horse, handsome, laughing—a young man not much older than himself. He had the fearless demeanor of a warrior, born to fight. Arthur had often noticed the excitement that flared in the faces of some of his own fellows, a raucous good humor as though the adventure of battle was no more than an afternoon's sport. He counted the number of the officers and their horses, drawing with a stub of charcoal on a bit of paper a rough diagram of the area. Then he followed his twig-marked path back through the woods, untied his horse, and led him across the frozen ground until both were out of view and earshot.

He was riding back to the garrison when he came upon a woman sitting on the bank, shrouded in the morning mist like some ghostly apparition, rocking back and forth, in a silent, keening motion. No ghost at all, he saw, slowing his horse, but a real woman, her clothing muddy and stained with blood, blouse torn, arm and shoulder smeared with filth. In her arms she cradled a small bundle. His first thought was that she could have been planted there to trap him, but he couldn't just ride on.

He dismounted, strode the few feet between them. He'd seen a woman's breast before—more than once—but he'd never seen one full of milk. He knew he was staring, but she didn't seem to notice. He watched in horror as the mother, crooning softly, tried to coax her unresponsive infant to take the distended nipple. He wondered how long the child had been dead. Could she not know? Its face had already turned blue. Whatever had happened to her in that town must have broken her wits.

'Oh sweet Jesus,' he said aloud. Captain Cromwell would have fined him for the profanity, but Captain Cromwell and his troops were way north and truly it was more prayer than profane. Sweet Jesus must not be listening anyway. What was he to do now? He couldn't take her back to the burning town from which she had fled with her newborn. He had no choice but to take her to the garrison. Maybe somebody there would know her. He knelt beside her. She cried out, her eyes wide with fright.

Holding out his hand, he approached her as one would approach a startled doe. 'Don't be frightened, ma'am. I am not going to hurt you. I'm going to help you.'

'He is not hungry. I'll feed him later,' she said, her movements slow and studied as she stroked the babe's face and fumbled with blue fingers to place her engorged breast back inside her torn blouse.

'Yes, ma'am. Let me carry him. I'll take you somewhere

safe. You can ride in front of me,' he said, placing his coat around her shoulders. It covered her down to her knees. Her feet were bare and bleeding, but she seemed oblivious.

'You are an angel sent from heaven,' she smiled at him. 'We are very grateful.'

Relieved at her gentle compliance, he assisted her to mount the horse. When she was settled he handed her back the lifeless child and climbed behind her.

'My husband's name is Godfrey,' she said. 'I am taking his son to meet his father.'

'Yes, ma'am.' He almost choked.

As they trotted off, he could feel her heart beating beneath his arms, and an odd little vibration. *Merciful Jesus.* She was humming a low, soft lullaby to her dead son.

'Ma'am,'—he started, but there was no gentle way to say it. Let Colonel Masters sort it out. Somebody at the garrison might even know her husband. The horse picked his way gently across the frozen ground. The woman, who had ceased her humming, slumped in his arms, but her hold on the child remained firm. Mother and child might have been carved from one piece of marble.

Despite the slow pace necessary, he arrived at the garrison by noon and gently handed over his charge to one of the officers' wives, who led the dazed woman away. She made no protest as following as gently as a lamb, she handed the child off. He gave his report about the Cavalier troop movements and the burning of the town to the commander of the garrison. 'She said her husband's name was Godfrey. I am sorry that's all I could get out of her. I found her on my way back to report. She was beside the river pretty much in the state she is now.'

After being assured that the commander's wife would see to the woman's welfare and they would seek out her husband— there were three Godfreys assigned here though he didn't know if he was currently in garrison—Arthur had a bit of food and fell into his bunk for a brief rest before receiving his new orders.

The next morning, on his way to the stable, he passed the officers' quarters where two women sat on the porch enjoying the morning sunshine. One of the women called out to him, 'Soldier, we would speak with you, please,' and beckoned him. He was in a hurry to be off and didn't have time for women's questions; he'd told them all he knew yesterday, but this was the officers' quarters, so he'd best not ignore them.

As he approached the porch, one of them looked up at him smiling. 'We want to thank you again for your kindness, sir.' She looked and sounded so normal he hardly recognized her, but, yes, it was the woman from yesterday, clean and wearing a borrowed dress too big for her. 'My son would thank you as well, but he has not yet learned to talk.'

He stared in disbelief; she was still cradling the child in her arms. Maybe he had been wrong. Maybe the child lived after all. He bent down to get a better look. She uncovered the child's face, so he could see it. 'Shh, he's sleeping.'

The officer's wife lifted her eyebrows and nodded at him, then raised a warning finger to her lips. But he could see from her expression that she was not warning him about waking the child. It was only a bundled ragdoll.

'They took him away for a little while, so I could rest. But they brought him back to me this morning. We are both so much better, thanks to your kindness.'

'You are very welcome, madam. I wish you and your . . . child well,' he said, not looking at the doll.

'Would you like to hold him?' At that moment, Arthur thought his heart would break. He could not imagine what had been done to her in that burning town to turn her wits so. What a devil's thing was war that it could change ordinary men to brutes.

The commander's wife nodded at him and smiled in sympathy. 'My dear, I expect our soldier here has gotten his new orders by now and is anxious to return to his regiment in the north. We should not detain him.'

Gratefully he tipped his hat and turned his back on the mad woman and her dead child. Behind him the fires of Cirencester still smoldered. The memory would be less easily left behind.

In London a cold, soaking rain had been coming down in sheets all day and Fleet Street was deserted. Early in the day the street urchins who hawked his news had returned the ruined papers to him soggy and useless, so James Whittier looked up in surprise from the press he was mopping to see a woman enter his print shop. He was even more surprised when she shook back the hood of her cloak and greeted him.

'So, Lord Whittier, The gossip is true,' she said, surveying the room with a half-smile.

'And what gossip might that be, Lady Carlisle?' He returned the ink mop to its pot and reached to help her out of her wet mantle. Holding it out gingerly, lest its dark green velvet rub against his stained apron, he hung it on a wooden peg by the door.

'The gossip, my lord, is that you have gone into the gossip business yourself.' She flashed him a smile, the same enigmatic smile she had worn the night she'd unwittingly donated her diamond earrings to his cause. 'Quite an impressive set-up,' she added, looking around his shop at the giant press, the stacks of paper. She picked up one of the engraved blocks from the nearest table and ran her fingers over its carved surface. It bore a crude likeness of the King. 'Such trifles surely do not come cheap. One wonders where one who has been known to plead poverty on convenient occasions could come by such a sum.'

Restraining a laugh, he reached out and took it from her. 'It is not a trifle, my lady, but you are right about one thing—it did not come cheap,' he said, wondering how a woman no longer young could manage to look so good. Maybe it was that irascible personality or the confident way she presented herself. A practiced flirt, to be sure, sometime lady, sometime courtesan. He returned the wooden block to its correct position on the table. 'To what do I owe the sunshine of your visit on such a day?'

'Well of course, it is always a delight to see you, my lord, whatever the weather, and I had hoped that you would call at Syon House, but alas I can see you have been very busy'—a flutter of her lashes, a pause, and then, 'but to get straight to the point, I have something you might be interested in. A little information. That is your stock in trade now, is it not?'

'Stock in trade? Yes. You could say that.' He pretended to

consider as he pondered her real purpose for the visit. He was busy, although a pleasant afternoon diversion was always welcome. He leaned forward, casually placing his hand on the doorpost behind her shoulder as if for support. Close. Close enough to smell the essence of summer roses in her hair. He said playfully, his tone low and intimate, 'I fear the cost may be beyond my meager means. What might my lady want in return for this . . . information?'

Her laughter reminded him of a piper's clear notes. In one fluid motion she slid from beneath his arm. 'In return? I had thought to offer it in friendship of course, but since you have turned tradesman I am not above striking a bargain.'

The way she lifted one perfectly arched eyebrow made him think she had more than money in mind. If not a little afternoon delight, then what? He was intrigued. Lucy Hay used gossip and the influence it gained the way powerful men used money. It had been the coin of courtiers like the Percy family for decades.

'Of course, Countess. I never turn down a beautiful woman, especially one who is as generous as you have shown yourself to be.'

'When have I ever been generous with you, Jamie Whittier—never mind.'

A few stolen kisses, some fumbling and heavy breathing in the clock courtyard once at Hampton Court came to mind. When Wentworth was in Ireland. She'd broken his courted embrace, reluctantly, murmuring something about other loyalties.

The sudden glow on her cheeks showed she remembered too.

'These news things you are publishing—who reads them?'

'I don't really care who reads them, as long as somebody buys them.'

'They are not partisan, I mean? Not carrying water for Parliament or King?'

'Oh, they are partisan. Toward my interests. And it is in my interest to give the people what they want to read. This is London, not Oxford. Londoners—the ones who haven't left or been clapped in prison—are solidly behind Parliament and they want to read about the atrocities of the King's soldiers and the extravagances and scandals of the court.'

'Every lurid detail, I suppose.'

'Well yes, human nature being what it is.'

'What about the Queen? Would your readers be interested in her activities? Nothing unseemly, as others of your ilk are reporting—Henrietta is not the whore she is represented to be.'

He thought he knew where this was headed. Lucy Hay had once been the Queen's favorite. 'My lady, if it's some virtuous little wife and mother story you wish me to print, I cannot oblige you. I would be run out of town, shut down by the godly magistrates who blame Henrietta Maria for the King's mismanagement of the kingdom. England might not have a Star Chamber anymore, but she has committees. I have too much invested in my equipment to see it trashed or confiscated.'

'I understand. But your godly readers would be interested in the Queen's whereabouts, surely—the possibility of her return even if their more salacious reading appetites are not fed.'

'You are privy to this information?'

'The young Princess Elizabeth and her brother Henry are under my brother's guardianship. Since Lord Percy's naval duties necessitate his absence, they are much in my care at Syon House. The Queen corresponds discreetly with them through me. That speaks to the coin I wish to exchange for a specific favor.'

'Which is?'

'I want you to print a story that the King's youngest children are being well cared for under Percy guardianship and that, through gentle instruction and persuasion, they are being schooled to turn against the evil of popery. They say their prayers nightly in English and have an English cleric who reads and interprets an English Bible for them. And I don't mean Archbishop Laud's Book of Common Prayer. The old King's translation is sufficient.'

'That's all? Just that story? Why do you care to see that in print?'

The Lucy Hay he knew was a woman with a survivor's instinct and wit and talent to act on that instinct. Necessary commodities, given the Percy history. What did she have to gain from this?

She said the name as though it tasted sour. 'Philip Herbert, Lord Pembroke, and his wife wish to take custody of the children. Parliament decides. I do not wish to inflict Lord and Lady Pembroke on the King's innocent children.'

'But surely their care is an imposition on a woman of your . . . sophistication.'

'They have a nurse. And demands on a woman of my 'sophistication' as you call it are much diminished since so many who would appreciate that trait have fled to the Continent or decamped with the King. Besides, I am fond of the children, and in spite of my religious differences with the Queen, I retain something of a fondness for her.'

The archness had left her tone. She might even be telling the truth.

He grinned. 'I am guessing you do not want that sentiment printed for our London readers.'

'Assuredly not. I will give you some details concerning what I know about the Queen's plans when I have seen your story praising the guardianship of the House of Percy. I wish to counter any issue which might be raised to the contrary by the Earl of Pembroke—before it becomes an issue with Parliament. You can help me do that by raising public interest in our favor.'

Lord Pembroke was a dour Puritan to be sure and capable of making all manner of trouble for a woman of whom he undoubtedly did not approve. Guardianship of the children would enhance his power with Parliament. And of course, Lucy would bear a grudge against him. He had argued mightily for the bill of attainder against Wentworth.

'What sort of details?' he asked.

'Nothing to compromise the children's safety—or the Queen's. But I think your readers will find any news of her interesting, since she is so reviled. Do we have a bargain?'

'Do you know where the other children are?'

'I have it on good authority that Charles and James are with their father.'

Whose authority, he wondered, but he thought he knew. There were rumors that John Pym had taken Wentworth's place in her affections, though much more discreetly, of course.

'Mary, the Princess Royal, has been delivered by her mother to her husband's household, Prince William of the House of Orange, and the Queen is lingering to see her well and safely established.' Then adding, 'In a Protestant household. Don't forget to print that.

'I will include that with a general story on the King's children. With a teaser that there may be more to follow.'

'You may say that the Queen misses her children. And that her health has not been good these last weeks. A sop to her enemies. They will be pleased to hear she suffers. You will not name your source.'

'I will not name my source.'

'And you will not say the children are at Syon House. Only that they are under Percy guardianship. A week hence then? How long does it take you to get your—?'

'Issues. We call them numbered issues. A week will suffice.'

'It would please me if you called at Syon House.'

He bowed, answering the invitation in her tone with a courtier's gesture more suited to a nobleman than a tradesman wearing a stained apron. 'It will be my pleasure, Countess. And I shall bring you the printed story to see if it satisfies. Before I print a run for distribution.'

She favored him with her coquette's smile. 'I am sure, my lord Whittier, that you always give satisfaction.'

'May I send you home in a hackney?'

'No, my groom is waiting for me.' She indicated the carriage with the Northumberland crest, waiting at a discreet distance on the other side of the street. He had not noticed it.

'Until next week, then,' he said as he helped her on with her cloak, marking how fine her face looked framed by the sable hood. 'Wait—' He dug to the bottom of a stack of damp news books. 'This one is reasonably dry. You might enjoy the story about the Irish rebellion. Like all such stories, it's luridly embellished. Tales of gore and rage draw keen interest—human nature being what it is—though the rebel fighting there is truly fierce, I am told.'

'Thank you, but no. I have already seen it. It was disgusting.'

'You still have Carlisle property in Ireland, don't you? I hope you have sturdy retainers.'

'My overseers are trustworthy. They have a stake in the
security of the property. Lord Strafford helped me find them.'

'That is good. For what it is worth, my lady, I knew Thomas
Wentworth to be a good and honest man who served the King
well.'

'Thank you, for that fine sentiment, my lord. He was—and
that's the irony of it.' She tightened the ribbons on her hood
and reached for the door latch.

'I will run your story about the Queen's children at the top
of the page. It will be less eye-catching than a story about a
burning Irish church filled with women and children, but there
is always sufficient interest in anything royal. Ironic, isn't it?'

'As you said, "human nature being what it is."'

He was still standing in the door watching, enjoying the
view as she hurried into her coach, when one of the urchins
who sold his papers ducked under his arm.

'Can I come in, milord? It's colder than witches' snot out
here, it is. We sold all our papers an hour ago.'

'Kicked out again? What is it this time, Ralphie? You been
misbehaving?'

'Nay, milord. Ye know better than that. It's me old stepdad.
'E got drunk mad at me mum, started yellin', came after me
with a stick of wood when I told him to shut his trap up. Best
for both of us if I don't go home. 'E won't remember in the
morning. Can I stay here tonight?'

James pretended to consider, then said. 'You may keep Little
John company. He's been sleeping here since his mother was
taken to Bart's two days ago with lung fever. I am going out,
but there's coal in the scuttle to keep the fire going and I'll
bring you both back some soup for your supper. Don't make
a mess with your roughhousing. I'm counting on you. Now,
finish mopping the press, while I set the paper in the frame.
If you boys are going to sleep here, you might as well learn
to print.'

Later, as the leaden sky faded to the color of ink, James
Whittier slipped his favorite dice into his pocket and went out
into a cold rain. A bad night to be sloshing through the muddy
streets, but last week he'd picked up a rumor that the King's
troops led by the upstart Bohemian nephew were laying siege,

burning and pillaging in the west. Amazing what secrets men divulged when they were in their cups. Besides even if he did not pick up any printable news, funds for the enterprise were getting low. His unwitting financial backers would be waiting at the George Inn.

RIPPED APART

I do more travail with sorrow for the grief I suffer for the ways that you take that the King does believe you are against him, than ever I did to bring you into this world.

—Susan Feilding, Countess of Denbigh and lady-in-waiting to the Queen, pleading with her son who joined Parliament's side, 1643

James Whittier entered the pub at twilight and nodded at the publican behind the bar. Squinting against the dark interior, he settled at his usual table at the back of the room where he could see the door. The pretty barmaid busy lighting the tapers looked up.

'Same as usual, my lord?'

'Same as usual. Got to keep my wits. Gives me an edge. But no hurry, Meg.'

The girl pulled his drink, topping it off from a water jug. 'Slim pickings tonight by the looks of it, my lord. Just that one in the corner over there. Says he's waiting for someone. Not much of a drinker.'

'Then I shall nurse my thinking man's drink and use my senses to enjoy the view.'

'Thou cannot see the river through that fogged-up window—oh.' She blushed with pleasure at his meaning, then put his goblet on the table in front of him and went to poke the smoky fire. Watching as she bent over, he stifled the remark that the view was improving. Sparks hissed and leapt up the chimney. His attention still on the girl, James barely noticed the only other customer in the tavern get up from his seat. She tossed her hair with a sideways glance at him and offered him a dimpled smile. The wench enjoyed friendly appreciation for her attributes, of which her shapely figure was not the least, but her rapier tongue would deflate any admirer who went too far. She seldom had to use it. The publican, a burly fellow, kept a club behind the bar and a watchful eye on the virtue of his sister's only child.

No matter. Profit, not dalliance, was Whittier's purpose. If custom did not pick up soon he would need to look elsewhere. But where? Damnable business this war. Cavalier dandies had fled north, most defaulting on their markers. Their lot often suffered from shallow pockets and deep expectations—always betting on 'the come.'

He heard a discreet harrumph from behind him and looked up with some surprise to see that the man who'd gotten up did not leave but was standing over him. 'Finally, Lord Whittier. I've been to your shop in Fleet Street twice seeking you,' he said. 'Thought I might find you here or at the George. About the only two places where a man can find a game these days.'

Whittier didn't immediately recognize him, though he looked vaguely familiar, but the voice? Yes. Resonant, confident, a speaker's voice. He was sure of it. Though this powerful Parliament man seemed to be worse for the wear of his burdensome job. He'd lost at least a stone, or maybe two, since last they had met.

'Mr. Pym. An unexpected pleasure. Please join me and tell me how I may be of service to you. Will you drink?' he asked, motioning for Meg.

Pym waved the barmaid off with what passed for a smile. 'My stomach is more Puritan than my appetite. It rebels against strong drink.' Pym took the offered seat, cleared his throat, and looked James directly in the eye. He liked that in a man, a strong, direct gaze. 'I will get straight to the point, Lord Whittier. It is my understanding your publishing enterprise is flourishing. As you are centered in London, I hope I may assume that you support Parliament's cause in this conflict.'

'Then you would assume incorrectly, Mr. Pym. I have no part in this war. However, you are partially correct. My readers are on your side and the market for my goods. I print the news my readers want to read. I would be a poor fool to do anything less.'

Pym frowned at this rejoinder. Whatever zeal was gnawing at his innards he naturally desired at least a pretense of sharing. 'Do you think your readers would be interested in coded letters written by the King to his French consort, letters which speak, among other things, of not only his tolerance for but his enlistment of Roman Catholics in his northern army?'

Whittier shrugged. 'I would think my readers already anticipate that circumstance. After all, isn't that what this is all about, another of the endless intrigues involving Rome and the English monarchy? Thing is I can't figure out whether this and all the others are really about religion or just political power.'

A flash of temper crossed Pym's face. 'It matters to your readers because some among them think, wrongly, that Parliament's reaction to the King's misappropriation of power is overblown, that this crisis will recede if we just seek compromise.' Pym rapped his knuckles against the table. 'I tell you, sir, it will not go away until one side or the other gains supremacy. This King will not share power with Parliament, though at the prodding of his wife he seems to have no trouble sharing it with the Pope. Should he emerge victorious in this conflict, there will be a purging of all non-Catholics the like of which has not been seen since the first Bloody Queen Mary. Political or religious—it will not matter to those poor people who will be kindling for the Roman fires.' He pounded the table with his fist, drawing the barmaid's wide-eyed attention. 'The King must be made to accede power to Parliament.'

When he had finished his polemic, James said quietly, 'I will not promise to publish toward that end, Mr. Pym. But I will publish newsworthy items that you are in a unique position to provide.'

Pym looked at him for a long moment, his small mouth pursing in thought, like one man taking the measure of another. You are much shrewder than you let on, Whittier thought.

Finally, Pym spoke. 'Well then, Lord Whittier, I only hope that you will maintain your neutrality for both King Charles and Parliament and not publish Royalist lies.'

'You may be sure, Mr. Pym, that I am beholden only to those who purchase and read my news. And since I am in

Parliament town that circumstance accrues to your side's advantage. Londoners love reading about their hated Queen, and with her absence there has been little to print, except unfounded rumors. A printer must keep some credibility lest he lose his custom.'

Pym considered this argument. When he spoke, his tone was more moderate. 'I think, Lord Whittier, that your readers might be very interested to hear that coded letters from the Queen have been exchanged with a prominent Scots lord. A more reliable source than rumor, surely?'

'You have my attention, sir. But aren't the Scots on your side?'

'Not this one. He is not a Covenanter. He is a Catholic.'

'His name?'

'Rand MacDonnell, Earl of Antrim. The Highlander conspirator who wed Buckingham's widow and conspired to raise an army of Irish Catholics. The letter contains proof of treason in the Queen's own words.'

'Proof, you say? Have you this letter in your possession? Have they been decoded?'

'They have. And I will show you the code. You can verify the content, provided you give your word as a lord of the realm that you will not publish the code.'

'I give you my word. I would hardly bite the hand that feeds me.'

'Indeed.' He reached inside his doublet and withdrew a tightly rolled parchment. Still clinging to it was the broken seal of the house of Stuart. 'For your immediate perusal. I will not leave the document or the code with you.'

Whittier glanced at the letter, which Pym spread out on the table before him, one hand holding a corner securely. 'May I write down the quote?' he asked even as he retrieved a traveling scribe's pen and paper from the same pocket satchel that carried his dice and, without waiting for an answer, began scribbling the particulars. He let escape a low whistle as he carefully copied the part where the Queen styled herself, 'her she-majesty, *generalissima*.'

'You were correct in your thinking, Mr. Pym. My readers will be interested. You do realize how incendiary this is?

You are fanning the flames of a war that will not end well. May I ask how you came by such a document, and are there others?'

'Does any war end well, my lord? And are you not fanning the flames? Perhaps with less principle than I. The King must be persuaded to see reason. As to how I obtained it, I will only say that it was found in possession of one of the King's heralds who was willing to relinquish it for his freedom and a bribe,' he said as he rolled up the scroll and put it back inside his doublet.

'Ah, the price of loyalty. Why did you just not take it?'

'Reasonableness begets reasonableness. The herald may find himself in need of money again. We know where he is quartered.'

Or he might feed you false information as well, he thought, thinking the Member of Parliament had the naivety of an honest man.

'I would be interested in seeing other news of this quality,' Whittier said, holding out his hand in bargain.

Pym, after the slightest hesitation took it, then said, 'We will speak again.'

Watching him walk away, Whittier ceded him a grudging admiration. There was something about his forthrightness. If James were going to pick a side, he'd lay his wager on Parliament, he thought. Then once more he took up his pen and hastily wrote at the bottom of the copied quote the numbers of the code he could remember from the cipher. What he could not remember he could probably figure out—if the need should ever arise. He had noticed that the page he was allowed to copy bore no fond signature in the Queen's hand. This suggested a second page whose secrets the wily Mr. Pym did not want to see in print. Not yet anyway. Sad in a way. Every *billet doux* passing between husband and wife was subject to leering eyes. Poor Henrietta Maria. Poor Charles Stuart. He was almost tempted to warn the King. Almost.

The smoke and the boom of the big guns frightened Mitte, frightened Henrietta too, yet it was not meet that a Queen should shiver and push her wet nose into the crook of a comforting elbow. Lord Denbigh's brocade sleeve did not look that inviting anyway.

'Algernon Percy surprises me,' Denbigh said into the fading echo of the cannon. From the balcony of the Queen's secret lodgings at Bridlington Bay—which had turned out to be no secret after all—they looked out across the open sea. 'I suppose I've not given him enough credit. I thought his ships would be lying in wait at Yarmouth in response to the false reports we leaked.'

'Perhaps you give him too great credit, my lord. He might have been unable to decode your false messages.' She reached out for the spyglass he was holding, put it to her own eye. 'A big man-of-war for a traitor admiral with so small wit.' A sharp intake of breath and then, 'Does Tromp turn? He does not retreat with my convoy of arms and men!'

'No, your majesty. Merely an evasive maneuver, I am sure. The Dutch ships are lighter.' Waving toward the promontory on the left skyline, he added. 'Percy is making for yon Flamborough Head, would be my guess. His heading was probably for Kingston upon Hull. His ship is bigger, clumsier. He'll lose valuable time trying to make the turn.'

Another cannon boomed and splashed, falling short of any target but wringing a whimper from the little spaniel in her arms whom she had just retrieved from his hiding place beneath the bed.

'Sh, shh, *mon petit,*' she whispered. '*Tout va bien.*'

Denbigh nodded toward her fleet. 'The Dutch ships are outfitted with some big guns of their own, though they may be hesitant to return fire against the King's frigate.'

'But it is no longer the King's if it is controlled by Parliament,' Henrietta answered indignantly. 'Tromp should sink it.'

'Ah, your majesty.' Denbigh smiled weakly, 'Such action might be construed as an act of war against England. The Dutch are pretty careful in matters of neutrality.'

Henrietta didn't have to be reminded of Den Haag *neutralité*. Experience had pressed that upon her more than once: their canniness about the crown jewels, the way they insisted on accepting envoys from both Parliament and Charles.

'The admiral is smart,' Denbigh said. 'His evasive maneuver

will delay the navy and divert Essex's cavalry north as well. Are you up for taking a ride in the wind and the rain, Majesty?'

Henrietta was wet, cold, and muddied from the ditch into which they had dived to avoid the cannon shot during what was supposed to be a secret landing. She longed for something warm to drink and a bed. But she wrinkled her nose against the acrid odor of gun powder and replied, '*Certainement*, my lord. How long a ride?'

She handed him back the glass. Gazing at the headland, he lifted it once again. 'Maybe two hours. If we ride quickly. A carriage will be waiting with an armed and mounted guard in Londesborough. We will overnight there.'

'And my ladies?'

'My lady wife is at the castle garrison at York. Your maid Genevieve is with her to prepare for your coming. We did not anticipate this ambush. But you should still make York garrison by tomorrow night or the next night at most. As to your other ladies, a troop of Cavaliers headed by young Percy and Henry Jermyn will accompany them in the opposite direction.'

'A decoy.' Henrietta did not like the sound of that. She was fond of both men. If her ladies were captured, Parliament would not dare mistreat them, but Jermyn and young Percy would wind up in the Tower.

'No worry, your majesty. Parliament might feel the need to place you under their 'protection' but they'll not bother your ladies.'

'Well at least they do not have to ride in the rain. Who will ride with me?'

'That honor has fallen to me. I am sorry you must suffer this indignity. But even if your royal carriage had not been lost on the first attempt at crossing, this would still be the more prudent. They'll not be looking for two lone riders in the rain.'

She smiled up at him in reassurance. 'I am not *sucre*. I shall not dissolve,' she said as a stable groom led two horses to them. 'It will be a comfort to ride again on the soil that carries my husband.'

Indeed, the sinking of the ship with her carriage and horses mattered little now that she was home. The knowledge that she was returning to her love in triumph made her heart flutter. Thank the Blessed Mother the cargo in the other ships had safely made the treacherous crossing. The gifts of arms and munitions she brought with her had already been secured in every barn and croft in York before her ship made Bridlington Bay—along with several hundred Catholic recruits from the Continent, all awaiting her command. She would help her Charles take control of his rebellious kingdom once and for all time. This devil's uprising and its perpetrators would be vanquished, and the King would be restored to his God-given kingdom. Then they would return rights to all Catholics in England as she had promised His Holiness all those years ago.

'Is this my cloak?' she asked, reaching for the plain peasant garment the groom held out to her. Denbigh shrugged apologetically and helped her into it.

She smiled at him reassuringly. *'C'est sans importance.* It is warm and dry and I am grateful to be in the company of such a kind and loyal lord.' She wanted to ask for reassurance. *You are loyal, my lord, are you not?* But she did not. 'You have procured for me a fine mount.' Then she took his hand as he assisted her into the saddle.

They did not try to talk above the pounding hoof beats. After a few miles the mist lightened. A bashful crescent moon flirted with coy clouds, making hulking shadows of the trees, but at least the path was better lit. Her companion rode only slightly ahead, watchful of her pace. She had to trust him. The way was not at all familiar, the muddy road hardly more than a narrow path. Were Roundheads hidden in the black hedgerows? Spies, watching her every movement?

Who could one trust? Even among one's closest confidants, the earth beneath one's feet shifted with each new day. Like poor Susan Feilding who cried day and night and wrote letters pleading with her son. Henrietta had not the heart to tell Lord Denbigh that she already knew their son had gone over to Parliament's side. Or like the Percy family—young Henry Percy so loyal, so kind to her, entertaining her, carrying her messages from Den Haag back and forth at his own peril, and Lady Carlisle his sister, who over the years had befriended her Queen and now somehow managed to wrest guardianship for the royal children from Parliament. She still trusted Lucy Hay, didn't she? But then there was the elder Percy brother, Northumberland, once the King's Admiral, now Parliament's Admiral and her husband's enemy, directing the very cannon fire from which she was fleeing.

Finally, the path opened out into a meadow, revealing a carriage in silhouette. Her companion waved and spurred his horse to close the furlong between. Here was refuge, she thought as Denbigh reined in his mount. The men spoke softly but she heard the driver of the waiting carriage say they were ready to receive her as best they could under these hurried circumstances.

Not waiting for assistance, she dismounted, then checked her eagerness. Charles had known about the original hiding place. She had written him. He had answered that he would be far afield and could not risk meeting her but the Earl of Newcastle could be counted on to protect her. 'Has his Majesty been apprised?' she asked as Denbigh helped her into the carriage.

'We are dispatching a message to him.'

'And news of Tromp's fleet? Did it discharge its cargo and my belongings safely?' she asked suddenly breathless.

Denbigh smiled. 'Yes, your majesty. All is well. The Earl of Newcastle has diverted all northern forces to protect your arms and your men are already under his command—until their Queen arrives, of course.'

'My ladies? Jermyn and young Percy?'

'Clean away. Roundheads gave chase, but they were too far behind. Except for our little side adventure all went as planned.'

'My accoutrements?'

'Your necessary possessions have already arrived at York. Henry Jermyn is in possession of the rest of your trunks. They will be delivered to Handsworth Manor with a small contingent of your guard and soon will also be under the protection of William Cavendish, the Earl of Newcastle. It should be safe for you to travel to Handsworth in Sheffield within the week. Until then, I shall be your most obedient protector and servant.'

This was a disappointment. She had hoped to join Charles in Oxford within the week. But at least Sheffield was south of here, closer to him. Ever closer. She was also anxious to see for herself the safety of her belongings. Packed away in various trunks of satins and household goods was a gift for her husband: a million English pounds. Pray God, it would be enough to restore his kingdom to him.

When she next saw John Pym, Lucy was in the salon with the children, reading them a letter from their mother, enjoying their pleasure in hearing that Henrietta would see them 'before Eastertide.'

'Stay strong my darlings,' the letter said, 'until that time. Obey Lady Carlisle. She is our friend. And do not worry about Maman. Jeffrey and Mitte keep me entertained and Henri and Jeannette see to my comfort. I pray for you each night and morning. I hope you are keeping up with your devotions. I am bringing gifts for you.'

A relief, Lucy thought, to read that the Queen still called her friend.

'Gifts? Madame, does she say what gifts?' Elizabeth's eyes sparked with uncharacteristic enthusiasm. 'Maman is bringing us presents, Henry.'

The child stopped banging his wooden horse against the floor and held it out to his nurse. 'Hungry,' he said. His nurse laughed and picked him up, offering him her breast. Lucy was thinking it must be time for him to be weaned, when she heard the large brass knocker on the door and old Carter's thump-slide walk to answer it. Seconds later, she looked up to see John standing in the doorway, smiling at them.

'This is a pretty domestic scene,' he said, with a smile. Whilst the nurse covered her breast with her shawl, he gave a half bow, 'My lord, and my ladies.'

'Mr. Pym. How glad I am to see you. Are you alone?'

'Quite alone.'

'Can you stay for refreshment? We can retire to my apartment to discuss our business. I'll have cook send up something.'

'That would be most welcome, my lady. If I could have but one hour of your time, perhaps? We have much to discuss.'

Glancing at the nurse, Lucy said, 'See that we are not

disturbed, Collette. Take the children down to the kitchen and ask cook for some bread and fruit and cheese. See if you can't coax Henry to some . . . real food. Mash some fruit with honey, perhaps, and give him a taste.' The girl nodded. 'Also, Princess Elizabeth should practice her letters. Her new tutor will be here tomorrow.' Then in response to a tugging on her sleeve, 'Yes, Princess Elizabeth, what is it?'

'The gifts from Maman, Lady Carlisle, did she say—?'

'No, my lady, she did not. You shall just have to wait and be surprised. Try to exercise some patience, dear. It is a virtue.'

And with that she led her visitor out of the salon and up the stairs to her bedroom where she quickly locked the door.

'But you promised me refreshment, Countess. No servant can get in,' he said in mock surprise.

'No servant is needed, my dear Mr. Pym,' she said as with eager fingers she began to remove his shirt, inhaling the smell of him, wanting to feel his skin against hers, his hands on her body, chasing away the memory of the long lonely nights.

As she pulled his head down to meet her lips, he said, 'But you just said, patience is a virtue.'

'If that is true then I have such a surfeit of virtue I can lend some to the devil. I have been patient long enough.' Suddenly clumsy, she tried to unfasten her skirt.

'As have I, my lady. As have I.' He moved to help her, but his need suddenly seemed as urgent as hers. Together they fell upon the bed in a tangle of silk and lace and garters, and only after their first passion was sated did they lie together, skin to skin, pounding heart to pounding heart.

When he was completely spent and sleeping, she marked how his body had changed. His collar bone was more pronounced and the extra flesh around his waist had melted away. As she studied his face, she noticed hollows in the once round cheeks and that his cheek bones protruded sharply. It was a wonder how a man so thin could muster such passion. Almost she regretted having pulled some life force from him that he might later need. Almost. She pressed her lips to the hollow in his neck gently, feeling his breath on her cheek. She noticed a sweetish smell like overripe fruit fermenting into rottenness. It did not repel her exactly, but his breath usually tasted of spearmint leaves.

She dressed and tiptoed down the stairs to get him some food. On her way back up she passed by the salon. It was empty. Collette would have taken the children back to the nursery by now for their afternoon naps. By the time she returned to her chamber with a repast of chicken with goat cheese and bread and a tankard of perry, John was sitting on the side of the bed, pulling on his leggings. She helped him with his boots, then he bent down to kiss her lightly on the lips.

'Later, my love, she said, laughing. 'You need sustenance after such rigor.'

But he ate little. Urging him on, she fed him a bite or two of the chicken from her own hand, ever playing the coquette, how could any man refuse such tender ministrations from so willing a hand. His Adam's apple moved as he swallowed and she lifted a cup to his lips. 'This too. It is a sweet concoction of cream and eggs and honey. It will strengthen you.'

Swallowing as she spooned it into his mouth, he said, 'Did I not seem strong enough?'

'Oh yes. Very vigorous. It is just that I can't help but notice that you are losing flesh. And I would keep every inch of you. You are too burdened with the affairs of Parliament.'

He took a couple more spoonfuls of the milky substance and then shook his head.

'It is enough to burden Samson. Parliament is so,' he paused to search for the word, 'disparate in its opinion and there are some very immoderate forces that are difficult to control. Where once we had a common goal to force the King to a more reasonable governance, now it is all splintered. The Baptists want a huge model army of godly soldiers to fight for individual freedom—every man his own priest—and the Presbyterians are pressing to align with the Scots Covenanters who want England's Church run by their bishopric. They think the fight is over what words we use when we pray. Then there are the Levelers, who just want to scrap all authority, no kings, no nobility, no ruling class, just agreement by the people—as if the *people* could ever agree on anything except free bread and ale.'

He stood up and started to pace with surprising energy, his voice strident. Lucy watched in growing alarm as he ranted.

'Even Parliament can't agree. My God they are all so unreasonable. Your cousin Essex has lost control of his troops. They conduct themselves more like brigands than soldiers and the treasury is being drained by the Trained Bands. The Mayor of London wants his own city state. He never stops pressing for money for a new bridge because the old one is so clogged with traffic and riff-raff that shipments are delayed. Hell's bells. Even if we could come up with the money, the Watermen's Guild is hard against it. Too many factions, too many voices. It is just all too much.'

And then suddenly he sat down hard on the bed, his head slumped in his hands. Lucy was stunned at the swiftness with which the storm bled out. He was a picture of dejection. 'Here, my dearest, take another sip.' She held the cup to his lips. 'I put a little sherry in it too.'

He pushed it away with a slow shake of his head and said in a low monotone, 'I can't take sherry; it gives me pains in the stomach.'

'It is worry that is giving you pains in the stomach, my darling. Do not let it trouble you so. Some things are simply beyond your control. Accept that and you'll feel better.'

He looked at her with an expression of intense sadness. 'It's all coming apart, Lucy. How did we get here? I don't understand how we came to this place.'

He sat like that for a long minute or two. The house was quiet, then a small thin cry. Baby Henry waking from his nap. Finally, he lifted his head and looked at her with a beaten expression in his eyes.

'Do you know what they did yesterday?'

They? But she just shook her head, waiting for his lead, knowing instinctively that he was not finished.

'Clotworthy and some of the others.'

Clotworthy. Her mind searched for the name then finally it came. 'Clotworthy. Isn't he your brother-in-law?'

'I am ashamed to own it. He is a brute. A stupid man.'

'What did he do, John?'

'He led a bunch of ruffians into the Queen's Chapel at Somerset House and vandalized it. Broke apart the alabaster saints, took away the golden trappings on the altar—they have probably already been melted into coin to buy weapons.'

Beneath the quiet utterance she could hear the clang and clash, the splintering of an iconoclastic rampage. She had refused to worship at that Roman altar, but Henrietta had taken her there once to admire the magnificent altar piece painted by Master Rubens. Henrietta loved that chapel almost as much as she loved her Charles and her children. Lucy felt her heartbeat quicken. John's voice was now so low she had to incline her ear.

'There was a painting of Christ behind the altar. A huge colorful piece, not plain enough for my taste, but well done. The suffering of the man on the cross was palpable, his agony transforming paint and canvas. The Word made flesh before our eyes. It was as though Christ himself was dying on that cross. But not to Clotworthy. Calling for a halberd, he struck the face, swearing at it, profaning it with words unfit for pretty ears.'

'You saw him?'

'I arrived just as he ripped the painting to pieces with the hook of his halberd.'

Lucy, being a good Presbyterian, had no particular love for images. But even she had been moved by this one. It possessed a physical kind of power that could draw even a Protestant into the passion of Christ's suffering. But apparently not a Puritan. 'Did you try to stop him?'

'It happened so quickly. Have you ever tried to interfere with an enraged Irishman? He was fierce, attacking that painting with a fury that approached madness, as if he were attacking a living enemy.'

'Perhaps it can be restored.'

'What his men could not rip up they threw into the Thames,' he said with a sigh.

Then he raised his head and looked directly in her eyes. 'I fear our righteous anger has spawned a fury that has opened the earth and loosed hell's demons. If that is true then God help us all,' he said. 'Next time it may not be paint and images but the blood of the innocent and the flesh of the saints.'

Shortly after, he left, pleading he must get back to his duties. A dark spirit settled over Lucy as she thought of the sleeping children and for the first time wondered if she could keep them safe from such an unrelenting hatred. She wondered too how Henrietta could bear being separated from them.

'I am managing well enough,' Caroline said, trying to put on a brave face. The Powells had enough problems of their own without being burdened by hers. 'Although last night I thought I heard musket fire.'

She did not say that William's farm manager had either run off or been conscripted; she didn't know which. He just failed to appear one day without notice of any kind. She didn't say either that she had to let the housekeeper go and the grooms had run away and she slept with William's loaded pistol at her side—when she slept. Most nights she just lay awake listening for strange noises, her heart pounding in her chest until the creeping, gray light. Then she would fall into a troubled half-sleep for an hour or so until her long day of trying to keep mind and body together started all over again.

They were outside St. Nicholas' church, Sunday services having ended—to Caroline's great relief. The preacher had droned on about supporting God's anointed until Caroline had begun to wonder if God's anointed was sitting in the back pew. She still had the chickens to feed and the sheep to tend. One of the ewes was about to deliver. *Lord help her. Lord help me too.* She had never been present at a lambing. She had thought to ask Squire Powell if he could help if there were problems, but he seemed so burdened she decided best not to trouble them. Maybe fortune would smile, and she would just go out to the barn and find the little lamb happily nuzzling at its mother's teat. And maybe the faeries had left her a pot of gold beneath a painted rainbow on the stall wall.

'Caroline, come stay with us. Richard promised William. He frets about your being there all alone. I do too,' Mistress Powell pleaded. 'Mary would love your company. It would be like old times.'

'Not to worry. I'll come if the fighting gets closer. But right now, William's prize Merino pair is all the stock he has left.

I need to watch out for them. He will need something with which to rebuild the herd when he returns.'

'You could bring them here, though I cannot promise they will be safe from the raids. The King's men come here weekly demanding resources. I cannot even promise the Squire wouldn't donate them in a moment of weakness. He is that besotted with the idea of putting down the rebellion. Have you heard from William?'

'Not for a fortnight. One of the King's scouts was passing on his way to Oxford and brought me a letter. William assured me he is safe and well. He's been put in charge of provisions for his garrison which is in Gloucester now but is soon to be made quartermaster and may be transferred back to Oxford.'

'That would be wonderful. He would be so close, he could come home once in a while.'

'Even if he can't, I'll know I could go to him in a pinch. But wherever he goes it is a relief to hear that he will not be in the cavalry or infantry. William is hardly fit enough for battle. Not like the younger men. How is everybody holding up? The Squire looks particularly distracted.'

'The children hardly know there is a war. I can tell you that though I am sorry for Mary's marital problems—I would like to put my sturdy hands around John Milton's throat—but right now it is such a blessing to have her here. It is the Squire I worry about. He seems to retreat into his stock of strong cider with alarming frequency. I don't suppose I have long to worry about that though, because it is rapidly depleting along with all our other foodstuffs. The King's commissar sent some soldiers from Oxford asking for grain yesterday. Richard gave them ten bushels of corn and a barrel of salt pork he'd cellared away for safe-keeping against hard times. When I questioned him about giving up the stores so easily he told me not to worry, just to tend to my business.'

As if whether they had enough to eat was not her business, Carolyn thought.

Then Mistress Powell lowered her voice almost to a whisper. 'Now he is saying that housing is short in Oxford. We might have to take in some of the King's retinue. I am a loyal subject, Caroline, but I have my limits.'

'You mean provide room and board to the King's servants. But surely you would be compensated.'

'Promissory notes. Like they give us for the food they take. I am surprised Richard even accepts that. Did you not see him nodding and smiling at the sermon?'

But Caroline was scarcely listening, distracted by the thought that maybe she could volunteer to take in a baker's family or a chandler. Even if the King provided no remuneration for boarding except his goodwill, surely, she could share in whatever goods were produced. Fresh bread that she didn't have to bake—or candles. She was running low on candles and didn't want to raid her little hoard to buy more. Most nights she sat by firelight, dozing and jumping out of her skin at the rattle of a limb against a window, the hiss and split of a burning log, or the barking of the dogs.

Caroline grunted in understanding as she untied her horse from the tree limb where she had secured it and climbed up into the cart. 'Tell Mary, I hope her fever is better so she can come to services next Sunday.'

Ann gave a wry little smile. 'I'll tell her. Though I think she feels uncomfortable . . . you know. Like people are gossiping, wondering why she is not with her husband, or he with her.'

'I know. She can ride over and stay with me if we get some warm sunshine. I would love her company.'

'Have you heard any news of how the war is going?'

'The King's messenger told me that the fighting at Maidenhead had been fierce and that the King had cut off the coal supply to London after he was denied access to Hull. At least we still have plenty of wood for fuel and are not like to run out.' She nodded at the Powells. 'I think the Squire is restless. He is motioning for you. I'd best get on too.'

Caroline flicked the reigns and the little mare headed down the muddy path away from the church. Thank God for the horse, she thought as they made the two-mile trek home, though she didn't know how much longer she could feed any of the animals. The butcher was a friend of William's and kept her supplied with meaty bones for the dogs. Though last time he'd apologized saying that excess bones were getting scarce as customers bought more meat bones than cuts now. She offered to pay, but he'd said not yet. Times were not so hard that he would deny the Splendid Pair.

Splendid and Pair—that's what the two mastiffs were called, after the entry in William's ledger. He always referred to the dogs as a unit asset until one day she'd demanded to know which one was Splendid and which one was Pair and, while she liked both the gentle giants, she preferred the one with the fawn-colored coat and wanted to know what to call him. 'Well the one you choose, my darling, must of course be Splendid,' he'd said with a smile. So Splendid became her friend and fierce protector. And now that she was alone on most nights he slept on the main hearth, though lately he was developing a nocturnal habit of waking her to be let out.

As the horse trotted homeward at a gentle clip, Caroline thought she saw something in the hedgerow. A flash of late sun caught in bare tree branches? A fleeting shadow seen out of the corner of her eye? Just an animal, she told herself, her heart beating a little faster. She heard sounds and saw shadows everywhere these days.

Approaching the yard, she saw no curl of smoke coming from the chimney. The whole place reeked of loneliness and neglect. What would William say, she wondered as she unhitched the mare and led her into the stall. Would he blame her?

'Go easy, Lillybud. Only half a nose-bag today, old girl,' she said, stroking the horse's mane. The pretty little mare had been a wedding gift from William—her favorite gift. 'We have to make this little store last until spring. I had to raid the puzzle chest to buy enough feed, but you have to share with the sheep or we will all starve.'

The miller had said he could no longer provide on credit, even Sir William's, now that he was gone off to war. Only barter: edible goods, labor—or coin. He'd thrown in a cartful of sweet hay when she produced the silver—whether out of compassion or an attempt to keep a paying customer, she could not say. At least the winter was almost over. Spring would come soon. If she could just hold on until the pasture greened, maybe she could even plant a bit of garden. She'd found some seeds in the shed from last year's harvest. Cook, who only came one day a week now, could show her how to get a start. But surely by then, either Parliament or the King would come to their senses, and the folly of this hellish war would be ended. Surely by then, William would be home. Surely.

That night, like most nights, Caroline slept fitfully in her chair, unable to sleep in the bed without the comfort of William's body beside her. She jerked awake at every imagined noise, getting up once to let Splendid out. 'You keep watch, now,' she said to the big dog, who raised his black mask to her as though he understood. She watched as he did nature's business to make sure he was not coming back in, but when he ambled across the starlit field, she closed the door and went back to her warm hearth. Once she thought she heard the dogs bark and got up again to look. But all was silent. Splendid was nowhere in sight. He'd probably gone to the barn to keep Pair company. The night was cold. She put a small log on the fire. That should hold until daybreak.

Exhausted, Caroline went to sleep and woke to a heavy silent dawn. Wearily she poked at the embers on the hearth, added some kindling and another log before swinging a kettle of water over the smoky flames. Her neck ached from sleeping in the chair. She stretched and looked out the window to fields covered with hoar frost. Maybe it would be a clear, bright day, Caroline thought, hoping for sunshine to lighten her spirit. She had not cried since she lost the baby and then only small, stifled tears lest she cause her husband more grief. Even when William left, her sadness cowered in a dry well. If sunshine could not lighten her spirit, it could at least warm her bones.

But the burden of those unshed tears was soon to be relieved, for when she entered the silent empty barnyard a few minutes later she called out to Splendid only to be met with silence. Ominous, unbroken silence. No rooster crowing, no barking dogs, no neighing horse answered her morning call.

Then she saw, slightly to the right of the barn door, the Splendid Pair. They lay inert, Pair's bloody entrails spilling out on the ground, Splendid's throat slashed, a bit of fabric still clutched in her massive jaws. That was when the crying began, first a trickle, old tears first, thick and heavy with the residual of clotted grief. Not knowing what second horror waited inside the barn, she staggered in like a woman in a dream. No horror. Only stillness making the space eerily unfamiliar.

The sheep were gone. And Lillybud's stall was empty. She stood for a moment in stunned silence. A stream of freshly loosed tears poured down her face. It was almost funny. The way she'd worried about running out of feed. The sound of choking sobs filled the cold dead air around her. Her legs gave way and she sank down on the bales of sweet hay, hay no longer needed.

She sat that way for a long time, staring at Lillybud's empty stall, wondering what she was to do now. Nothing left. No hungry sheep. No greedy pony. Not even a chicken left pecking in the yard. Only a neglected barn with a sagging roof.

With sudden fury, she seized a shovel leaning against the slats of the stall and, running outside, started to dig. Eyes averted from her beloved mastiffs, blade against unyielding ground, she pushed hard, like a woman in labor, until the ground began to give, slowly at first, then whole shovelfuls.

Flying over her shoulder.

Exploding into the air.

Thud. Thud. Thud.

Like the beating heart of the earth.

As the hole deepened, her fury mounted.

King. Parliament.

Soldiers. Marauders. Thieves.

With each dive of her blade, she punished them all. And when she was finished, she half-dragged, half-carried the Splendid Pair into the giant hole in the barnyard. She would have buried all of them: all the evil ones who murdered and crushed and pillaged—if she could. Instead she buried innocence.

She was sweating when she finished, and the air was chilly. But the frost that had promised a clear sky did not lie and already she could feel the warming rays of the sun. She went to check in the hen house. It was as she supposed. Nothing was left except the walls and the poles on which the birds roosted. Scarcely a feather. She ran her fingers into the nests.

They had not even left one shit-speckled egg.

She remembered the flash and shadow she'd seen from the hedgerow, yesterday. Animals. The two-legged kind. With a slowly building rage, the kind of rage that builds false courage and dulls reason, she went into the house, retrieved the pistol from the mantle, and strode purposefully across the fields.

But when she entered the hedgerow, all she found were fresh footprints and, beside a dead campfire, one of the little bells from Lillybud's harness. She snatched up the bell, swiping at the dust and ashes, and polished it on her skirt. It tinkled a sad little sound in the thin air. As she listened to that solitary tinny sound her rage gave way to a solid determination.

She would not be alone for long.

Tomorrow she would go in search of her husband. She would inquire first at the Oxford garrison. He might be there by now or they might know if he'd been posted there. It was not that far away. And unlike him, Caroline did not have to ask leave of anybody. If he knew how bad things had become at home, he might get leave to come home. Or make provisions for her to stay with him. Some wives did, she'd heard. Especially now that there was so little left to guard.

She returned to the house and straightaway began to plan. Her legs suddenly weak, she sank down beside the cold hearth and rested—but not long. She would have to write a note to Mary. There was no time to go by Forest Hill: not if she had to walk, and besides they would only try to talk her out of it. Going to William's desk, she paused at the memory of him there, straight back slightly bent over his neat ledgers, pen in hand, his brow furrowed in concentration.

Tomorrow was cook's day. She would need a note of explanation also. Caroline carefully removed two small cut pieces of paper and dipped the pen into the ink. When she had finished, she folded the notes, heated a blob of wax over a candle flame and pushed William's monogram into it. She put Mary's note on the little table beside William's chair, propping it up prominently with her name on it. She knew cook could read. She'd given her lists before. She wrote COOK in large letters and placed hers on the kitchen table where she would be sure to see it. With cook's note she would leave a few coins and a key asking her to check on the house from time to time until her return.

But first she needed something to eat and to gather up something to take with her. There were half a dozen eggs in the egg basket that she'd gathered yesterday. As they were boiling over the cookfire that she had to stoke, she opened the puzzle chest, retrieving all the coins. When she had eaten two of the eggs and the last of the pear preserves on a hunk of bread, she sewed some of the coins in the hem of her skirt. Others she sewed into a little belt that she would wear around her waist, next to her skin. What was left she placed in her token box along with the little harness bell and buried the box inside the almost empty cellar. Then a second thought sent her to her cupboard to retrieve Letty's best pieces of silver— William would hate to lose these memories of his first wife— and buried them there also.

It was late afternoon by the time these tasks were done.

One more thing she had to do. Rumbling around in a clothing chest, she found an old pilgrim's scrip of sturdy leather and broad strap, large enough to accommodate a fresh smock and skirt. The old pilgrim's cloak she decided against. Nobody dressed as a pilgrim these days. It only invited harassment—or worse. She wrapped the pistol in a clean shift and put it in the bottom of the satchel. The cupboard offered the remainder of the bread, the other four boiled eggs and a bit of old cheese (with a knife to scrape the mold away). When she buried the box, she had discovered one lone withered apple and one more jar of summer pickles on a dusty shelf. These she tied with the other foodstuffs in a kerchief and placed all in the bag, weighing the bag in her arms. She could carry it easily enough with the strap over her chest to distribute the weight.

By this time the sky had turned to deep indigo. A woman alone dared not travel at night. Caroline sat down in her chair beside a dying fire and waited for day to break.

JOURNEYS

. . . [T]he joy I shall have in going, hoping to see you in a month . . . I fear to become mad with it for I do nothing in the world but think of this, the only pleasure which remains to me in this world, for without you I would desire to remain in it not one hour.

—Letter from Henrietta to King Charles I in
February 1643

7 March 1643

By the time they reached the hunting lodge in Londesborough, Henrietta's strength was failing. Her head ached from the jostling of the coach, and the small brazier at her feet did not chase away the numbing cold. An ageing groom, sheltering a torch, hastened out to take charge of the horses and carriage as Lord Denbigh helped her alight.

She recognized the lodge, a shadow of the one in memory. She and Charles and the children had hunted here once in midwinter. It had been alive with light and laughter and music.

'We are honored to receive you, your majesty, but we are embarrassed by our poor hospitality. We have not opened the lodge this season. When we received notice a few hours ago that your secret lodging had been compromised, we thought only of your safety. I fear you find us short-staffed and ill-provisioned.'

'Do not think your hospitality less than sufficient. A roof over our heads and succor from our enemies—is all that is required. Be assured that your courage and your loyalty will be rewarded by the King.'

As they entered the hall the smell of disuse made her nostrils flare. Dust hovered everywhere, on the stairs and in the corners,

coating the great mantle and painting the rich woods of the
furnishings with a gray patina. Cobwebs decorated the mounted
antlers of proud bucks, which in her memory had been adorned
with greenery and bright candles. Faint with weariness, she
sucked in her breath, dragging the musty air of neglect into
her lungs. But as she gazed into the shadows of the great hall,
she almost gasped in delight.

With wide staring eyes she watched as Charles, still in his
hunter's garb, descended the stairs with a ghost-like grace.
He raised his glass to the success of the hunt, gesturing at
a feast laden with succulent pheasant and confectionary
delights, then held out his hand to her. So real was her
vision she smelled the scent of his hair as he bowed before
her. She reached out her hand. He faded into the stale air. A
little cry escaped her lips. Not Charles. Just some figment of
her weary brain, mere image conjured by a longing so intense
she could not name it.

'Majesty, are you unwell?'

With scarcely breath enough to answer, she said, '*Je vais bien.
Un moment, s'il vous plaît.*' She shook her head, shutting out
the images, as she tried to regain her composure. When she
opened her eyes, Lord Denbigh was holding out a glass taken
from the meager board set only with a flagon of wine and a
platter covered with a linen cloth.

Beside him the steward spoke apologetically. 'Your majesty,
please forgive this poor hospitality. The house has been unused.
You will find England much changed in the year you have
been away.'

'*Mon Dieu. C'est un changement triste.*'

'*Oui*, it is a very sad change,' Denbigh said gently.

A woman who looked vaguely familiar offered a deep curtsy
from behind the small table. 'I am Constance, your majesty.
I would be pleased to attend you in the absence of your ladies.'

'*Oui*, Constance. I remember. You are married to the
seneschal.'

The woman's smile showed her pleasure at being remembered.

Denbigh held out his hand. 'Come, sit by the fire, your
majesty. Let Constance give you food and drink before you
retire to your chamber. It is the one you shared with the King

when you were here before. Constance has cleaned it and prepared fresh linen. I think you will be comfortable.'

Henrietta remembered that chamber, a love nest in a forested glade. Charles had been in a convivial mood at the evening fête. But the child they conceived that afternoon had been stillborn. The bleakness of the place recalled that early sorrow.

She sat down by the fire, and took the food and the drink, letting the warmth from the fire ease her aching body. When she had finished the bread and cheese, the bit of candied fruit that had probably come from Constance's own kitchen, she asked, 'Has the King been informed of our safe escape? Will he be at Sheffield to meet us?'

'I am afraid not, your majesty. Not immediately. He is at Oxford, preparing for a cessation of hostilities negotiation. The fighting in the Midlands has been fierce. Heavy losses on both sides. Parliament has taken Litchfield by blowing up the wall around the cathedral close. A marvelous feat of battle engineering—from the enemy unfortunately.'

Mon Dieu. Charles must not give in to the negotiations because of one defeat. She must get to him soon to convince him.

'Don't despair, your majesty. There is good news. Lord Brooke was killed.'

'Lord Brooke? He was their general in the North, *n'est pas*?' At Denbigh's nod, she said, 'That devil deserved to die. He called the Holy Father the Antichrist. This is to Parliament a great loss. It will give the King a stronger footing in the talks with Parliament, *oui*?'

'*Oui.* They will feel his loss keenly. Brooke's death was an inglorious one. He was spying on the fortifications surrounding the cathedral when he took an arrow to the eye delivered from none other than the village idiot.'

She shrugged. 'A merciful death for a heretic. Many have suffered worse deaths. Where is my convoy and men at arms?'

'Your army is under the direction of the Earl of Newcastle. He will accompany you to Oxford as soon as Rupert of the Rhine or his brother Maurice is free to provide cavalry escort. Rupert is presently fighting in Bristol and Maurice is in Gloucestershire.'

'His mother told me that Rupert was here, but I did not know Maurice had joined him. This is good. They bring with them many skills learned in the wars on the Continent. With their help and the resources I bring, I am sure the King will put an end to this insurrection soon. Now, I wish to retire.'

'Constance will attend you. Your maid Genevieve is already at Handsworth, your next stop. I am sorry there was not enough time to fetch her.'

She nodded, and tried to smile through her fatigue. She didn't really care if she had to sleep in her clothes.

'One more thing, your majesty,' Denbigh called as she ascended the stairs. 'The Queen's Guard are on their way. We can leave for Sheffield tomorrow, if you wish. Will you be ready, or do you want to rest here another day?'

'I will be ready,' she said.

Lucy Hay eyed her guest with a mixture of desire and appreciation. He was a fine specimen of manhood. She must be getting old, she thought, for somewhat astonishingly, his lustful gaze on her cleavage as she poured the wine was satisfaction enough. Almost.

'The proofs as you call them are satisfactory, Lord Whittier. Indeed, you seem to have included a morsel or two that I do not recall sharing. Have you another source of information about the Queen's children?'

He laughed, lifting his glass in a salute. 'That was direct. But just as I would not reveal your name to my other source I shall not disclose his name. It seems that is the easiest way to build trust among those providers upon whom I rely. Would you not agree, Countess? I mean a man must have integrity in matters of business.'

Reluctantly she ceded the point. There were more ways to trap a fox than one. She abruptly changed the subject. 'Rumor says that Lord Brooke has been killed at Litchfield and the Queen is in Yorkshire.'

'Indeed, I heard the same rumor, which at this stage, I can neither confirm or deny. Many rumors swirl in a vortex of misinformation.'

'But if this one is true, it is quite a blow to Parliament. I once visited Litchfield with my first husband,' Lucy said wistfully. 'It was beautiful then with its towers reaching to Heaven.'

Lord Whittier smirked. 'I suppose it is now reduced to a pile of rubble. Parts of it at least. The gods of war are blind to beauty.'

'As they are also blind to goodness and mercy. Why traffic with them at all, I wonder.'

'Why indeed?'

'Who holds Litchfield now?'

'That appears a muddle. But the story emerging is that the King's nephew had to withdraw his cavalry from Litchfield to shore up the Crown's main garrison at Reading. Without Rupert, if Parliament hasn't already taken the fortress at Reading, it soon will.'

'Is that the story you are going to write?'

He considered for a moment. 'I think not. At least not until I investigate further. I like to think I have more integrity than the other broadsheet and pamphlet-pushers who will publish any rumor as fact.'

'Speaking of that. How is your little enterprise doing?'

'Surprisingly well. The pace of the war feeds hunger for news in isolated London. I have a ready audience. Too much work for a one-man shop. I have hired a young man, a veteran from the war who lost his arm. He helps run the shop and manage the press.'

'With one arm?'

'He is smart and resourceful. And able-bodied young men are hard to find.' Then changing the subject, he asked, 'Have you more news from the Queen? Parliament intercepted a letter from her saying she is returning in May when the storms recede. But it was not in code, so they are skeptical of it. The rumor is that she is returning sooner than that, perhaps alone and in disguise. Is she coming to London to see the children?'

'I am sure I do not know. But that would be very foolish of her, would it not? I suspect her spies have already informed her that Henry and Elizabeth are with me. I hope that gives her some ease, given our history. Her appearance in London would only endanger herself and them. I expect wherever she is, she will eventually seek the temporary court at Oxford.'

'You have not heard from her, then?'

'I have not heard.' She shook her head and sipped her wine. A smile, a lift of the eyebrow—the courtier's expression of one who traded in secrets.

'May I see the children?' he asked. 'I would like to report on their good health.'

'You mean you wish to report that you have seen them? That seems foolish.'

'Not at all. Parliament knows they are with you. Leader Pym reports to them about the children's welfare, I am sure. My information is for those who are less invested but no less curious. Frankly, it may even engender some sympathy for them, should things take a more dangerous turn. Poor little lambs abandoned by their parents, etc.'

'Very well. You may see Elizabeth. She is with her tutor. But I warn you. Bathshua Makin is a dedicated scholar and considers Elizabeth a protégé. She will not welcome the intrusion. Henry is in the nursery. He still naps in the afternoon. But I grant permission only on one condition. You do not ask Princess Elizabeth any questions about her mother. It will avail you nothing and will only upset the child.'

He nodded his agreement, as rising, she led him down the hall and into the salon turned schoolroom.

'Excuse us, Mistress Makin,' she said opening the wide doors.

The woman frowned. 'This is an untimely interruption, Lady Carlisle. Princess Elizabeth was reciting her Cicero.'

'We will be only a moment,' Lucy answered apologetically. She was more than a little intimidated by the woman said by scholars to be the most learned lady in England. Lucy would have thought that title would surely go to Lucy Hutchinson, but she was young yet. Quickly turning to the princess, Lucy said, 'Your royal highness, this is my friend and yours, Lord Whittier. His name is James, like your grandfather's name. He wishes to convey his good wishes to you.'

Whittier bowed deeply, a bow worthier a queen than a child. The little girl's shoulders straightened and she lifted her chin confidently at the homage. Bless, you James Whittier, Lucy thought.

The girl's voice was high and excited. 'Did you know our grandfather, Lord Whittier?'

'I did indeed have the honor of meeting his Majesty. You have his intelligent eyes, if I may be so bold.'

Here at last was a family friend, the girl was thinking. Lucy could see it in her eager eyes. She almost feared the child would rush into his arms. Apparently, he had that effect on females of all ages. Royalty though she was, she was still a child who missed her father. And he was not above taking advantage of that.

'Have you any news of our mother?' the girl asked.

'Alas, I'm afraid not,' he said. Have you any—?'

Lucy steeped closer, grinding her heel as hard as she could into his boot. 'We must interrupt your Cicero no longer, your grace, lest Mistress Makin become annoyed with us. Lord Whittier has to depart. He is going on a journey.'

'A journey? If you see our father or our brothers, will you tell them to come and visit us? Our mother has promised to—'

'Lord Whittier really must leave, now, your grace. We would not want to delay him, would we? There are sometimes brigands on the road at night.'

James bowed again. 'I wish you a good lesson, your highness, and I hope to see you again soon. Perhaps I will have more time to visit when I return. You can recite your Cicero for me. And if I should encounter your father on my journey north I will tell him how much his daughter misses him.'

'And Henry too. He cries out for him at night. He loved to pull on Papa's beard.'

'And Henry too,' he said clicking his heels and backing out of her presence as though he were Raleigh and she the old Queen Elizabeth.

'You rogue. You have quite enchanted her and given her false hope. Her nagging will not cease until you visit us again. But that was your intent, wasn't it? I am warning you, James Whittier.'

He laughed and chucked her under the chin as if she were no older than the child whose chin he could not stroke, then said soberly, 'You have nothing to worry about, my lady. The girl's plight arouses my sympathy. She looks to be quite frail. I suppose she takes after her mother in form. If you should need help with her protection from either side, you have only to call me. Children should not be pawns in men's ill-begotten schemes of war.'

'I almost believe you, my lord,' she said as she reluctantly removed his hand from beneath her chin. 'Now what is all this about a journey?'

'See how prescient you are. But it was not a lie. You put the thought in my head with your maneuvering. I need to invest-igate rumor for myself instead of relying on rumor. I have to go to Reading anyway to order supplies.'

As he was putting on his cloak and hat, she followed him to the door. 'Do be careful. Rogue that you are, the world would be a much duller place without you.'

'I shall keep my eye out. I have been told there are brigands on the road at night,' he grinned.

She watched him ride away. The man was an enigma. Whatever he was, he was not a man to be trusted, and yet oddly enough she did.

LONGINGS

The night of the battle . . . I was obliged to walk about
all night, which proved very cold by reason of a sharp
frost . . . when I got meat I could scarcely eat it my jaws
for want of use having almost lost the natural facility.

—Parliamentarian Edmund Ludlow describing the
aftermath of the battle of Edgehill, October 1642

C aroline was relieved to see the sign of the Lamb, the
coaching house in Oxford. For three days she had
camped outside the Oxford royal garrison waiting for
an audience with the Captain of the Guard. At night, for three
pence, she had slept, or not-slept as was more often the case,
on a foul-smelling straw mattress in a smithy's forge. The
banked fires of the furnace conjured a ghostly warmth against
the damp and chill, but the nights were filled with heart-jolting
sounds: drunken soldiers cursing in the street, the occasional
burst of musket fire, and the ever-present rats scurrying behind
the coal stacked against the back wall. She passed the nights
with her mantle as blanket and her pilgrim's bag as pillow,
grateful for the reassurance of its hard center.

How foolish she had been to think she could just walk in
and demand to see William. Each morning she had gone to
the guardhouse asking to be admitted. Each morning she was
turned away. On the fourth day, she sat down on the prisoner's
bench behind the makeshift desk and told the young guard
that his captain must surely appear sooner or later, or some
other person in authority. She would remain on that prisoner's
bench until someone listened to her. It was an appropriate
enough place to wait she said, for she too was in a sense his
Majesty's prisoner. The lad had looked discomfited in the
extreme, but he made no move to have her forcibly removed.

Bye and bye, her patience was rewarded. No ragtag recruit this time, but a real soldier clad in helmet and breast plate, sword dangling from his belt, darkened the threshold.

'Captain,' the young man said, jumping to his feet and saluting.

The captain said nothing at first, just glanced at her and frowned, then raising one eyebrow, looked at the guard.

'This woman is waiting to see you,' he stammered. 'I tried to send her away but she would not leave. This is the fourth day she has been here.'

'What does she want?'

'She asks for admittance, sir.'

'Admittance. To a garrison of hardened soldiers? Now why would any respectable woman want that,' he said with a smirk. 'We have enough of her kind here already.'

'She says she wants to see her husband. She says that he is garrisoned here in the King's service and she must speak to him.'

The captain did not even give her the courtesy of looking at her as he dismissed her. 'I'm afraid that is impossible. I've been dealing with Madame Brome Whorwood and her demands to see the King all morning. I've no time for this. Send her away.'

'I've tried, sir. But she will not—'

That name filtered through Caroline's anxious fog. Whorwood from the manor of Holton Park. She had met this woman and her husband once at a dinner at Forest Hill. She had come soliciting funds for the King, boasting of her family's long-time connection with the court. The woman was charming enough, more enthusiastic in the appeal than her husband, a rude upstart squire , who was said to have fled to the Continent when the fighting started. The captain had said he'd *dealt* with her. Jane. That was her name. Mistress Jane Whorwood. Caroline doubted he had dismissed her as rudely.

She stood and stepped between the desk and the man who could give her entry, forcing him to look at her as she said, 'His Majesty would not be pleased to know that the wife of a knight in his service has not been offered this small courtesy. Please check your lists. Sir William Pendleton. You don't have to admit me. I am content to wait here until you fetch my husband. I must speak with him about his affairs. His last letter to me said he was being posted here. He was serving as Master of Provisions for the King's troops. The King's own herald brought the letter.'

The captain scowled at her as if he'd never seen such a disagreeable woman. 'Sir William Pendleton. And you say you are his lady.'

'Here, I'll show you. The letter bears the royal seal.' When she produced the frayed letter from the pilgrim's scrip, he glanced at the ragged seal and sighed, still eying her suspiciously. And why not, she thought. She must look more like a camp follower than a knight's wife. He gestured for her to sit on the bench, mumbling under his breath, 'All these women, all their needs urgent with no idea what it means to be at war.' Then he turned on his heel and left.

'Is he going to come back?' she asked.

The youth shrugged. 'Who can tell. When he gets his back up—it's a good sign that he didn't yell at you like he does everybody else who crosses him.'

She bit back her frustration and sat back down on the bench. Close to an hour later, her feet aching, her throat parched, and her bladder begging for relief, he returned. His countenance had softened. The skepticism did not come back with him. But neither did William.

'Yes?' she asked, her heart stuttering.

'My lady,' he said, expressionless. 'You were correct, Sir William was posted here but I am sorry to tell you that Sir William—'

Sorry. Sorry? Why sorry?

'I am afraid your husband is no longer here. He—' He paused for what seemed to her like an eternity.

What could he not say? Not that. She would not hear that. 'Not here?' she asked quietly. 'What do you mean, Captain, not here?'

'He left three days ago for the garrison at Reading with supplies to relieve the King's loyal subjects who are under siege. I cannot say when he will return. It may be a fortnight. Maybe longer.'

Weak relief washed over her. Not here. But not killed. Not wounded. 'Reading? That is south. I know that road.'

'Then you also know it is too far for a lady to travel alone even in peace time. We are a nation at war, my lady. There is heavy fighting around Reading.'

Heavy fighting around Reading. William's destination. But I am not a woman alone, she thought. Not completely. She still had two lead balls and a vial of black powder tied in a kerchief and bound with the other rags she'd brought for her personal needs. Every night before she closed her eyes she'd rehearsed what William had so carefully instructed the day before he left: *take the rod secured to the bottom of the pistol barrel and ram the black powder and one of the lead balls in. Ram it hard as you can, Caroline.* And then he had demonstrated how to set the dog latch. *Don't walk with the pistol half-cocked. You'll have to wait. When you release the dog latch and the flint strikes the frisson there will be a tiny pause. Keep the pistol pointed at your target.* And he had made her practice, again and again, scolding her when her attention wandered. All she could think about that day was that he was leaving. She would still have the overseer; why would she ever need to fire a pistol? If William really thought she would have to defend herself in this way, how could he have left her?

'How did you get here, Lady Pendleton? On foot, I'd say,' the captain said glancing at her muddy boots, then he tapped the shoulder of the young guard who leaned against the door frame, listening.

The soldier assumed a more appropriate posture. 'Captain, sir.'

With a sudden stab of longing, she thought of William's son. She had not heard from Arthur for months.

'Obviously, Thompson here has nothing better to do. He will accompany you back to the inn. You can rest there until you decide what you want to do. I will be sure and tell Sir William Pendleton of his wife's visit when he returns. In the meantime, I strongly recommend you return home and await your husband's instructions.'

'Thank you for your concern, Captain. I know the way. I

don't need an escort.' And then looking at the boy, she relented, 'But I will enjoy the company.'

She released the young man as they came into the court-yard of the inn, but not before ordering some refreshment for him. The homesickness he spoke of, the fear leaking from beneath a thin veneer of bravado, moved her almost to tears. He said his mother had cried when he left. As Caroline had cried for Arthur, but not in front of William. Never in front of William, who was much too angry at his son to tolerate her tears.

The innkeeper greeted her warmly. She and William had on more than one occasion hired horses from him. His wife brought her bread and warm broth and wine and offered her a room. She wisely made no comment on Caroline's disheveled appearance. 'If thou be wanting to go to London today, my lady, I fear we let the last private coach an hour ago.'

'I am not going to London. Is there a public coach to Reading tonight?'

'A public coach?'

Caroline heard something akin to disapproval in her tone. 'Yes, Mistress Betty. Quite sure.'

'There is no public coach tonight,' she said quietly, chastened by the firmness of Caroline's tone. 'But one is due in from Coventry about sunset. Overnights here. It will leave at daybreak. Bart is the regular driver. He's a goodun too. I'll put a peep in his ear. He'll take care of thee, he will.' Then she seemed to consider before adding, 'Will thou be wanting a room? With the coach leaving so early and all. Thou can have one all to thyself. Traffic is slow.'

A room to herself would mean a good night's rest, and she would not have to greet William so travel-stained.

'Bart always stops for fresh horses and relief at Tokers Green and supper at Benson. You could be in Reading by day after tomorrow midday, the good Lord willing.'

'What is the cost of the room?'

'Two shillings. But that comes with a chamber pot, a bed warmer, a fresh towel for bathing—and a sturdy lock. A cake of soap is four pence,' she added apologetically. 'And I'll fix ye a bit of breakfast on the house.'

'That sounds reasonable, Mistress Betty. And I will take the soap.' She could at least wash her hair and put on the clean skirt she was saving. 'How much is the fare to Reading?'

'Will that be round trip?'

Caroline suddenly felt her mind go numb? Round trip? The bloody image outside the barn flared and died. She had not thought past finding William. A swift and cutting longing covered her. His solid strength had been her strength. But what if she could not find him? Or what if—? What would be her strength then?

'My lady?'

'I am . . . I am not quite sure. I am seeking my husband. He will tell me what to do when I find him.'

'I understand. It must be very hard to be alone. It is my greatest fear. I will pray for thee, my lady.'

The offer of those prayers was somehow the last straw. Caroline blinked back tears. 'Thank you, Mistress Betty. Just book a passage for me one way, and I think I would like to retire to that room now.'

Mid-afternoon and the tavern room at the Reading inn was empty. It was early yet. James Whittier chose his seat carefully, his back to the wall facing the door. He pulled out a deck of cards and, placing them on the table in front of him in open invitation, signaled the publican to bring him a pitcher of beer. Two Royalist soldiers glanced over at him, one nodding in recognition before turning back to his companion with a smirk and a muttered comment. A reluctant contributor to James's enterprise the evening before, this one would need to be seduced by the sounds and sights of the game to repeat his loss. James sipped his beer. It was early yet.

The only other occupant of the room was a woman sitting with a plate of cheese and ale, chatting with the barmaid. A regular from her easy familiarity—but not a common woman, he thought. She was tall and fashionably dressed. A pretty round face with smooth skin was marked subtly with a large round pox mark on her cheekbone and another to the right of her nose, but all in all the disease had touched her gently. She talked animatedly, her smile contagious, and with a good-humored manner that showed a woman at ease in this common setting. An abundance of flaming red hair suggested Scots heritage. James had employed many Scots at his court. And King Charles still entertained some, but fewer since the Covenanters had risen in protest at the imposed English prayer book. This one might still have currency at court—if there was still a court—a younger less pragmatic Lucy Hay but probably more loyal. She glanced his way. He nodded and smiled. Tempting. Maybe later.

He had lingered outside the walls of Reading an extra day. The coaching inn and stables were located on the main road and reasonably comfortable. In addition, it offered easy plucking of bored pigeons—though, trouble was these birds were a little sparsely feathered. They had complained of the King's paymaster being churlish and sluggish. James had made a mental note. A sign of Charles's rapidly depleting treasury? That might be a bit of news a Parliament town would enjoy.

Although the town was preparing for siege, he felt safe enough. The commander of the Royalist garrison of two thousand soldiers, the newly appointed Governor of Reading was Sir Arthur Aston and an old friend of James's late father. He felt sure he could talk himself out of any tight situations and besides, his paper supplier was a staunch Royalist and would vouch for the neutrality of a good customer.

No real threat from Essex's gathering forces on the perimeter either. When he'd entered the town yesterday, the respective armies had been too preoccupied with digging ditches and shoring up stonework defenses to bother him. If the cannon started firing in earnest, he was sure he could get safe passage back through Parliament lines. He would just drop Lady Carlisle's name or John Pym's. He had planned to leave today but as he sipped his beer he decided one more night wouldn't hurt. Last night's pickings had been decent, and though the regulars had already been cleaned out, one of them had a handsome pistol in his belt that James coveted.

The flintlock had a dog-latch barrel that was only about twelve inches, small enough to carry in the pocket of a coat. The handsome checkered carving on the walnut handle and the shorter-barreled snaphaunce, not standard issue even to officers and gentlemen, argued that this was a personal weapon with which the soldier might part for a price—or perhaps a gambling obsession. One more night just might be worthwhile. Also, he might be able to glean some real news about the siege. Reading was close enough to London to be a threat to the city. London's readers would be interested.

As he twirled the beer in his mug he wondered idly if the pleasing redhead would be staying overnight at the inn. Unescorted? Odd for a woman of quality. Perhaps she was meeting a lover. A secret assignation. Intriguing thought. When his game was finished he might seek out the pleasure of her company. No pressing need to rush back to the shop anyway. In exchange for room and board, he'd recently taken on a disabled young soldier to mind the print shop. Ben, the youth had said his name was, after a small hesitation, Ben Pender.

'How can you mop an ink press with only one arm, Ben?' James had asked.

'Give me a chance to learn, and I'll show you,' the lad had said.

James had wanted to ask how he lost his arm, but he thought that might be too close to the bone. 'Who were you fighting with?'

'Cromwell in the North. I was sent to Edgehill to scout out the rumor of Royalists planning battle action there. I found out too late that it was no rumor.' He took a deep breath. 'I didn't make it back to report. Maybe that's why Cromwell's men got there too late.' Then the boy gave a half-grin, too sardonic by far for a man his age and added. 'But Rupert was late too. They said the battle was pretty much just a bloody draw.'

'You didn't actually see the battle, then?'

He looked down. 'No, I was ambushed the day before the fighting started. All I saw was a field of black. It was a frosty night for October. I remember feeling so cold as I lay on the ground trying to staunch the flow of blood. Then I blacked out. A friendly shepherd found me. The barber surgeon who relieved me of my arm said I was lucky. The cold was all that kept me from bleeding out.' He gave a bitter little half laugh. 'Funny thing, I don't feel lucky.'

'Well, you've got one good arm. And a head on your shoulders. You muster out or just walk away?' He didn't want to use the word desert. That would be a hanging offence.

'Medical discharge. Unfit to serve.'

'Do you have family hereabouts, Ben?'

The youth studied the toe of his worn-out boots. 'No, sir. No family. Army sent me to Bart's as soon as I was fit to travel. After I recovered they let me keep on sleeping there so I could help with the wounded. But they—the wounded—just kept coming. Every day. Every night. They just kept coming. After a while I just couldn't stand the screaming anymore.' He looked James directly in the eye. His gaze was straightforward and a little empty as he said, 'I need something else to do.'

It had only taken James a moment to decide. He liked the boy's nerve. Admired his initiative. 'You can sleep here. Room and board. Though I've no cook. The fare is what I provide from street vendors and cook shops: mostly bread and cheese, milk and apples when we can get them. The occasional roast joint from the tavern to celebrate a successful issue.'

'I can cook. Basic stuff—stews and porridge,' Ben said, with a nod at the two ragamuffins binding the papers into stacks, pretending not to listen. 'Enough for the boys there, too. If you'll supply the victuals.'

'They'll think that's an improvement, I'm sure. There is a coal stove you can cook on. Probably needs a good scouring. I'll expect you to help with the press to the extent you can. I'll show you how to set the type. You should be able to do that with one arm. If after two weeks you're more than earning your keep,' he shrugged, 'a shilling a week to start. You can bunk here in the press room with the boys on straw mattresses. I sleep upstairs—with my door open so I can hear any devilment that might go on down here.'

'You will not be sorry, I promise. And I'll keep these two over here out of mischief,' he said, turning, grinning at them.

'Ye'll be right welcome. Gets half scary down here some-times in the dark,' Ralphie had said, his mouth a round *o* and his eyes wide.'

James remembered noticing then the difference in their

speech. The youth's words were coherent and clear of any trace of the street accent of the London boys. That had made him curious. 'What did you do before the war, Ben?'

'I was a student. First year at Cambridge. But I gave it up when my tutor went off to join the cause. I guess I followed him. To the wrong side, according to my father.'

'Ah, the father you do not have.'

'Yes. The father who no longer owns me.'

He might be hardly more than a youth, James had noted, but he had a man's full-grown pride. 'Just one more question, Ben. Was it worth it?'

'Worth it, sir?'

'Your arm, I mean. Do you think this power struggle between the King and Parliament worth the loss of your arm? The loss of your family?'

Ben studied the toe of his worn-out boot a minute before he answered, then he directed that empty gaze on James once again and said, 'Can't say now. I'll have to wait and see what comes of it all, won't I? But the way I see it, it's not the King's Parliament. It's ours.'

After two weeks, Whittier had felt comfortable enough to leave him on his own. The news boys were in awe of him, with his tied-up sleeve and stories about his scouting expeditions. Stories Whittier was sure would find their way into some of the broadsheets. But that was a good thing. Parliament needed to know what it was doing to its youth. Young Ben was not the only limbless discard he'd seen recently: sleeping in doorways, picking through garbage, begging.

The sound of a coach and six interrupted the quiet of the tavern. Business would pick up, now, he thought, taking another sip of the beer. He watched out the broad-paned window as the passengers began to unload. Five of them. Two looked as though they had not tuppence between them. But the other two he judged well-heeled and jolly enough. One looked in his direction, saying, 'Give us a chance to slack this road thirst.'

James nodded and looked up to see the fifth passenger enter. Another woman. This one alone as well. Strange times, he thought. War just didn't fracture policy and loyalty to country but families as well.

She paused in the low doorway and frowning, looked around, as if she were sizing up the room. Looking for an easy mark? No. More like looking for safety, he thought as she settled with her bag in a shadowy corner. As still as a statue, she just sat there, staring out the window, clutching the large bag in her lap. Pretty in a weary kind of way. Good body, tall and thinner than the redhead but strong square shoulders and nice firm breasts. Damp tendrils had escaped a chestnut-colored bun at the base of her slim neck.

Her gaze met his then turned quickly away.

No invitation there. On the verge of his mind something stirred, almost startling him into recognition. But his attention was suddenly directed away from the woman as the two new arrivals approached him.

James stood up and bowed slightly. 'How about a friendly game?'

'I don't know, shall we risk it?' the older of the two asked his younger companion. Then he addressed James. 'Soldier over there says you're a hard man to beat. But we'll give it a try,' he said sitting down. A scraping of chairs and his fellow followed suit.

'Come on over and join us, friend,' James called. 'Maybe you'll recoup your losses and then some. Landlord, bring my friends here three mugs. Cards or dice, gentlemen, your choice.'

'Cards,' the sullen loser from last night grunted.

'Cards it is,' James said, picking up the deck and shuffling.

The disgruntled one reached out, grabbed his hand. 'A fresh deck from the landlord. If it's all the same to you.'

'Were it not for the fact that you are the King's soldier—and for that splendid pistol you are carrying in your belt, I might take offense. But I shall choose not to.' He smiled affably, 'Landlord, may we borrow a deck of cards?'

'Tuppence, rental only,' the landlord said, slouching over and slapping a worn deck of cards onto the table. James dug into his pocket, mentally putting that to the newcomer's account. He slid the cards forward. 'I think our skeptical friend here should make the first cut, just to show we are all men of good will. What do you think, gentlemen?'

They nodded, and the game began. They played in silence

at first with James careful to see that he did not win right away. As his 'luck' increased, the two playing on each side of him were at least staying alive. But scarcely twenty minutes had gone by before the soldier threw in his cards. 'I'm out. Nothing left to lose. Should have learned my lesson.'

James smiled at him as affably as he could. 'Evening is young, friend. You deserve a chance to get your money back. I much admire that pistol. I'll buy it from you and you can start all over. It's not King's issue, is it?'

'King's issue?' the soldier grunted. 'You must be joking. I took this off a dead man.'

'One you killed?'

'No. His uniform said he was one of ours. An officer. I didn't think he'd be needin' this fine weapon.'

'But why would whoever killed him not take a valuable gun?'

'Do I look like a bloody mindreader? Roundheads ambushed a convoy of supplies three days ago. Took a couple of prisoners, must have wounded this one before he ran and bled out. Clothes were all bloody. His body was in a ditch. Poor bastard. Buzzards had worked on him pretty good.'

He paused in the telling of his tale. 'He had some fine boots, too. Too small for me though.'

'Did you bury him?' one of the other card players asked. 'He was one of your fellow soldiers.'

'What was the point? Nature does it well enough. I imagine his bones are picked clean as a toothpick by now.' He shrugged. 'Besides, I didn't have a shovel.'

James could see the print header in his mind, *Death of an Unknown Soldier and the Spoils of War*, as his companions grunted in disgust. Then a scraping of chairs as the story-teller stood up and looking directly at James said with a sneer, 'I'll keep the gun. Might be luckier than your cards.'

As he walked away, his hand caressing the curved handle of the pistol, a player commented, 'Why would the fool think that? It didn't bring much luck to the dead man.'

'Bloody fools, all of them,' the older man said.

They played another few rounds after that, but it was as though the mention of the dead stranger, who had been so carelessly relieved of his gun and his life, cast a pall on the pleasure of the game. After a small profit, James let his companions win the last two rounds and then stood up and throwing in his cards made his excuses. As he walked away, he glanced at the corner where the woman had been warming herself by the fire. The bench was empty. So was the table where the red-head had been sitting. On his way to his room he asked the barmaid about the woman who had arrived on the last coach.

'No, sir. I don't know her. I've not seen her here before. She left about an hour ago.'

'Did she say where she was going?'

But what did he care where she was going. Pretty, lonely women were two for a penny these days.

'She asked for directions to the garrison,' the barmaid answered.

A glance at the window showed the thin April twilight had turned to indigo.

'At this hour? The gate will already be locked.'

'Mistress Whorwood offered to share her quarters with her, but she was most insistent on reaching the garrison tonight. Lady Jane gave her good directions, told her which gate to enter, and gave her a letter of recommendation for the gatekeeper.'

'Was she traveling on foot?'

'Yes, but she left before dark. It's not more than two miles, she'll most like be there by now.'

What prompted James Whittier to his next action, or the nature of the impulse goading him—a news printer's curiosity or some greater, genuine concern—he would not ponder until much later. He was halfway up the stairs when he suddenly had the urge for a moonlight ride. He turned around and going back to the bar asked the publican to call for the groom to fetch his horse.

SIEGE

The Governor returned answer that he would not deliver the town, until wheat were come to forty shillings a bushel, and as for the women and children they could all die with him . . . whereupon the Lord General made his cannon to play upon the town all the whole day . . . until 6 o'clock this morning.

—a report of Sir Arthur Aston's response to surrender from the *Mercurius Aulicus*

James had been right in his assumption. The main gate was closed. He had not passed the woman on the road, so she must have made it safely inside, but as he was here, he might as well ask for an audience with the governor of the garrison. Sir Arthur Aston would be a good source of information, and even if he should not be forthcoming, James could judge for himself the man's reaction to the large number of troops massing outside the town walls and glean somewhat his strategy for defense.

He guided his horse around the curtain wall to the small postern gate behind a rise of brush. This rear entrance was cunningly located adjacent to a hidden path leading down to the river, well out of sight of Parliament's forces. His horse picked his way carefully through the thorns and into the narrow opening, manned by a lone guard—hardly a soldier from the looks of him, more likely a local conscript, a tanner by his odor, who had abandoned his enterprise for refuge inside the city walls.

'Halt. Who goest there?' the man growled.

James saluted him with a respectful nod and a show of open hands. 'Lord Whittier to see Sir Aston,' he said, reaching with careful movements into his doublet's inside pocket in a two-fingered retrieval. When he held out the coin, the tanner's eyes squinted with greed. He would have to scrape a lot of hides to earn half a crown.

Holding out his hand and jerking his head to the right, the guard said, 'Ask for the Governor at the main gate. Somebody there will escort thee and take care of thy horse. I daren't leave me post. A reckoning must be kept of all who pass.' He thrust a slate out to James. 'Scratch thy name in the 'after sunset' line and the purpose for thy visit.'

After writing his name, James trotted his horse around the inside of the wall to the portcullis, dodging casks and barrels stacked high. It was obvious the town was preparing for a siege, but if this was all the excess they had, they would not last long. Two laughing children, chasing a hound through the street, prompted him to hope the grain bins were full. A prolonged siege was a terrible thing. A musket ball through the heart was quick, but in a siege the weak and innocent slowly starved to death on poor rations. The defenders would be fed first, a cold logic of war. The man at the pub had mentioned a stolen convoy of supplies. A strategic move by Essex. Soon enough the stone walls, which now defended the inhabitants of Reading, could become a prison to be escaped only by surrender or starvation.

A couple of lanterns swung from the entrance to the guard-house. From within their circle of yellow light two men, each armed with a blunderbuss slung from his shoulder, distributed axes, pikes, and a few carbines from an unhitched wagon. A few cobblestones closer to the gate another soldier harassed a cart driver.

'Spy!' the indignant youth driving the cart protested. 'This is the third wagonload I've brought today from the mill. Check with the commissar. He'll tell ye.'

But the guard plunged his dagger into one of the sacks to be sure. About a cupful of precious flour spilled out. Satisfied, the guard let go the reins of the nag pulling the cart and jerked his head sharply in a motion to proceed.

Holding securely to the reins of his horse, James dismounted and approached one of the men handing out arms. 'Lord Whittier to see the governor,' he said in a businesslike tone. 'I have important news for him. Please be so kind as to direct me to him.'

The soldier just looked at him, a half-smile on his face. This was no rustic volunteering for protection.

'He's expecting me,' James lied. 'And where is the nearest public stable?'

After a brief pause, the soldier responded, 'We'll see to the horse for you.'

And it will suddenly go missing, part of the King's cavalry, James thought. He said, 'That is kind of you, but your duties are deserving of your full attention. Carry on as you were. Just tell me where to find Sir Aston.'

Another considered pause and then the slightest shrug of his shoulders. 'His lordship is probably on his way here. To the guardhouse. He was called to an interrogation.'

'Is that usual? I mean for the Governor of Reading to involve himself in questioning strangers?'

'No, not usual. Just being extra-careful I guess. Dangerous times.'

Did this man have any understanding of just how powerful a storm was gathering outside the walls? James had known Reading was too close to London to tolerate a Cavalier garrison, but as he skirted their encampment two days ago, even he had been surprised by the thousands of Roundhead dragoons and cavalry, the big cannon brought up on river barges, waiting to be rolled into position. Essex's mighty war machine against the kind of paltry arms being handed out from this wagon? No cannon mounted on the walls, just a few sniper holes in the ramparts and some large pots of oil waiting on the battlements, ready to be lit and tipped. Yet, from what he remembered of Arthur Aston, he did not seem like the kind of man to surrender easily. He was a man who wore confidence like a mantle embroidered with arrogance.

'Which way is the nearest stable?' James asked as though permission had already been granted. 'By the time I get back the Governor will probably be finished with the interrogation.'

'Maybe.' The soldier shrugged. 'Maybe not. He is questioning a woman. Came in alone just before the gate closed, demanding admittance. Refused to leave until she spoke with someone in authority.

'Did she give her name?'

He shook his head. 'Can't remember. Lady something or other. I guess that's why they didn't toss her out. Just trot your horse along the curtain wall. The stable will be on your left behind the smithy.'

As the guard turned back to his work, James noted that the armaments wagon was almost empty. That was good. And as he had hoped, by the time he walked back to the guardhouse the two soldiers were gone and even the wagon had been rolled away. The street was deserted except for a young guard sharing his rations with a cat on the lip of the stone railing.

Voices spilled out of the half-open door into the now quiet street. Aston's, he recognized. The woman's voice was pitched low, exasperated, breathy. He was wondering if he should enter the guardhouse when her tone began to rise in pitch, indignant, protesting, treading memory. Somewhere he'd heard that voice before. Curious, he entered. The subject of the interrogation was seated at the table over which a scowling Aston towered in a posture of intimidation. Spread out on the table between them were the contents of her bag. On the top of the sundry assortments rested the object that had occasioned such scrutiny from the Governor.

James recognized the woman. He also recognized the pistol. He had seen both just hours before. The woman looked up at him, her eyes wide with something, not fear exactly, not resignation, but something closer to frustration and even anger. He did not know her name. But he knew this woman; he had seen her at the inn tonight.

And once before.

On a lonely road outside Rickmansworth.

And now he was wondering just how she had achieved what he could not, the possession of that fine weapon. 'Perhaps I may be of service, Sir' he said.

Aston looked up with a frown.

'James Whittier. You were often at our house in Kent when my father was living.'

'Whittier? Ah yes. I remember. You were the younger one. Though now I suppose you are Lord Whittier. How can you help? Do you know this woman? She says she is the wife of a knight in the King's service.'

'I have made her acquaintance briefly. She was in the company of her husband. He was certainly a gentleman. I did not know he was a knight as we were not formally introduced. He was from Oxford, I believe.'

The woman was staring at him with puzzlement, but she said nothing.

Aston looked thoughtful. 'That would be consistent with her story and the document she carries. Can't be too careful with Essex's Roundhead dragoons swarming. Speaking of which, how do you come to be here? Are you the King's man?'

'I will be honest with you. I am neither King's man nor Parliament's man. I am only a humble printer seeking the truth of this war in the hope it will shine a light on reason and might just save England.'

Where had that come from? But it sounded good, if a little grandiose.

He continued. 'I came to Reading to buy paper and to discern truth from self-serving lies. My print shop is in London. As you can imagine, information gleaned from sources there concerning outlying events are less than trustworthy. I can show you my bill of sale and you may verify with the supplier. He is just outside the walls, riverside. Not far from the mill. Behind the earthworks your men are digging as an outer ring of defense.'

'I will take your word for it.' He paused before adding, 'I was sorry to hear about your brother's misfortune. I thought you were at Cambridge studying for the priesthood. Did you abandon a vocation to manage the estate after his death?'

'Hardly. There is nothing left to manage. As for my vocation,' he shrugged, 'I disliked being beholden to king and archbishop for my living.'

'It is not too late, you know. We are going to win this little skirmish. We are going to win the whole goddamn war. And when we do, it will go hard for those whose allegiance was not pledged to his Majesty. I can commission you right here, right now.'

'That is more than kind and please don't think me lacking in gratitude, but I am afraid I am as ill-suited to soldiering as I am to preaching.'

Aston frowned. 'Suit yourself. I hope you do not live to regret it.'

'My lords, may I please reclaim my belongings?' the woman interrupted, already gathering the contents of the bag. 'May I have the gun back also? It is one of a pair brought from Spain. My husband left it for my protection when he went into the King's service.'

So the gun was one of a matched pair. The mate to the gun he had made a bid for? Or the weapon itself?

She continued, 'I have come from the Oxford garrison seeking news of my husband. William is Master of Provisions there. He was dispatched several days ago with supplies and food-stuffs to aid your garrison during the siege.' She paused, and he noticed when she resumed the slightest quiver in her voice. 'He should have arrived by now. I am in desperate need to speak with him.'

I took it off a dead man. That's what the other soldier had said. *One of a pair*, she said. This desperate woman was looking for her husband with no understanding that she was already a widow.

'Please. Take me to him.' More a command than a plea.

Yes. He was sure of it now. *Don't you dare hurt him.* And something about the eyes, ringed with shadows now, but glaring anger and determination. *There's three of us and one of him.*

This was no shy violet. This was a strong woman, strong enough to challenge an armed criminal on an open road. A sudden surge of sympathy surprised him and a twinge of guilt, remembering the ring he had kept as a souvenir of his short-lived criminal enterprise. This woman might just survive this war, if she could get back to a place of relative safety, back to her home and family and friends. She did not need to learn the futility of her suit. Not here. Not now when she was worn out from her travels and trapped inside a town about to explode. How could he even be certain her husband was the dead man mentioned in the card game? The source of his information was hardly reliable.

'Where is your home if I may ask, my lady?' James asked.

She looked at him with irritation as if to say what difference did that make and answered, 'We live about seven miles east of Oxford, close to Forest Hill Manor. William's last letter several weeks ago said that he was being posted permanently to Oxford. I was glad because I thought I would hear from him more and maybe even see him occasionally. But that was my last letter. I urgently need to speak with him, so I inquired at the garrison and they confirmed that he was posted there.'

'Sir Aston, giving the lady back the gun would be an honorable thing to do,' James said quietly. 'She may need it. As long as her husband is away in the King's service, what other protection will she have? I think I can get her safely back to the inn where she can catch the next coach back to Oxford before the siege begins.'

'I am not leaving until I see my husband,' she said.

Aston turned to the woman, his exasperation showing in his tone. 'Madam, your husband is not here. I am sure of it. We have received no supplies from Oxford. Would that we could. Even if he is on his way, he will not get through. He has probably already turned back. You may keep the pistol, Lady Pendleton. And you may stay within these walls for safety. We are aware of the forces massing against us, but we have received news that Rupert of the Palatine has been diverted from Litchfield and will come to our defense, though I will admit he is some days away.'

The woman opened her mouth to answer but was interrupted.

'Sir Aston,' The young guard who had been feeding the cat hurtled through the door.

Aston looked up at him annoyed. 'What is it?'

'Begging thy pardon, but there is a trumpeter at the gate demanding to be let in. He says he brings documents from Lord Essex.'

'Documents? What sort of documents?'

'I asked. He laughed and demanded to the see the commander about surrender terms.'

'Surrender terms! Whose? His or ours?'

'Don't open the gate for him. I will come myself. Stay with her,' he barked at James. 'This won't take long.'

And it didn't. Though awkward attempts at small talk and the resulting silence between made it seem longer. After no longer than five minutes, Aston came back, white-faced. No documents in hand.

'Arrogant bastards,' he muttered under his breath and then he addressed the woman. 'My lady, under the circumstance your wiser course might be to accept Lord Whittier's offer. A siege can be a hard thing to suffer for a woman alone and unprotected.'

'If my husband is not here, I have no wish to stay. I shall seek him elsewhere.' She turned to James. 'I am grateful for your offer. I shall go with you gladly.'

'Wise choice,' Aston said, handing her back the pistol.

'Have you any objection to riding astride with me? I doubt that Sir Aston can spare a horse.'

'It will be better than walking. I shall ride behind you.'

'It's settled then,' he said. Wait here and I will fetch our ride.'

It seemed an eternity to Caroline before he came back. Sir Aston had excused himself abruptly, saying his scouts had reported the big guns were now within battering range and that he hoped she would be able to catch the public coach early in the morning before the firing began.

When her escort finally came back, he did not even dismount, but put his arms down to help her up. She was used to riding astride. After a small hesitation, she put her arms around his waist.

'Don't be shy,' he said evenly. 'Cling a little tighter. We need to try to get you out tonight if we can.'

'Won't the public coach be coming from London tomorrow? Can't I go then?' she shouted above the pounding hooves.

'It may not be able to get through tomorrow. The firing may start in earnest, it being Sunday.'

Caroline had not thought of that. She'd almost lost count of the days. 'But surely not on the Sabbath. Aren't they mostly Puritans?' she asked as the gate closed behind them.

She could feel his disdain for her naivety in the tightening of his stomach beneath her clasped hands. They approached the place where the lane narrowed between two hedgerows. He reined in the horse briefly and answered, all the while searching the moonlit hedges for movement.

'That's what the good citizens of Reading will think too. But if you are one of the godly intent on rooting out the idolatrous Papist, you might think Sunday a propitious day. Not only will you have God on your side but the element of surprise. You'll need to hang on tighter through this patch.'

A clicking of the rider's tongue; a snap of the reins, and the horse bolted forward, Startled by a flash of light and the sound of musket fire, he pawed the air as Caroline gripped— *what had he said his name was*—around the waist so tightly her arms strained. He whispered something in the horse's ear, dug in his heels, and the horse leaped forward in a bone-jarring gallop that slowed only when they reached the open expanse of the inn yard. They halted beneath the circle of lamplight. Feeling as though her legs would not support her, Caroline accepted his arms to help her down.

'Go inside and wait for me. I will be in as soon as I have seen to the horse.'

Still trembling, she went in and sat by the smoky fire. The room was empty compared to the night before. The barmaid nodded at her as she wiped the tables with a wine-stained towel. 'Looks like we have it all to ourselves tonight. Can I get thee aught to eat or drink?'

'Not now. Maybe later,' Caroline thought, thinking about the shrinking weights in the hem of her coat, and how it would lighten more if she had to stay another night.

Lord Whittier came in, acknowledged her with a nod, then went to the bar and spoke briefly with the landlord. The landlord glanced at her. *They are talking about me.* She wished herself somewhere far away. She wished for the quiet assurance of William. How was it that she could not find him in Oxford or here or on the road between? It was as though he had vanished, leaving her at the mercy of strange men.

'Is Mistress Whorwood still here?' she asked the maid.

'No, she left this morning. In a bit of a hurry. A messenger came for her. I heard her order her coachman to take the north road toward West Riding.'

No help there. Nothing for it but to spend the night and catch the morning coach—if there was to be a morning coach. Surely there would be a morning coach. He was wrong. Even Parliament would not begin their siege on a Sunday. Anyway, she had enough money to stay here a week or two. The siege would end by then. Or William would come looking for her. He would hear from the guards at Oxford that she was desperate to see him.

Whittier strode over to her, his manner less convivial than before, a curtness in his tone when he called for the barmaid to bring her a pasty. 'Wrap it in a bit of cheese cloth. She will take it with her.'

'But—I . . .'

'Unfortunately, the public coach has already come and gone. He told the innkeeper that he would circumvent this stop until the siege is ended. I have hired a private coach and driver who is willing to leave tonight for Oxford.'

She opened her mouth to protest, but he shook his head and held up his hand. 'I am afraid you have no choice. I have paid the driver for his risk and time and ordered him not to leave you until you are delivered into safe hands—not the Oxford garrison but all the way to your home. The innkeeper assures me this driver is safe and resourceful, a gentleman of middle age who knows the road well.'

'But I cannot leave. Not until—'

'You cannot *not* leave.' His voice rose, his black-winged eyebrows lifting. 'Why do you think this inn is so empty? I have no doubt the firing will begin at dawn. I cannot make you leave, but—' He paused and then added, 'Consider your husband. He would not want you to be in danger.'

Almost too weary to breathe, she thought of home and how bone-tired she was. She should have done as William instructed. She should have gone to Forest Hill in the first place.

'You are a good man, my lord. My husband will repay you for your kindness. Where can we seek you to repay you?'

'I need no repayment except your word that you will let the driver deliver you to a place of safety. But if you ever are in London I would like to know you survived this night's adventure unharmed. I have a print shop in Fleet Street. I live above it. There are usually street urchins in the area hawking my wares. Just ask one of them. It would give me pleasure to know you made it safely.'

'What about you?'

'I will be fine. I am leaving as soon as I see you safely away.'

The innkeeper approached. 'The carriage is outside. John is the driver's name,' he said, Then, looking at Caroline,' added. 'Thou needst not be afraid. He is a godly soul. He'll see no harm comes to thee,' he said as he handed her the pasty.

Whittier opened the door and the night air blew in with a dampness that presaged rain. Shivering, she pulled William's greatcoat around her. He ushered her into the coach as though he could not wait to be rid of her. She opened her mouth to speak, but he interrupted her, pointing to her bag. 'This is not a long journey under normal circumstances. But less safe than it might be. Give me the pistol,' he said, 'and the powder and ball.'

She had no choice but to hand it to him. He loaded it and handed it back to her.

'Place it at your feet with the muzzle pointing toward the door, just in case the driver needs your help.' His eyes locked on hers and for a moment her heart skipped like a stone over still water. 'I think you will know what to do.'

'I will pray for your safety—'

But before she could get the words out, he waved to the driver and the coach lurched forward.

NETWORK OF SPIES

. . . exceedingly loyal, understanding and of good judgment . . . the most loyal to King Charles in his miseries of any woman in England.

—description of Jane Whorwood from the Diary of
Anthony Wood, Oxford

Caroline jolted awake, blackness all around. Her neck, stiff from sitting, hurt when she moved it. How long had she been asleep? Why had they stopped? The only sound was the creaking of the springs on the coach and then in the distance a cock crowed. Heart in her throat, she reached for the gun and pointed it toward the door. The door opened. Her fingers groped for the trigger of the pistol.

'Whoa, mistress. Hold up. It's me John, thy coachman. Thou be home. At least I think, from the directions I remember, though it looks deserted and as dark as a witch's heart out here.' He held out his hand for the gun. 'Best let me carry that.'

'Careful,' Caroline said, handing it to him. 'It's loaded.'

She retrieved her scrip from the dusty floorboard, not even bothering to brush it off. What was one more layer of muck? The satchel was light without the weight of the pistol.

'Glad thou caught a bit of shut eye. We made good time, we did truly. Guess every soul and even God's critters was hunkered down, waiting for the guns to start.'

An overwhelming gratitude welled up inside her towards this good man whom she had never met before another good man brought him to her rescue.

'Is this it then? Home?' he said, uncertainty roughening his voice.

He had stopped on the road, short of the drive—not wanting

to raise an alarm in case he was mistaken, she supposed, but close enough she recognized the hulking configuration of the Forest Hill outbuildings. No light in any window, not even in the kitchen, but she could just make out the arched doorway and the familiar roofline with its seven chimneys.

'This is it,' she said.

'Then I'd be obliged if we could get thee in and safe, so I can head back to Reading afore daybreak. A while ago I heard the distant sound of cannon fire out of Reading. Probably practicing for the morn.'

The sounds of war ushered in a Sabbath profaned by the sound of gunfire. All in the name of God. She took his rough hand and stepped down.

The dogs began to bark as they walked up the stone path. 'I'll see if I can rouse somebody to give you some refreshment before you go,' she said. 'That is the least I can do.'

'Aye, mistress. Ye'll need to wake somebody so I can see ye safely handed off. Lord Whittier paid me extra for that duty, but I'll not linger once that's done.'

'You are a righteous soul, good sir. I will pray for your safety on the road and I will be sure to tell my husband of your kindness. He'll look you up at the inn outside Reading and thank you personally, when this horrid war is over.'

'Righteous,' he laughed softly. 'I'd like my wife to hear you say that.'

Three times Caroline lifted the heavy knocker and let it fall. 'Late-night interruptions don't usually put Squire Powell in a good mood,' she whispered.

A light appeared in an upstairs window, framing a bulky silhouette, then heavy footsteps on the stairs and low cursing as a dog inside joined the chorus of epithets. 'What is so blasted important that could not wait for a decent hour—' More ferocious barking.

She leaned her face against the door and called, 'Squire, are you there? It's me, Caroline.'

'Hush, Festus. It's Caroline.'

The barking diminished to a welcoming whine. She could almost see the dog behind the door, tail beating back and forth, ready to spring in welcome.

'Sorry to disturb you so late but—'

The door jerked open halfway, revealing a disgruntled Richard Powell in nightdress, holding a night lamp up to inspect his intruder. 'Girl, is that really you? Where in the devil have you been? We have been sick with worry. Get away, Festus. Go on, git.'

The dog slunk under the hall bench, but his tail still beat a muted welcome on the stone floor. Caroline quickly banished the vision of her own Splendid Pair—not now. Not when she was so worn and weary, she could not hold the weight of that memory. 'I left you a note. Did you not find it?'

'Aye. We found it—four days ago. We went looking for you when one of the King's soldiers came inquiring about requisitioning the empty house for a garrison.'

The coachman cleared his throat impatiently, reminding them of his presence. He handed the gun to the squire, who looked up at him with a startled expression. 'This belongs to the mistress. Best handle it carefully. It's loaded. We've had a worrisome journey from Reading this night. That city is tighter than a—well it's about to come under the big guns of Parliament men.' Then he straightened his shoulders and continued in a no-nonsense tone. 'Now that the mistress is safe, I'll be heading back if thou givest me thy pledge, sir, that thou knowest this lady and will offer surety for her protection.'

'Know her!' He reached forward to embrace Caroline. 'Like my own daughter, and right glad I am to see her.' The squire offered his hand.' I am Justice Richard Powell, good sir. You wait here whilst I fetch come recompense for the service you have rendered this night.'

'No need. I've been well paid,' the coachman said.

The Squire did not press the matter of material compensation but said heartily, 'Well, if you should ever be in these parts again and run afoul of the law for some petty misunderstanding, tell the constable that Justice Richard Powell will stand for you.'

The coachman nodded and then disappeared beyond the circle of the candlelight. Moments later she heard the crack of a whip and the hollow echo of hoof beats.

'Come in, girl. I'll rouse the scullery maid and fetch Mistress Ann and Mary. We'll get you something to drink and you can tell us how you found William.'

'No, don't wake them. Please. You go on back to bed too. What I really want is to just go to my old room—is the bed still there? I need to close my eyes under a safe roof.'

'Yes, of course. I'll have the maid send you up some clean clothes and a wash basin. You can tell us about your adventure tomorrow. But first just tell me about my dear friend William. Where is he? Is he well?

The realization of what Caroline was about to say and what it might mean suddenly stunned her. The admission of the truth. 'I did not find him, Squire,' she said dully.

'But I thought—we'd heard he was at the Oxford garrison. Did you go there?'

'I went there first. He had been there but left on a mission to Reading. I—I don't know where he is, and the commander at Reading said he never arrived. Now Reading is under siege.'

She paused fighting back the tears that had threatened all night as he said nothing. Just a wide-eyed stare of disbelief.

'But I'm not giving up hope. We would have heard if . . . if some calamity had befallen him. Wouldn't we?'

Squire Powell hesitated a second too long, a little too much assurance in his answer.

'Yes, girl. You can be sure of it. It's just the confusion of war. He's probably hiding out until it's safe to either go back to his garrison or complete his mission. You go on off to bed. We'll hear from him soon. I'll make inquiries at the garrison myself. I should have gone with you in the first place.'

'Do you think it's possible that he was taken captive on the road? William was well known in London. He had friends in Parliament. They would not mistreat him, would they?'

'They are all honorable men. All Englishmen. Try not to worry. You are exhausted and anxious. Everything always looks bleakest just before dawn. You are safe. That's what William would want. We have a squadron of the King's soldiers quartered here. They'll check on him for us. They owe us that much for all the ale they drink and the beef they eat. Now go quietly off to bed and try to sleep. Things will look better in the morning. We'll make a plan. Here, take this light. If Mary or Ann call out, don't answer. They'll only smother you with their tears and hugs and questions.'

Caroline fell upon the little attic bed she'd slept on as a girl, removing only her skirt and not bothering to wash. She lay there in the dark, inhaling the comforting smell of the rough-hewn rafters, unable to fall asleep as she waited for the dawn to come creeping.

Henrietta did not have to suffer the austerity of Castle York's fortifications for long. It was the second stop on her journey south and judging from its meager hospitality an unexpected one. Within the week William Cavendish, Earl of Newcastle, came with an enhanced contingent of the Queen's Guard to escort her to his fortified manor at Handsworth where the Queen's apartment had been hastily but at least adequately prepared. Cavendish bowed stiffly and informed her that since the fighting in the Midlands was too fierce for either Rupert or Charles to come for her now, it would be his great pleasure if her majesty would remain his welcome guest in Sheffield for the time being. If she desired, she could inspect her troops now integrated with Newcastle's army in York, but she would be better served to postpone that activity since her enemies knew that she had returned. When it was safe to travel to Oxford, he would pull her mercenaries and Catholic recruits out to join the King and Prince Rupert.

This was a disappointment. 'His Majesty sent no personal letter for me?'

'No letter, your majesty. But a verbal message. He said to tell you that he was very impatient to welcome you home properly and you may expect to hear from him as soon as the negotiations with Parliament have ended. He also instructed me to tell you he has added a new symbol to your private cipher. The letter N. He wisely did not say what it represented but that you should be on the lookout for it soon. He also pressed me to assure your majesty that Prince Charles and his brother are with him and his lieutenants. They are safe and well and anxious to be reunited with their mother at Oxford.'

Then the commander bowed abruptly and without waiting to be dismissed excused himself.

After he left, she sat very still, willing herself to parse what he had said, both in word and manner. The specter of betrayal ever loomed. She could easily be captive here, held to gain some private advantage. But if Charles had chosen Cavendish as his general in the North, Charles trusted him. She would have to trust him too. With Parliament's spies everywhere, she had no other choice.

She was safe enough here, surrounded as she was by Nottingham's fortress and her own Queen's Guards, but the rebels knew where she was. Almost before she was settled in, messages came from Parliament, John Pym personally beseeching her to use her considerable influence with the King to persuade him to 'reasonable and efficacious' negotiations, lest more English blood be spilled. *Efficacious for Parliament*. She answered carefully: she was flattered by their confidence in her . . . she did not think it her duty to instruct his Majesty in policy . . . he would not be swayed by her opinions in any case. This last was a calculated reply. Pym was astute enough to discern how much influence she really wielded over her husband. She knew what Parliament feared most was the influence of their hated Catholic queen.

Parliament's harassment, this crushing disappointment at Charles' delay, and the fact that he had sent no personal message drove her to the hastily contrived *prie-dieu* in her chamber. There she prayed for the safety of her husband, for the safety of her children—the Holy Mother was a wounded mother too. But most fervently she prayed for an Old Testament wrath to rain destruction upon John Pym and his Parliament allies. God's enemies, King's enemies—one and the same. She knew their names and she called them all, staying on her knees until they were bruised. By the time Henrietta heard the commotion outside, the altar cloth was damp with her tears. Making the sign of the cross, she got up stiffly and went to see what was afoot.

'Your majesty, come and see. It will lift your spirits. The grooms have brought your trunks.'

Henrietta clasped her hands together in delight. It was a

sign from the Virgin: seven great hulking chests, filling up her bedchamber. Lord Denbigh's wife, Susan Feilding, along with her faithful Genevieve, were bent over the first chest, cooing with admiration as they unpacked French silks and embroidered laces and velvet sleeves with colorful ribbons, all purchased at wholesalers' cost from the Dutch traders. Henrietta's eyes discreetly searched each trunk for signs that the false bottoms with their cache of Florentine gold had not been disturbed. All appeared intact.

'Do not unpack them all,' she instructed as she probed the bottoms, releasing the smell of lavender into the air. 'The King will come soon to escort us to the new court at Merton College. We will save the best until we are safely there. This rose-colored damask will be sufficient for tonight's entertainment.' An attempt at an entertainment she thought, watching Genevieve shake out the gown. 'No jewels for my hair. I shall wear no other ornament, only a plain cap and my necklace, until I am reunited with my husband.'

It would be a sober affair by Whitehall standards, yet better than the dreary feasts provided by the Dutch for their royal visitors, she thought as she considered herself in the mirror. How loosely the gown fell around her. 'Genevieve, before I next wear this I think you must employ your needle.'

'The Dutch food did not settle with you, I fear.'

'Sometimes it was more than just not liking the food,' she said pinching her pale cheeks.

Genevieve nodded and smiled in sympathetic understanding. 'There will be a fine feast tonight. The company may be riotous, but it will not be dull, like the Dutch—or pretentious, like the Winter Queen—and the food will be hearty.'

'*Oui*, it is good to be rid of that one.' She turned sideways for one last look at her reflection. 'You always know how to cheer me, Genevieve. Elizabeth's beloved late husband, instead of planting a garden atop the old battery in Heidelberg, should have bought his bride a cannon. Her tenure might have lasted longer than one winter.'

Smiling, Genevieve stooped to smooth her skirts. 'You are almost home. Eat well. And I may not have to get out my needle.'

Noise from below filtered up—hearty laughter and music. It had a welcome celebratory sound, and Lord Denbigh would be there by her side. But sweet Jermyn and young Henry Percy, gone to join the fighting, she would sorely miss. The stiff William Cavendish of course was hosting the Scots Catholic lords who supported the Royalist cause. *Trés judicieux*. It would give her a chance to bind their loyalty to their Queen through their shared religion. A bulwark against the Scots Presbyterians. Charming them into releasing some of their gold for Charles would be an easy night's work.

Though Henrietta had difficulty with the Scots' thick brogue, she smiled often and invited the visitors to celebrate vespers in the small chapel. Later as they feasted on venison and good English beef, she listened to the dirge of their groaning bagpipes and applauded prettily. But she applauded more enthusiastically when, after much good whisky and flattery, they emptied the little pouches strategically adorning their kilts. Before departing they swore fealty to her and Charles and left her with good profit and a feeling of accomplishment. She could not wait to tell Charles how his beloved Scots lords responded.

But as the days passed and still no word came from the King, this small triumph was soon forgotten. Why was Charles in no hurry to send for her? They had never been separated this long before. Was he not as eager for their reunion as she was? Had Hyde and other ministers of floating loyalty poisoned his mind in her absence? Or horror of horrors, had he found some other source of comfort? She remembered how easily she had wooed him away from grief after his cherished Buckingham was killed.

The relentless spring rains made her body ache and the news of the fighting depressed her spirit. The fact that the Earl of Newcastle, despite the additional troops and arms she brought him, had not been able to retake the armory at Hull from its traitorous commander infuriated her.

It was mid-morning when Susan Feilding tiptoed in. The sun was already flooding across the counterpane. 'Your Majesty there is someone to see you. She says she has a gift for you.'

Henrietta started to wave her away.

'She says it is from the King.'

'Do we know her?'

'I don't remember ever seeing her at court. She calls herself Jane Whorwood, Mistress Brome of Holton. She says that she has come from Oxford where she is in charge of the royal linens.'

'Receive the gift on my behalf and send her away.'

'I tried that, your majesty. I told her you were indisposed. But she says that she will wait. Her instructions were to give the gift into your hands only. Here is the letter of surety that bears his Majesty's signature and seal.'

Henrietta sat up in bed and examined the document, drawing in her breath sharply. Sketched almost like a flourish of the end was something unfamiliar, the letter N perhaps? Or it could be just a slip of the pen from a man writing hastily under hurried conditions. She considered for a long moment.

'Grant her an audience,' she said. 'In the presence room. Give me half an hour and send Genevieve to help me dress.'

Why would Charles not send one of his heralds? Was the war so short of men he could not spare one to take a message to his wife? Not bothering with her complete toilet Henrietta assumed her place in the draped cross chair set up for her in the anteroom to her private chamber and signaled to Susan that she was ready.

When she was ushered into the makeshift presence room outside the Queen's bedchamber, the woman dropped to the floor in a strong curtsy, not the slight perfunctory sort Henrietta too often experienced at court.

'Thank you for seeing me, your majesty.'

Henrietta did not recognize the woman. She would have remembered such a creature if only for her tall stature, and bold, blue-eyed gaze.

'You have come on a service for the King? You are lately of his household? I do not remember you at Whitehall or Hampton Court.'

'No, your majesty. I serve him at the King's court in Oxford as mistress of his linen closet and laundry. I am Mistress Brome of Holton. My family has long been in the linen trade and we have a wide network of individuals well placed among the King's friends. That happy circumstance allows me to perform double service for him.'

'Double service. How so?'

'Here is one small example.' She held out a parcel, wrapped in silk and tied with a crimson cord. 'This is a welcome-home gift for you from some of those friends who have been generous in their support of your husband. Please forgive the little white smudge on the silk wrapping. We smuggled it out of London under watchful eyes of Parliament—in a barrel of soap.'

'London. I doubt my husband has many friends left in London,' Henrietta said as she accepted the parcel. It weighed lightly in her hands.

Jane Whorwood—although she had announced herself as Lady Brome, Henrietta thought the name Jane Whorwood suited her better. A common Jane, who when she tossed her head, revealed a pock mark hidden by a well-placed curl.

'Parliament has not routed all the King's friends, I assure you,' the common Jane said. 'Though they must show their friendship carefully for fear of Parliament's thugs and spies. The same wagonload of soap and trade linens carrying that little parcel you hold in your hand, also carried a goodly amount of gold for his Majesty to Oxford, which I delivered to him this past fortnight.' Pointing to the parcel in Henrietta's hands, she said, 'Please, your majesty, I would truly like to see you open it. I have come a long way. It is a welcome-home gift. I should like to tell the King and your loyal subjects in London that you delighted in it.'

Henrietta unwrapped the parcel as those it might contain a serpent, but her subsequent gasp was one of appreciation.

'They are from his Majesty's loyal servants in Cripplegate. The King commissioned the gift, but the Glovers' Guild would not let him pay. They have not forgotten the royal charter that he signed for them.'

'*Exquis coutoure.*' Henrietta caressed the gloves lovingly, white kid stained cream. Tracing a fingertip over the embroidered gauntlet, she whispered more to herself that the messenger, '*Tres belle,*' then added, 'my husband has exquisite taste.'

The edging and lining were of sky-blue silk. Raised silver wire chain-stitching in heart shapes and scrolling arabesques surrounded crimson lilies. Yellow silk French knots formed the flower heads.

The common Jane sighed with pleasure at the Queen's response. 'Yes, his Majesty does have wonderful taste,' she said. 'You are fortunate in your husband, your majesty, as I am fortunate in my King.' Admiration, a slight shade below worship, colored her tone.

Henrietta looked up sharply. 'You have met the King, then? Personally, I mean.'

'Only briefly, your majesty. When I took him the gold. He was most gracious to accept my offer of help—when I explained my family's network of connected manor houses and shopkeepers.'

'Your offer of . . . help.'

'As a messenger, your majesty.'

'Although I thank you for coming so far, Mistress Brome, I am sure you need not have troubled yourself in these unsafe times. The court has many messengers.'

'Oh, but your majesty, I wanted so much to meet you. Surely so great a man must have chosen for himself a worthy queen. It is my honor to serve you as well. Shall I take a message from you back to your husband?'

'No, but thank you.' Henrietta tried to keep her tone polite. 'I already have a trusted messenger. But you may express my delight to the glovers and say how much the Queen admires their gracious and beautiful gift.'

The woman just stood, apparently unaware that she was being dismissed.

'You may go. If you would like I will order some refreshment for you to be sent to the hall.'

'I thank you your majesty, but being admitted to your presence is refreshment enough.'

'God's speed then.'

'Right. May God be with you as well.' And then the woman curtsied again and backed away.

When she was gone, Henrietta turned her attention to the gift. She tried on the right-hand glove. A perfect fit. But when she tried to pull up the gauntlet on the left-hand glove, a slip of paper fell out. She recognized the signature. So, the woman had seen Charles, and he had seen the gloves or he had given her the note to place inside the glove. It was written in their private numerical code. The only letter in a string of numbers was the letter N. *Holy Mother how she missed Jermyn.* He always decoded for her. It was such a tedious process. Concentrating hard without retrieving the code from her private hiding place, she could just make out the numbers next to the N. The number 3 for J the double 6 would be oo and the 9 for W. Jane Whorwood. She would check it later, but the empty feeling in her stomach told her she didn't need to.

Charles had another woman besides his absent wife who adored him, a beautiful and willing woman. A younger woman bearing gifts. It didn't mean that he had bedded her. He was slow to attachment, not abandoning one too eagerly for another. Even she—and God knows she had tried, urged on by her mother—had not been able to capture his attention as long as the favorite Buckingham lived. But adoration was a strong aphrodisiac. The weaker the man, the stronger the spell.

Holy Mother, let me find a way to him and soon, she prayed. She traced the beautiful beadwork on the glove. She would write to him tonight, if she could find where she'd put the damnable cipher.

UNDER PRESSURE

*I find by all the Queen's and her people's discourse that
they do not desire an agreement between his Majesty and
his Parliament but that all be done by force and rail
abominably at the Parliament. I hear all and say nothing.*

—From a letter written by Elizabeth Stuart,
the Queen's sister-in-law

June 1643

James Whittier looked up from the press to caution his
visitor. 'Careful. The ink may still be wet.'

'You were there, then? Inside the walls at Reading with
Sir Arthur Aston? This reads like an eye-witness account.'

'I was there. I got through Parliament's lines just as the
bombardment began, but I lost a good horse. I had to trade it
for passage downriver.' His hands never paused as he positioned the small blocks into lines of type.

The leader of the most influential party in Parliament
gingerly replaced the proof sheet on top of the stack of papers
beneath the drying ropes strung along the wall. 'Have I come
at a bad time, Lord Whittier?'

James shook his head in reassurance and indicated for his
visitor to sit on the high stool beside the long worktable. The
most important man in Parliament, second only in name to
Speaker Lenthall, stared in fascination as James continued
picking and placing the lead rectangles: letters into words,
words into sentences . . .

'Tomorrow's broadsheet. What can I do for you, Mr. Pym?'

'It is more what I can do for you, Lord Whittier. I have
some news from Parliament and a packet of the Queen's letters.'

He paused to let the words sink in. 'Letters that detail trea-sonous activities while abroad.'

James placed a large square block, a sketchy carving of a cannon, strategically pointed opposite a block of clay etched with crossed lines that, when filled with ink, might transfer into an approximation of a stone wall. Without looking up, he stepped back to survey the effect and muttered, 'A crude rendering of a city under siege, but it will do to catch the eye.' Then, looking up at his visitor, 'Treason, you say. That is a serious charge, Minister Pym.'

The leader returned his bold, direct gaze and corrected him, 'Charges. Plural. Trying to raise a Catholic army against England. Correspondence and conspiracy with the Pope to intervene in English affairs. Bartering the crown jewels.' He paused. 'I could go on.'

James let out a low whistle. 'Have these charges any evidence to back them up?'

'There is proof aplenty in the Queen's correspondence.'

'How do you know this correspondence is not forged by her enemies in Parliament?'

'Our best spymaster has authenticated them. They are too specific not to be authentic. And in her own hand, of which we have many samples.'

'Well, yes. In that case, I think I would like to see them.'

'All in good time.' John Pym cleared his throat.

He looked like a man carrying a too heavy burden, James thought. 'Would you like a drink? Water, or something stronger?'

'You are very gracious. Water would be good. Herding sheep and goats together is wearying business.'

James didn't have to wonder who were the goats. Moderate voices had emerged in a parliament already wearying of war.

'Ben,' James called to the next room where the boys were busy folding the papers. 'Could you bring my visitor some water, please.'

Pym looked up when Ben brought him a drink. If Pym noticed his empty left sleeve, he made no comment except to thank him. He sipped his water slowly, giving Ben time to leave the room before he spoke again. 'I read a pamphlet recently—picked it up in St. Paul's Churchyard—calling for peace, reconciliation, even concessions, deep concessions to be offered to the King.' He frowned. 'A litany of complaints against the hardship visited upon the good people of London, not by the King but by Parliament's struggle with the King.'

'Let me guess,' James said. 'The embargo on goods from the Midlands. No vegetables from the country. No fresh meat to be found in Smithfield. No coal for the cook fires. What will we do if the war drags on until winter? The merciless conscription. The growing number of widows and orphans.' One widow in particular crossed James's mind but he pushed it to the margins of consciousness, where it hovered. 'And last but not least, the burden of taxation to maintain the army, the navy, and bribe the Scots Covenanters for their "loyalty to the godly cause."'

Pym's half smile carried no amusement. 'You didn't mention the great number of limbless young men returning to London, unemployable, begging on the street. But I am glad to see that one at least has found employment. You seem very knowledgeable regarding the paper. Did it come from your press?'

James laughed. 'It could have. Those are the kind of complaints I hear on a daily basis. Parliament with its sequestered, purpose-laden noise may not be aware but in the pubs and markets and shops there is a growing weariness with the war. But, no, I didn't print what you read. Anything that comes from my press bears my mark.'

Pym raised his eyebrows in question. 'Which is?'

Whittier plucked one of the carved rectangles from the bottom left-hand corner of the form. 'This,' he said, holding it out for inspection.

Pym squinted to make out the mirror image. 'A pair of crossed swords?'

'Meant to imply impartial news as far as I can glean it. Two swords. Two sides. Something approaching the truth.'

'And you think you are wise enough to discern truth.'

'Do you? Think you are wise enough? And what about those partisans with whom you engage. Are they wise enough?'

Pym's shoulders dropped. More of a sag than a shrug. 'Some

men are wiser or—at least privy to certain pertinent facts, which allow them to more closely discern the truth.'

'Then shouldn't all men be privy to these facts and be allowed to judge for themselves whatever greater truth such knowledge may lead to?'

James was surprised to hear this coming out of his own mouth. The idea of common people, anybody who could read having free access to those things which were revealed to only a privileged few was not something he had ever worried over.

But he was not as surprised as Mr. Pym. 'What an appalling idea. You quite take my breath away. It is—it is a preposterous idea. We would never find peace. There would be endless wars of words.'

'Wouldn't endless wars fought with words, informed and sound opinion, wars fought with spilled ink instead of spilled blood be better than what we have now? A free unlicensed press. It might happen. Now that Parliament has abolished the Star Chamber. Might it not?'

A look of satisfaction crossed his visitor's face. 'Don't bet your future on that circumstance, Lord Whittier. It might interest you to know that the day after tomorrow Parliament is voting on the establishment of its own licensing board policed by the Stationers' Guild and enforced by the courts. Under this jurisdiction Parliament will have the right, dare I say the responsibility, to assure a responsible press. This will include search and seizure of enterprises falling under suspicion and destruction of any publications found to be offensive with the publisher thereof subject to imprisonment and/or fines.'

James stood up straight and looked his visitor directly in the eyes. His hovering hands stilled. 'Offensive to whom, Leader Pym. Who gets to decide what is "offensive?"'

'Only God gets to decide that.' Pym shrugged. 'And the Stationers' Guild, of which you are a member I am sure.'

'And if I'm not?'

'You are a smart man, Lord Whittier. And maybe a prudent one. I suggest that it might be in your best interest to petition the Stationers' Guild for membership, if you have not already. Parliament trusts the recommendations of such civic bodies to help provide guidance in matters of governance.'

Then the leader stood up and handing his empty water glass to James patted the left breast of his coat, a reminder, James thought, of the proffered letters. 'Perhaps, Lord Whittier, we would be wise to reconsider the matter of the Queen's letters at a later time.' Then with a brusque nod of his head, he took his leave.

James was not surprised when he did not hear from the Parliament leader again regarding the Queen's letters. He didn't need to see them anyway. He was listening outside Westminster on the twenty-second day of June when the charges were read aloud in Parliament. Not knowing the provenance of the letters James printed only the fact of the charges unaccompanied by any damning argument or screaming header of condemnation. He knew full well what his stubbornness would cost him. Parliament would only find a more willing mouthpiece, and he would be frozen out or worse. But if ever London needed a free exchange of opinion it was now. James determined to ride that horse as long as it had legs.

By the middle of June, Henrietta had lost her patience. The King's nephews, Rupert and Maurice, were too busy fighting in Buckinghamshire to provide safe escort for her and her convoy of gold and arms to Oxford. But what else could she expect from the sons of her hateful sister-in-law and Protestant husband? By some contrivance of the devil—and Charles's blindness—now Elizabeth's upstart son was Charles's most trusted general in the west, who for all his experience fighting with his father in the failed Protestant wars on the Continent was hardly more than a brash boy. Elizabeth and her heretic husband had prejudiced both Rupert and Maurice against her, probably even blaming her because Charles never provided aid in their Bohemian campaigns. Perhaps they even blamed her for their downfall and exile. It was becoming apparent that Rupert was in no hurry to fetch her. He would put her home-coming off as long as he could, if for no other reason than to please his mother.

Then, adding to Henrietta's *ennui* and burgeoning resentment, came appalling news that intensified her discontent and heightened her anxiety. Parliament had dared to do what they had threatened. Not only had they impeached her, but—*le Diable-emporte-leur-âme*—they had charged her with treason. She would not sit here in this dreary northern outpost one day longer. Henriette Marie de Medici, Queen of England, Ireland, and Scotland would not wait for them to come and arrest her. She would meet them in the field with an army of her own.

After he had signed the bill of attainder condemning Wentworth to death Charles had cried like a helpless child, but she had held him to her breast and told him kings had to make hard decisions for their kingdoms. Charles loved her, loved her more than the long dead Buckingham, loved her more than the more recently dead Wentworth. She believed that truly. But was he strong enough to defend her? Did he still love her enough? Had absence really made his heart grow fonder as he promised in his letter? Possibly not. Not with women like Jane Whorwood around to offer whatever comfort he might accept.

She needed to get to him. Now.

Her protector, the Earl of Newcastle, whom she now thought of as a well-mannered gaoler, did not give in on the first day. Nor the second. It took almost a week whilst her spies scoured the countryside for any sign of her impending arrest. The intelligence they offered bought her a few precious days. John Hampden, one of the five Parliamentarians who had escaped arrest, had died within the week of the impeachment action taken against her, thereby providing great satisfaction to her— and welcome distraction for Parliament. But his timely death would not distract her enemies long. So, she began her campaign of alternately pestering and harassing William Cavendish with veiled threats and pitiful tears until she prevailed.

Finally, no longer able to hide his impatience with her badgering, the Earl summoned his son Charles from the battle-field and ordered him to provide escort to Henrietta as well as her convoy of men and arms. The young Cavendish accepted his mission with puppy-like devotion. Unlike his father, he was utterly charming. She might have lingered longer had she not already dispatched her coded message to Charles that she could not bear this separation any longer and was on her way to meet him regardless of the danger to her person.

On the day her convoy headed south, the sun was bright, and a June breeze wafted the royal flags. Refusing the carriage, she said a curt goodbye to her tight-lipped host and mounted her horse, a strong, swift stallion from Cavendish's own stable. As she rode out of the fortress gate, hope surged. She was surrounded by men at arms, her soldiers—recruited by her— and proud to serve this Catholic Queen. They would fight for her with more enthusiasm than they fought for the Earl of Newcastle. And she was confident that when Charles got her message, somewhere along the way he would meet her, and all would be well again. She longed to see his face when she offered him the chests of gold buried in the provisions wagons.

They rode south for two days. The first night they camped in a pleasant copse of old oak trees. By the second night they had come to the River Trent, where her mercenaries spread their bedrolls in a nearby wood while Henrietta, accompanied by her young cavalier, was well entertained by the lord of the castle. With her treasure wagons and Queen's Guards secure inside the castle ramparts, Henrietta was tempted to linger in this pleasant place one more day. But at daybreak, which was rosy and fair she gave the order for young Cavendish to summon her troops. An auspicious breeze fluttered her colorful banners in the fine June morning as Henrietta—who was quite enjoying the military role she had cast for herself as leader of the troops—followed the winding river. At midday they approached an already scouted, less conspicuous river crossing. But the fickle June morning had changed its aspect and black clouds were giving chase—as well as rumors of a company of Roundheads shadowing the royal progress.

As they prepared to cross the bridge, young Cavendish reined in his horse at her side. 'It's a small force but big enough to cause trouble if they make the crossing. Your majesty, we must ride hard. Can you do it?'

'*Oui.* I am ready, Captain. Even *le diable* could not slow me down.'

Thunder rolled in the distance as he shouted in her ear. 'My scouts have already strapped barrels of gunpowder to the braces. It will be for them like the Egyptians following Moses across the Red Sea.'

This image made her smile. She nodded enthusiastically.

'When you hear the explosions, don't stop. Just keep riding. Hard. The men will follow you.'

She leaned forward, silently blessing the bravery of the young captain as she whipped her horse and prayed that the provision wagons would make it across. The sound of musket fire punctuated the thunder. She could feel the heat from the horse as he responded to the pressure. *'Mon brave cheval,'* she whispered, then remembering he was an English horse murmured, 'Run. Run like the wind.' The horse's hooves barely skimmed the ground as they approached the bridge. When the first loud boom exploded, he whinnied skittishly. Another whisper from her and a gentle spur from her heels and they were off again.

Exerting all her strength she finally reined him in, then looked back to see the last of her wagons lumbering out of a cloud of smoke. She crossed herself and patted the horse's neck. *'Mon brave cheval.* You are a French horse now, you belong to me.'

As raindrops began to fall, the young captain trotted up. 'We should not linger, your majesty. Some of the Roundheads might know how to swim.'

But from her side of the river they looked ridiculous, shouting and cursing like a flock of startled geese, floundering for the shore. She shouted *'bon jour'* over her shoulder as they resumed their journey. But she was well out of earshot and the sorry looking brigade had already begun to retreat. Henrietta took it for an omen.

PRINTER'S DEVIL

[I]t may yet befall a discreet man to be mistak'n in his choice . . . and who knows not that the bashful muteness of a virgin may oft-times hide all the unlivelyness and natural slothe which is really unfit for conversation.

—from *The Doctrine and Discipline of Divorce*,
by John Milton, August 1643

On the Southwark side of the river clouds piled high, portent of a simmering summer storm. Water from the Thames sloshed against her silver-buckled shoes as, right hand holding up her lace-edged hem, left hand holding down her high-crowned hat, Lucy Hay ascended the water stairs to Westminster. A puff of wind climbed with her carrying the stench from the river. Why had she not been disgusted by that rotten odor when she was at Whitehall with the court? Maybe it was because she was now accustomed to breathing the untainted air of Syon Park. Then as she thought about it, she remembered the court had seldom been at Whitehall during the summer, and when it was Inigo Jones created a world apart for them; a kind of pretend Eden—when Henrietta was in the mood for Eden.

Lucy's hold on the little *copatain* kept it securely on her head, but she watched in dismay as its dislodged feather swirled away on a current of wind. A pity. Lucy had chosen the little black sugar-loaf hat because its saucy adornment, perching above her right ear, shivered and teased when she tilted her head in the mirror. Probably just as well it was gone. The feather would be an ostentation amongst so many prim Puritans.

She paused on the top stair long enough to watch the feather float toward the opposite shore where detritus washed up. God forbid the innocent little avian plume should snare on the corpse of some poor woman from the Southwark stews. In her hair maybe, or on her sodden bodice, wet and gleaming like a ruby brooch, a bizarre adornment celebrating a life unmarked by any other. She tried to banish the unwelcome image, but her imagination continued its conjuring—the crimson feather pinned by the current in a water-logged mass of brown hair, hair the color of her own. Was that a body floating face-down on the tide? *Foolishness, woman. It is only a bit of flotsam stuck on a rotting log. You have been too long alone in the company of children.*

She turned back to her own, more respectable, shore and strode across the yard, heading toward the first door she saw. Her determined gait was only partially prompted by storm threats to her *ensemble*. Lucy Hay was a woman with a purpose. Due to the press of 'Parliamentary business' (or so he pleaded), John Pym's visits had become less frequent and of unsatisfactory duration and substance, so Lucy approached the door to St. Stephen's Chapel determined to confront her friend and lover concerning his neglect. Well, maybe confront was too strong a word. Gentle persuasion was more her style. Sometimes a distracted man didn't realize he was starving until his eyes settled on a feast.

She had dressed carefully, choosing a gown of deep crimson that he'd once said suited her, except this time, not to offend his godly colleagues, she had prudently laced the bodice higher and covered her cleavage with a broad collar of white lawn. An appropriate choice, she thought, for a good Presbyterian woman. But her hair smelled of rose water, the same scent with which she perfumed her bed, and she had rubbed Spanish paper on her cheeks and reddened her lips with a brush of cochineal paste. Beneath the collar, a strategically placed crescent-moon patch concealed the pock mark above her left breast, upon which the light of day could be counted to shed no mercy. Lucy was confident that when she took off the collar John would remember the crimson dress—and the occasion upon which he'd last removed it from her body.

As she stepped inside the cooler, dim interior, she looked around uncertainly. Somewhere within the warren of rooms that made up Westminster Palace was a closet where John had taken her—literally—and on more than one occasion. But which way? She had come in by another door the last time, meeting him at the visitors' entrance. The first time she had sought him out at Westminster Palace to petition for Wentworth's life she had snared him as he came out this same door to hail a waterman. This must be the members' entrance, and the Commons not in session. That was the reason it was deserted. The large room at the end of the hall must be where they convened. Her steps echoed as she walked toward the room that had once been the King Edward III's Royal Chapel.

She listened at the door. The chamber was as silent as the hall. Tentatively she pushed on the right side of the double doors. The room was empty; the members' seats unoccupied. Curious, she entered, thinking how few women had ever stood where she stood and how it didn't look much like a royal chapel with its whitewashed walls and plain wooden chair where the altar used to be. But of course. Under old King Henry, the Protestants would have long ago stripped the paintings and changed out the Catholic stained-glass windows. All those beautiful paintings. All that jeweled glass. All those golden vessels melted down to fund schemes of war.

She was thinking about Henrietta's gilded chapel and how it had so recently been looted when she heard the door open. Startled she whirled around to see whether friend or foe, though these days it was becoming harder to tell the difference.

The voice was blessedly familiar. 'Cousin. This is a surprise. Why have you decided to invade this unhallowed chapel?'

She smiled, a genuine smile of relief that she was not confronted with an angry sergeant-at-arms to whom she would have to plead sweet innocence. 'And you, my lord Essex? Have you deserted your troops in the field for Parliament's austere halls?'

He entered the chamber and looked at her thoughtfully.

'Ah, my dear Lucy. The true battles are fought here.' He waved at the rows of benches facing each other. 'Where monks once intoned their prayers in unison from these opposing choir stalls, now MPs sit on these same wooden benches, and with shouts and argument quibble over the fates of men—much as the devil and his demons are thought to quibble over souls,' he said.

'And what of your voice, cousin Devereux? Does yours quibble too? What have you to argue about? Come to think of it, why are you here at all? If your voice is to be raised should it not be in the White Chamber?'

'The Lords' Chamber is becoming—' he paused for the right words—'increasingly irrelevant. So many are in exile or have gone with the King. As Captain-General of the army, Parliament's army now, I have come to deliver a petition for back payment to John to be read out in Parliament. If my men are to be expected to fight, then they must be paid. They have not been paid in three months and they are growing restless.'

'If you handed the army over to Parliament could you not as easily hand it back to the King—if you should choose?'

'I could but I won't. Charles Stuart, I hear, is no better paymaster for his troops. Besides my place is gone. His Majesty has given the commission of Lord General to another. I shall remain chief commander for Parliament's troops. Though I think Waller is angling for my place. He blames me for his defeat at Oxford, says I did not support him with troops.'

'Why did you not support him?'

'We were otherwise engaged,' he said sharply.

'But you and John are friends. Surely he sees your side.'

'John has cooled towards me of late. He does not like that I and Algernon and others are pressing Parliament to try another round of negotiations.'

All were names among the original five whom she had warned of the King's plan of arrest. It was a little surprising they still would want to sue for peace in spite of the recent failure of negotiations. 'John says Charles will never accept any agreement that cedes even a grain of power to the Parliament. You must know how hard he has tried, Robert; he told me he even wrote conciliatory messages to the Queen, pleading for her intercession with the King.'

'John is wrong,' he said. 'If we do not negotiate, this conflict will bring only more death and destruction. It will tear England apart.'

'The Puritans are dead set against sharing power with the King as long as he has a Catholic queen. They say too much blood has been shed to turn back now. They say we have crossed the Rubicon, that any concessions will make Charles into a more perfect tyrant, and the Queen will restore the tyranny of the old religion. How do you answer that, Robert?'

Distant thunder rolled—or was it the roar of cannon? Hard to tell these days.

'I say one more try. Let us try some new negotiation tactic. We might even have more leverage now that the Queen has been charged with treason.'

'They have charged the Queen of England with treason? That will only make Charles Stuart more resolute, less inclined to give an inch.'

He shrugged carelessly, 'Whether she lives or dies—could be part of the new negotiations.' His tone was as casual as if he were discussing the price of beef.

She was suddenly looking at him as though she had never seen this Robert Devereux before. But she had. She remembered how, though he had not been as certain as John, he had lent his voice to the decision to condemn Wentworth with damning words. '*Stone dead hath no fellow,*' he had said in agreement, even though he had been friend to Wentworth. She had tried to put that behind her, told herself she had to put it behind her to survive and blamed Charles Stuart's cowardice for Thomas Wentworth's death.

'This is not some King's advisor whose fate you treated so lightly, Robert Devereux. This is an anointed Queen, for God's sake, even Parliament would not threaten to harm her person.'

'Lower your voice, please, cousin,' he said. 'I understand your reference to the King's advisor. I see you still harbor a grudge though you have forgiven John Pym for his part apparently. Further, Henrietta de Medici is not an *anointed* queen. Remember. She refused to be crowned or anointed by an Anglican archbishop.'

'She is the sister of the King of France, Robert. Do you think Louis would not seek total revenge?'

Another of his casual shrugs and a wave of his hand as if war with France was some small matter, he said, 'We could negotiate her exile if she turned herself over. Charles is not a brave man. He would give her up with maybe more tears and *mea culpa* than he gave up his dearest and most loyal friend, but he would give her up.'

Lucy could not refute the possibility of that. She had decided long ago that stubborn though he might be, Charles Stuart was a weak man.

'The Queen is back on English soil, holed up in York for several months now, and she has brought back with her an army of three thousand men. An army raised with money from her Catholic alliance, which our spies say is on their way to Oxford. This is our last chance to sue for peace before the inevitable.'

'And that is?'

His eyes were cold when he answered. 'This is a hard world, Lucy. When the fighting is over the victor will totally vanquish the loser. You once warned me and four others of our impending arrest, so I am warning you now. Use your influence with Pym. Try to talk him into this last chance at negotiations. Do not try to contact the Queen or warn her in any way—or offer comfort to her even for the sake of your past friendship.'

Another roll of thunder, closer this time. Lucy suddenly felt the chill of the approaching storm, chill like a fever, as she remembered how Henrietta had risked her own life to offer her favorite lady-in-waiting comfort by visiting her in her pox-contaminated chamber. Rain beat against the courtyard windows. Footfalls echoed outside the chamber. Essex waited for them to subside.

'Since Wentworth's death you have managed to walk a fine line. Others who were at court with you are now in exile, confined within the perimeters, or killed on the battlefield. Do not make public your relationship with John Pym. There are those who suspect, but they can prove nothing. Stop frequenting the Puritan services—yes, there is some notice of your sudden piety. Do what you can to keep the younger children safe. If the two older boys flee to the Continent, then young Henry will become valuable to them. They can set him up as a puppet king with a Parliament-controlled regent.'

'Like who? The Earl of Pembroke?' There was derision in her voice.

Her memory conjured the little boy who only this morning had pointed to her and said *maman* when his sister Elizabeth had asked about their mother. She had not corrected him but caressed him. 'Henry is not even three years old.'

'All the better. Controlled by a regent—a fine English precedent: under-age king, a magnate for the machinations of the greedy and power-hungry—and this regent appointed by Parliament.'

'John truly believes the only way England will ever be relieved of the tyranny of 'divine right' is the King's removal.'

'The King's removal? Think what that might look like, cousin. Charles in exile? Raising a Catholic army. Do we want another endless war on English soil like the one on the Continent?' He glanced away then, lowered his voice to a whisper, then led her by the hand to a bench with a clear view of the door. 'It will not end in the King's exile. If all negotiations fail, exile is not the solution they will seek.'

She could not suppress the little gasp that escaped from her lips.

He continued with urgency in his voice, 'Use your influence, Lucy. Try to persuade John to join with us. They are already calling us the Peace Party. The factions are lining up. John is the bridge between. We need him on our side.'

'But what if the King wins?'

'What do you think will happen if Charles Stuart wins? At court you saw: Charles the good father; Charles, the loving husband; Charles the sovereign, gracious King who rewards those who serve him—as long as it's convenient. But have you ever known him to blink at the shedding of blood.' He had not let go of her hand and gave it a slight squeeze. 'Think on it, Lucy. If he let Thomas Wentworth lose his head what do you think he will do to the rest of us. If he wins.'

For all his lack of masculine swagger, Essex was a cunning general. He argued strategy. He argued common sense. And he knew how to reach Lucy by invoking Thomas Wentworth.

He let go her hand and stood up, then pointing toward the empty benches said, 'If you could sit in this place and listen to both arguments, you would see that Pym's insistence on cutting off negotiations is madness. If you love him, if you love England, you will try to persuade him to reason. I only succeeded in angering him. This madness is eating at him from the inside. He is not the reasonable man he was in the beginning. Make him see that re-opening negotiations would be to his benefit and England's. Make him see it is the only way.'

'I will try. Truly, Robert, I will. I also am sick to death of this war. But I doubt that I can make him understand. You said you just left him. Where can I find him?'

'Just cross the courtyard, first door,' he said. He smiled at her then, an old teasing look she remembered from so long ago, before his first wife had ruined his reputation by publicly divorcing him on the grounds that he was *incapable of consummating the marriage*. 'I am sure you'll recognize his hidey-hole at the end of the hall.'

He stood up and departed with the same quiet with which he had entered. Lucy sat there for a few more minutes, trying to sort out all that he had said to her. Taking out her expensive little pocket mirror—a gift from her husband? Or was it her first lover, George Villiers, the Duke of Buckingham? She had been married to Jamie then. Hardly more than a girl. But James Hay hadn't really minded. Yes, she thought, looking at the mirror, it was Buckingham. He'd given it to her before he went to France to fetch Charles Stuart's bride—so many years, so many admirers.

In the mirror she practiced her coquette's smile, but today the smile did not come easily. Maybe it was the absence of the quivering little feather flirting back at her.

When the rain outside stopped, she crossed the courtyard to go in search of John Pym. Her mission had changed; her tactic had not. She had only one kind of coin. It suddenly occurred to her that in that regard she was not so very different from the poor unfortunate women of Southwark, one of whom who lay at the river's edge, face down, with a weeping red feather in her hair. But apparently Lucy's resources, like the currency of England, had been debased by war. She failed to accomplish either her initial purpose or the newly adopted one. John was far too worn out with the affairs of state to care about the affairs of the heart. When she mentioned that she met Robert Devereux on his way out, he frowned and said, 'He wants new taxes on London, money for the troops.'

'That seems a reasonable request.'

'The House will comply. But there are many in the Lords who wish to sue yet again for peace. Your brother is among them. Parliament is splintering. Percy has absented himself from the parliamentary councils and is at his estate at Petworth.'

'Plotting or pouting?'

John shrugged. She had never seen him so on edge. Or so haggard looking. 'The former, I would guess. Considering his options if the peace party, as they are calling themselves, fails.'

'Will it?'

'As I draw breath.'

He turned back to his writing. Lucy read dismissal in the gesture. 'I miss you, John,' she said. And then a thought occurred to her. 'Is Mistress Pym back from Ulster?'

'No. And with both my daughters married and gone, Derby House is quiet now. But I spend most of my time in this little cell sending and receiving, petitioning and planning.'

'A visit from you would be a diversion for the children.'

'Are they well?'

'They are well. Henry hardly misses his mother at all. And Elizabeth fills her days with study. Bathshua Makin is turning her into a formidable scholar.'

'Good. Keep them safe. They are a valuable commodity.'

She let herself out then, wondering if that compassionate man who'd first brought the children to her had departed or was merely in hiding.

'I miss you too, Lucy,' he said without looking up. 'This will all be over soon.'

But she feared that time was not soon enough.

The printer's devil was so intent he scarcely noticed the muscle strain in his working arm. It was the first time Lord Whittier had allowed him to print a project from typeset to finished broadsheet. Thirty times he pulled the press down onto the type bed until finally he lifted the lever to remove the last page. Maybe a bit paler than the one before. He would mop more ink before doing the next batch, but no faint spots or blotches. *Good job, Ben, if I do say so.* Funny how one could get used to things—even a new name, he thought, as he hung the papers on the line to dry. Like putting on a new skin, a spur of the moment whim, not wanting to be Arthur Pendleton, not wanting to be a disappointing son, an unfit soldier, a cripple. He rather liked it. It was a good, solid name.

This thought process of self-congratulation and reinvention was interrupted as a whirl of dusty energy disturbed the quiet of the shop. Ben didn't even have to look in the direction of the door to know the source; Ralphie's signature arrival. Everything the boy did vibrated with noisy enthusiasm. That was why he sold more papers than the other newsboys. Still squinting at the drying sheets to catch any missing line or distorted margins, Arthur acknowledged his arrival. 'Surely you haven't sold out already. It's scarcely midday.'

'Sold out my lot by ten bells,' the cocky lad said. 'I been helpin' Little John with his. I keep telling him he just needs to speak up more. The customers don't know they want to buy until he tells them they do. If one of them looks at him, he don't even look back, just shuffles his feet and mumbles in his little-boy squeak, "You wouldn't want to buy a paper today, would you, sir?"'

Ben stifled a smile at the almost-hitting-the-mark mockery. The boy did not need to be encouraged in his merciless teasing.

Ralphie wiped the sweat from a freckled face with the crook of his arm. 'I swear he couldn't give away free guineas. But I'm teaching him. You can count on me, Master Ben.'

The newsboys had taken to calling him Master Ben. They didn't exactly know what *Master Ben's* status was in the shop's hierarchy, but they had an instinctive knowledge of their place in the chain of things. Arthur, less certain of his own, would have envied them that surety. Ben did not.

'Haven't had time to get you rascals any victuals. Been a mite busy.' He nodded at the printed papers hanging around the room's perimeter.

Ralphie showed his appreciation by pursing his lips and delivering a low whistle. He'd just lately learned to whistle and practiced it at every opportunity—some more appropriate than others. Ben laughed, his spirit lighter than it had been in a while. It did a man good to work.

'You'll be taking over milord's place afore long, to my reckoning. Anyways, I didn't come back to eat. I just left my partner long enough to bring this customer who was asking about the whereabouts of a free printer.'

The boy stepped aside to reveal the outline of a woman silhouetted in the open door. 'Why didn't you say right away we had a visitor? Step inside, madam. It is somewhat cooler in here.'

As the visitor stepped beyond the light and into the room, he saw that she was a young woman—tall, with an upright posture and a high forehead. One black curl had escaped her bonnet to paste itself above dark brows.

'The printer and owner of this shop has gone down to the docks to see about a shipment of metal type. I expect him back soon,' he said.

Beside him, Ralphie piped up, 'I told her milord wasn't free but he was cheap.'

Ben wanted to shake the grin off his face. 'I don't think that's exactly what she meant by free, Ralphie,' he scolded as he noticed the light flush on the young woman's face. 'Please excuse this rogue's cheekiness, madam.'

The boy hung his head in mock shame, but the grin on his face remained.

'Best you be getting back to work, Ralphie.'

Reluctantly, he headed toward the door, but before he was out of earshot, his momentary scolding forgotten, he was whistling again, a tavern song about old barley corn, a tune he was way too young to know.

'I fear these boys get their learning and manners from the streets. It's hard to keep them out of mischief. I am assuming that by free you mean independent, and yes we are in some respects an independent shop. We provide the content for most of what we print. We sell it ourselves.'

When she spoke, her voice was low and gentler than her

bearing and manner presaged. 'Might thou be open to printing someone else's work? For hire, I mean.'

'I can't make a contract on the owner's behalf, but if you would like to, you may wait for him.'

'Thou art very kind, sir. I have had a difficult time, trying to find an 'independent' printer. I will sit for a bit, and I thank thee for the offer.'

'Please,' he said, looking for a surface that wasn't covered with drying papers and then, in the absence of same, indicated the high stool beside the press. As she stepped closer, he could see her more clearly. The blush had started to fade, revealing a creamy complexion. She was younger than he was by a couple of years, scrupulously neat in her appearance, her plain dress suggesting she was a servant. Perched on the stool like an uncertain bird who might take flight at the slightest shadow, she looked around the room, nodding as if she approved the evidence of industry. With a small graceful movement of her hand, she untied the strings to her bonnet, then reaching up and removing it, fanned herself before placing it primly on top of the leather folder in her lap. This she clutched as though it held some treasure.

'Please, sir. Do not let me keep thee from thy labor.'

He picked up a rag and wiped at the edges of the type where it had collected and would smudge the next lot, if it were not removed. 'I was just finishing up,' he said. 'Is it a big project you wish printed?'

'Not me—my master. It is several pages.' Tucking her brown skirt around her legs, she hooked her shoes onto a brace at the bottom of the stool and straightened her back—as if it could get any straighter. 'I hope the printer will agree to print it. What is his name?'

'Whittier. James, Lord Whittier.'

Her eyes widened as she muttered, each word more laden with breath than before, 'I've never asked a favor of a lord before.' One brow furrowed as if she was wondering if this day could get any worse. 'I've never met a lord before.'

'Don't be put off by the title. He barely claims it. He is nice enough, sometimes a little abrupt. But he means nothing by it. Don't let that alarm you. He scratches out a living just like me and you. Anyway, think of it like this, you are not asking him for a favor. You are offering a mutually beneficial arrangement. He prints what's in that pouch, and in return you pay him. Simple as that. Although I'm guessing that the content might be a little of a sticking point. That's why you're asking for a 'free' printer.

A lift of her expressive brow told him he'd hit the mark. 'Don't let that stop you asking,' he said. 'There's a reason why Lord Whittier is an independent printer.'

After an awkward silence in which he pretended to be studying the print bed she said, 'I heard thee mention feeding a meal to thy newsboys. I hope Lord Whittier returns soon. I too have boys that need feeding. How many dost thou feed?'

Her old-fashioned language had distracted him at first. Many of the working class—especially the Puritans—still clung to the language of the old King James Bible even though some had scorned it as old-fashioned even at the time of the translation. Usually, he found it irritating, as though the people who clung to it were trying to call attention to their holiness. But suddenly, he was finding the cadence and the archaic pronouns not off-putting at all.

'We have two regulars,' he said, 'they sleep here too. But for the midday meal the number sometimes grows. They find hungry friends.'

He swapped his inky apron for a cook's smock, hanging from a hook beside the stove, and began to chop, with one practiced hand, while holding the vegetables in place with the stub of his upper arm. He could feel her staring at him. Why didn't she just ask like everybody else? He had a ready answer, a muttered, *Lost it in a skirmish in the Midlands; at least it wasn't my leg like so many poor devils.* But she said nothing. Just sat there silently, clutching her package. He reached for an onion and fastening it against the chopping block with the point of a thin knife peeled its papery skin.

'We make the porridge a little thinner,' he said. 'The boys seem to find hospitality extended to their friends well worth the trade-off. I try to feed them heartier for dinner, since they've been hawking their wares since soon after daybreak.

Supper will be a light ale and some cheese. I found some cherries in the marketplace yesterday. I still have a few of those.'

Should he offer her some cherries? Or a drink? He didn't really have anything except some ale or cider. The barrel of sweet rain water he strained through a cheese cloth had been empty for a week.

Suddenly he felt her beside him. 'It will go faster with three hands,' she said. 'You chop, and I'll scoop. If I can keep up with your flying hand with my two.' Her laugh was soft and rhythmic like her accent.

The forthrightness of her manner distracted him from an immediate response. No condescension in her offer and not a spark of pity or curiosity in her eyes, a gaze so still and blue it must have sprung from a crack in a frozen lake. 'Well, I suppose three hands are better than one,' he said nodding.

'Or even two,' she said.

'How many children do you have? Are they all boys? You look too young to have many,' he asked.

'I also have four. But they're not mine. I have no husband. The gentleman I work for is a schoolmaster, scholar, and a famous poet.'

Chop. Chop.

Scoop.

'Tell me,' he said. 'Why is it that a schoolmaster, scholar, and poet has need of a free printer?'

Chop. Chop.

'I'm sure I don't know. I cannot read well enough to read his handwriting.'

Scoop.

'Not that it is not a perfect script. Everything he does—well almost everything—is to a very high standard.' With a question in her eyes she nodded toward a pot of herbs in a window.

He nodded.

Snip. Snip. 'And I would not presume, even if I dared ask. It is not my place.'

The fragrance of parsley and thyme and rosemary filled the room. 'And what is your place?'

'I am his housekeeper.'

'Would it not make your task easier if you could read his scrawl? Do you know your letters?' Wiping his hand on his smock with more than usual industry and trying to appear as nonchalant as she had when she offered help, he did not look at her, as he added like an afterthought, 'I could teach you all your letters. Both the block and the cursive. I deal in letters every day. Only if you would like of course? I don't mean to presume.'

Gazing out the window above the herbs on the ledge, she said, 'It is a long way for me to come.'

He wiped at the cutting board without looking at her. 'I understand—'

'But I will think on it. Especially if we could come to an arrangement that could be, how didst thou put it?—"mutually beneficial." If there is some way my two hands can assist with some of thy chores.'

'We can come to some arrangement. Three hands are better than one. And it will be good to have a friend in London— besides my employer, of course,' he smiled and looked up, the tone in his voice going up an octave, 'who is just coming in the door.'

'My lord, this is—I am sorry, mistress—I don't think I remember your name.'

'I don't think I told thee my name. I am called Patience, my lord.' She turned her direct blue gaze on Whittier who seemed too preoccupied with the boxes he was carrying to notice. 'Patience Trapford, housekeeper to Mr. John Milton. I have come at his request. He asked me to seek out an—' she paused and smiled shyly at the man who had suddenly just appeared to become aware of her presence—'an independent printer.'

Lord Whittier only nodded at her, then turned back to his cartons and motioned for Ben to unpack them. 'The new type is lighter weight than the old and more finely chiseled. I think you'll approve the simpler font: it would print cleaner than the old lead type, which was worn.'

When he stood up, he scarcely looked at Patience, before reaching abruptly for the folder, extracting the document, and handing the leather packet back to her. He quickly scanned the title page. 'John Milton. I know that name. Some ecclesiastical and political opinions. Some poetry. Is he in search of a new printer?' he asked, surprise in his voice.

'If it pleases thee, my lord, he requests thy services for this particular document. Because of the unorthodox content his usual printer has refused to print it,' Patience said. 'He asked that thou read the first two pages, and then if thou shall agree, to please write down thy price. I will deliver thine offer to him.'

Ben watched as his employer scanned the pages, the expression on his face unreadable. 'You may tell Mr. Milton that I will print his unorthodox opinion.'

Relief showed on the young woman's face.

'Mr. Milton has asked that thou putst thy terms in writing, if thou pleases, sir.'

Ben was offering him a paper and pen before he asked.

As he wrote Lord Whittier said, 'These are my terms: I will not print it for money. I will print and publish Mr. Milton's piece on shares. That is to say, I will print one hundred for Mr. Milton at no charge, to use and distribute as he sees fit, and in return he will grant me the right to publish one hundred copies of the *Doctrine and Discipline of Divorce* to be distributed by me, profit to accrue to me as the publisher.'

Ben was taken aback. *Doctrine of Divorce*? Was that what he said? There was no doctrine of divorce. The Church forbade it and the Puritans abhorred it. No wonder the man could not find a printer. Certainly not in Puritan London.

When he had finished writing, Whittier handed the offer to Patience, but did not return the manuscript.

'Mr. Milton asks that I not leave the manuscript with anyone, my lord.' And then she added almost apologetically, 'He is very particular.'

'Of course. I completely understand,' he said, handing the paper to her. 'Tell Mr. Milton I shall look forward to hearing from him at his earliest convenience,' and he returned immediately to examining the contents of his boxes.

Patience Trapford started to leave but turned back at the door, smiling at Ben. 'Good luck to thee then and I thank thee for letting me wait.'

'You are welcome any time. And by the way, Mistress Patience, my name is Ben.'

Ben watched her walk away thinking he hoped he would see her again, but he didn't have long to linger on that thought. Outside he heard the boys coming back. And it sounded like their numbers had multiplied.

'Don't worry, printer's devil—' that was the nickname recently assigned to him, his employer's way of letting Ben know that though they had no real apprenticeship agreement, he regarded him as such—'I stopped at the bakery and picked up some fresh bread and a round of cheese to go with your savory smelling porridge. Now let's look at your completed task.'

But he was already looking at the sheets Ben had printed. And to Ben's great relief he was smiling.

There was still no word of William, but Caroline could not fault Squire Powell. He had scouted out the garrison himself, confirming that Sir William Pendleton, Knight Bachelor, had volunteered to accompany relief supplies for Reading, suggesting that perhaps the wagons might be less conspicuous if they did not have a large escort. They would stay off the main road; he knew a way to go around. The commander had apologized saying that at the time he had thought this decision made sense: the two accompanying officers were well armed, and all possible troops were needed at the front. But the supplies had never arrived, nor had they been turned back.

The commander also confirmed that after Lady Pendleton had come looking for her husband, he had made diligent inquiries and sent out a recovery party. They had found only one empty, wrecked wagon and one body, a youth who worked in the scullery as an orderly. The commander's assumption was that William and the two other officers had either been taken captive or they had deserted.

'I set him straight in that,' the squire had said, his face reddening in anger at the very thought. 'I let him know straight on that if any man is loyal it is William Pendleton, and he has never lacked for courage.'

Caroline remembered then how William's hand shook when he opened his orders. How he'd had to get drunk just to face the truth of what he had to do. But she was sure in her heart that he would have faced a volley of bullets before he deserted. He was dead, or he was captured. Though some small part of her wished he had deserted—he could join the community of the many who had fled to the Continent— and one day, if Parliament gained the day, he would return to her none the worse for having chosen the wrong side. But she knew her husband. Caroline's only real hope was that he'd been taken prisoner.

One of the soldiers quartered with them, a Captain Potter from Nottingham, had become overly fond of Mary Powell— Mary Milton, Caroline mentally corrected herself. The winsome young soldier followed after her like a lovesick puppy.

'Simon—Captain Potter will help us find William. He is such a kind man,' Mary said as they went about the endless chores that war had visited upon them.

The young captain did try, making the trek the few miles back to the garrison every day to check the roster for the dead and injured. But every day it was the same. It was as though William had vanished into thin air. Until one day when Caroline had come upon Captain Potter strolling with Mary in the orchard, he had told her reluctantly that her husband's name had appeared on the missing list. No other information could be gleaned but, he assured her, he would keep making inquiries.

'Simon is not the sort to give up, Caroline,' Mary said as they opened the door to the henhouse. This was a chore that was becoming shorter each day. The layers who occupied the Forest Hill henhouse had no liking for the noise and confusion of the new tenants who, Caroline suspected, raided the chicken yard with impunity. They didn't even bother to give a reckoning to pay for the pilferage with the worthless promissory notes the King gave for their billeting. At least their presence offered some protection from Parliamentary forces and opportunistic outlaws. That was something, she supposed.

The squire had said it was Roundheads that had raided William's holdings, and that in her absence he had sublet the farm to the Cavaliers, lest the Roundheads come back and burn it to the ground. She'd started to protest that he should have at least consulted her, but in all fairness, she had been gone, so how could she gainsay his decision. But of course, that meant she could not go back home. Indeed, he forbade her to go unescorted. Mistress Powell had packed a trunk for her when they came looking for her and found the destruction and her note. Thinking of the box in the cellar, the silver plate and her personal items, she protested. Squire said he would go back with her when he had time. So far, he had not had time.

'Don't worry, my dear. The court provost has assured me they will do no harm to furnishings and personal items. We've not let the whole house, only the outbuildings for stables. I have allowed a small contingent of soldiers to shelter in the main hall and kitchen. The library and study and your bedroom are all boarded up.'

Bone-tired from the extra duty they'd had to pull in the brew house because Ann Powell was down in her back—and no wonder—Caroline sat down on one of the empty nesting benches in the henhouse. Mary ran a practiced hand under the first hen, who jerked her beak suspiciously even at this familiar groping. 'Tsk, tsk. For shame, Prissy, you lazy girl. Just one,' Mary said, handing the lone egg to Caroline, who placed it in the large breast pocket of her apron.

Mary moved on to the next hen. She smiled. 'Two eggs this time,' she said as though she had just plucked a prize from some secret hiding place.

How beautiful the girl looked, how fragile; the fine white curve of her neck, the gold of her hair highlighted in a dusty sunbeam. That little smile, glimmering with a soft hope that belied the circumstances of the world around them.

Suddenly Caroline felt very old.

'Does Captain Potter know you are a married woman, Mary?' Caroline asked as she cupped her hands to receive the eggs.

The girl quickly looked away, but her face flushed crimson. Her gaze deliberately not engaging Caroline's, she demanded, 'Why ever would you ask me that, Caroline? It is cruel of you to remind me. What does it matter anyway?'

'What does it matter? How can you say that? Don't you see the moon-eyed way he follows you about?'

Mary tossed her head as if she was shaking off a gnat. Maybe she was. There were plenty swirling around the chicken-feed bucket, but Caroline thought she was shaking off something she didn't want to face—as she herself didn't want to face the fact that William might never come back.

'Why are you scolding so?' the girl primped. 'It is just a harmless flirtation.'

'Harmless?' Caroline heard the harshness in her voice, lowered it to a gentler tone. 'My dear, innocent girl. It is a wonder to me how you can be so unaware of the effect you have on men. They fall in love—or think they do—so easily. Think what effect on Captain Potter when he learns you are married, Mary.'

'Oh, Caroline, I don't know what I am going to do. I can't go back. I think he hates me. He thinks me stupid,' she wailed.

The eggs that Mary was still holding fell to the earthen floor, thudded and split apart, their yellow centers spilling out. The alarmed hens cackled and fluttered, nest to roost, pole to floor, and back to roost, stirring up feathers and dust and droppings.

Caroline jumped to her feet and took the girl in her arms and hugged her to her, ignoring the crackle of eggshell against her breast pocket and the yellow mess running down the front of her apron.

'Oh please, don't cry. I cannot bear it.' She buried her face in the top of Mary's head. Her hair smelled of dust and straw and the faintest odor of decaying chicken shit. The girl's shaking subsided into muffled sobs. Caroline held her out at arm's length.

'If you don't stop crying, I'm going to cry too,' she said, wiping at Mary's cheek with the skirt of her apron. 'I'm sorry. I was too harsh. Just look at the pair of us,' she said, then she swiped at the dripping egg yolk and wiped her hands on her apron, leaving another yellow stain. Picking a feather out of Mary's hair, she said, 'Haven't we made a fine mess. Let's forget about the eggs. Let's forget about John Milton. What we need is a good soak with some sweet-smelling soap in a tub of hot water. You can go first.'

'We'd have to heat the water. Cook wouldn't have time. She's helping Mother.'

'Come on. I'll heat enough water to break the chill.'

'Maybe we can get Captain Potter to carry it for us,' Mary said sheepishly. 'But you'll have to ask him, Caroline. I heard what you said. I'll be more . . . circumspect. Is that the right word?'

It felt good to laugh. 'That's exactly the right word, Mary.'

But in the end neither of them had the energy to heat more than a little water, and Captain Potter was nowhere in sight to carry it for them if they had. So, settling for a wet rag and a basin of water, her body aching with fatigue, she fell into bed.

But sleep did not come. She stared into the darkness, listening to Mary's deep, even breathing, and wondered if she would ever see her husband again. Fatigue and hopelessness tore at hope like a hungry dog. Numb in body and spirit, she lay unmoving on her bed. Despair is a sin, she reminded herself. *Our Father who aren't in heaven, hallowed be thy name.* The darkness in the little attic room was so close it took her breath. Darkest before the dawn. Was He there? Did He even hear? Was He asleep? *Lead us not into temptation.*

St. Peter's rooster crowed again. Three times.

Deliver us from evil?

She could not even remember the rest. She tried to breathe. *The Power. The Glory.* The Creator God would return with the morning to fix His broken world. Tomorrow she would go to the church of St. Nicholas and light a candle. Kneel at the altar. Put a coin in the poor box on the altar. If she could find a coin. Tomorrow she would be kinder to Mary and she would help Ann more with the chores. If she could find the strength. Tomorrow she would kneel at the altar and thank God for past favors, counting them for grace, and beg more grace from His well of mercy. Tomorrow, the good Lord willing, she would hear from William.

REUNION AND SEPARATION

. . . a sober man [rather than a worldly man] may easily
chance to meet, if not with a body impenetrable, yet often
with a mind [impenetrable] to all other due conversation
and to the superior purposes of matrimony useless and
almost lifeless.

—From *The Doctrine and Discipline of Divorce*
by John Milton

London
July 1643

Just before sunset Henrietta's entourage came to the River
Avon. Its broad expanse was shaded by willows leaning
in as if they too thirsted for its cooling waters. Captain
Cavendish galloped up beside her, expanding the cloud of
dust that surrounded her. He slowed his horse to match its
pace with hers.

'We shall rest here, if it pleases your majesty.'

'Inviting as it looks, don't you think we should press on,
Captain? This is enemy territory,' she said, though she longed
to bathe in the clear stream—she had done nothing but wipe
herself from a basin for a week, had not changed her chemise
in three days.

'You are well informed, your majesty. This is enemy territory. But our intelligence says the fighting is west of here. We
have just received word that the King's nephew and his troop
of cavalry are going to meet us here.'

Reflections from the setting sun caressed the shadow pools
beneath the willows, gently painting them orange and purple.
'How long?' she asked.

'The herald said they are less than an hour away. The Prince is to escort you to the King's encampment at Edgehill.'

'Edgehill. How far is that? Does this mean you will leave when the Prince comes?'

'I must, your majesty, as much as it grieves me. The King has ordered me back to Bristol. To help my father keep the peace gained there. I am relieved of duty here as soon as the Prince arrives.'

This was not how she had planned the longed-for meeting, not how she had dreamed it in the lonely nights. She did not want Charles to see her, after so long an absence, dusty and disheveled, worn out from the road, more *generalissima* than queen. Such a sight would dampen any man's ardor. She wanted to rush into his arms unadorned by the stink of the journey. There had been such sadness in his eyes when she sailed away. She wanted to see joy there now—and not just for the goods she was bringing.

She reined in her horse. At her signal, he reined in his as well. 'Captain, I thank you for your service to me. It has been beyond compare, but I would be pleased if you would do one more thing for me.'

'Anything, your majesty. Just name it.'

'While you keep watch, I am going to bathe in that little cove behind the willow. As soon as you fetch a few things from my private carriage. Tell Genevieve and Lady Denbigh. They will know what I need.'

'Your majesty, I don't know if—' but she did not wait to hear his objection.

She spurred her horse in the direction of the weeping willow. By the time the captain returned with Genevieve and a satchel, the Queen's horse was tied loosely to the willow, head down. The beast flicked his tail against a swarm of gnats and continued drinking greedily. Henrietta, already chin-deep in the cool clear water, swatted at a dragonfly that had dared to rest its jeweled wings on her streaming hair and shouted a greeting at them. Blushing, he retreated, her laughter floating after.

*   *   *

James Whittier assessed the progress of the Milton project and said to Ben, 'Looks as though we'll finish this print run before the Sabbath and that is much to be desired. The church wardens will be on patrol. St. Bride's has already fined me once for working on the Sabbath, but the vicar vacated it with a warning.'

Ben grinned. 'But it's probably still on their book. Next time he might call the bailiff to lock you up. I'd hate to have to bail you out,' he said as he removed the last page from the press and handed it off.

James cast his critical gaze on the page he was inspecting and said, 'My turn to press. Your arm must be sore by now.'

Ben did not argue. His right bicep had begun to twitch with the strain. 'Patience said that Mr. Milton seemed pleased with the first lot.'

'He is not lavish in his praise, so I assume he was satisfied. But regardless, I am pleased. We struck a good bargain. I have already taken orders from several booksellers. This lot will sell out quickly. Apparently J.M.'s *Doctrine of Divorce* has caused quite a stir in godly London.'

'It is a radical stance for a Puritan to be sure. Patience and I talked about it, though she was reluctant to discuss her employer's personal affairs. She did say that truly she had never seen a more ill-suited pair in her life. Brooding tension all the time except the storm never burst. At least in her hearing, though Mistress Milton cried in her chamber—which Patience said she did not believe her husband shared—' Ben paused to hang two more of the big sheets that would be folded into a pamphlet-style codex before continuing—'and Mr. Milton kept to his study or the schoolroom most of the time. The misery in that house was as *oppressive as summer lightning.* Her words.'

'What finally happened to make her leave?'

'Patience didn't know. She just came to work one morning expecting to see her new mistress 'fumbling about in the kitchen,' as Patience put it, with that dazed look of a cornered animal. One day she just wasn't there. Not the next day either. When Patience asked if she was indisposed, Mr. Milton said that she had gone home to attend her father who was ill.

And that was his last word on the subject. He just carried on as before with his bachelor routine.'

The press groaned as James pulled the lever down. 'Well, that's a dreary little outcome,' he said. 'But if you read the essay, it makes some sense. One can assume husband and wife were dismally incompatible. Milton likened an unhappy matrimonial bond to being chained to a corpse.'

'I didn't read past the introduction. The language was way too high-blown for a poor one-armed printer's devil. But Patience conceded the girl was fairer than most and gently spoken so I'm thinking she was not a scold. What possible complaint could a bridegroom have with a prize like that?'

Ben's accompanying grin was a welcome sight. James admired the way he treated his loss as something to be overcome, a challenge to be mastered. Remarkable really, James was thinking as he answered, 'From my reading—and yes J.M. is overly fond of words—it seems he just did not find his bride a fit intellectual companion. But having met him, there is a pomposity that rankles—one would be interested to hear her side.'

'If you don't want to see her eyes flash pure temper, don't let Patience Trapford hear you disparage her paragon, though she admits she felt sorry for the girl. She said she would have liked to see Mary Milton stand up for herself. Just once. So that he could see she was not just an empty-headed doll.'

Ben turned his attention to removing and stacking the dried sheets, his one arm working rapidly. Then suddenly he paused and looked up at his employer with a look of curiosity as though he had just stumbled upon a puzzle. 'Why did you never marry, my lord?'

The press stilled.

When James did not answer, the boy blushed to the roots of his light hair and shook his head. 'I am sorry. I overstepped. It was an impertinent question.'

James waved him off as if the question were of no consequence. 'I came close. Once. But it's a tedious tale.'

They worked on in silence for a while. James pressing, Ben retrieving and hanging, retrieving and hanging, Ben embarrassed and James, for his part, still pondering the question and thinking about how terribly wrong it all had gone. The two other players in that sad little drama were gone now forever. Best not to think about. And certainly not to talk about it.

The atmosphere grew heavy in the room as the fading light slid away through the western-facing window. James peeled the last sheet, handed it off, and wiped the press.

'How are the reading lessons progressing?' he asked to lighten the mood.

'Surprisingly, quite well. Patience is a quick learner, but for a woman she has some strong opinions and is not afraid to express them.'

'Opinions? About what? Besides the domestic failings of her employer's household?'

'Religion mostly. She has plenty to say about the Church of England and some of the Independents as well. She doesn't like the Queen. She thinks the King is a power-hungry tyrant. But she says some in Parliament are "too bull-headed to see that war is going to bring nothing but more war."'

'Maybe she should sit for Parliament,' James said, immediately repenting the sarcasm in his voice. 'What opinion does she have of you?'

'Me?' The blush returned. 'Well, she calls me a friend.'

'And you?'

He paused, considered, as if thinking about the question for the first time. 'A friend is a good thing to have. Sometimes she makes me laugh to hear such unorthodox observations come out of her mouth with such certainty. Yet she never takes offense when I laugh. Just throws it right back. But you need not worry that my time with her hinders production. We work as we spell and recite. She practices her reading on the headers. She sewed most of the pamphlets in that last lot we sent out.'

'Maybe I should put her on the payroll. How does she have the time?'

'She gets a half-day every other week and all day on Sundays. Course Sunday mornings she goes to church.'

'Do you go with her? You seem to be keeping the Sabbath with sudden regularity.' James finished cleaning the press and handed the rag to Ben who deposited it with the others in a basket in the corner.

'I make sure that Ralphie and Little John get up when they sleep here. I make them scrub up good before I deliver them to the new Sunday school that one of the Independent congregations has opened for the poor children. Patience shamed me into taking them. But I think it's a good thing.'

'They go willingly? Even Ralphie?'

'They like it. They get a crust smeared with honey or jam, instead of the dripping I give them, sometimes a cup of milk, and they say the teacher tells awesome stories with giants and battles and big fish that can swallow a whole man.' He shrugged, and the grin was back. 'The way I figure it I don't have to give them breakfast and a little religion might help keep them out of trouble. Keeps the Church police away from your door, too.'

'I've noticed some of the Independents' rules are in some ways more lenient than Laud's ever were.'

Ben nodded. 'Can you imagine the old archbishop letting parishioners take Sundays to work on the earthworks? But the independent preachers say the 'ox is in the ditch' when the godly kingdom is under siege. Even Parliament has declared that the Lord will understand if the able-bodied take a Sabbath to work on the earthworks that protect it.' The grin grew wider. 'As long as we chant a psalm or two to keep the rhythm while we shovel on the big ditch.'

James didn't dare raise an eyebrow at 'the able-bodied,' but he didn't have to.

'I know what you are thinking, my lord. That maybe I am not so 'able-bodied.' But pulling on your presses has built up a powerful strength in my good arm. Besides sometimes Patience works with me. I put my foot on the shovel while we both push, and then I pitch the load into the bucket. We have three hands instead of two to carry it and empty it onto the pile.'

'And I guess the two of you are chanting the psalms the entire time.'

'Sometimes,' Ben said. 'And sometimes we have this little rhythmic spelling song we've made up.' And then the lad must have caught the sarcasm in his employer's remark about the psalms. His face flushed, but he lifted his chin and looked straight into James's eyes. 'You should join us sometimes, my lord. You'll have an excuse when the church wardens at St. Bride's come calling. How about tomorrow?'

'On the morrow, if the church warden bangs on my door, he'll get no answer. I'll be at the private chapel of the chop house down by the river. I'll try to remember to bring you and the boys a morsel for your supper.'

How could Ben argue with that?

'Maman, hold.' The child held up his chubby arms for Lucy to pick him up.

'Do not call her that,' Princess Elizabeth said. 'She is *not* Maman. Maman is in France. She is Lucy Hay, Countess of Carlisle, Henry. You must not call her Maman.'

'Maman,' the child insisted, his mouth set in a pout.

Lucy picked him up, inhaling the sweet smell of him. His clinging incited in her a longing she had not felt in many years. 'Don't scold your brother, my lady. Let him take his comfort where he finds it. He doesn't remember his mother. But he will. It will not be long now. I believe your mother has arrived back in England and will soon be at the new court in Oxford.'

'She is not coming here to see us?' Elizabeth's mouth flew open, her forehead crinkled in disbelief.

'It is not yet safe for her to travel to London.' And then seeing the tears threatening, Lucy added, 'Maybe we can visit her.' Doubting, as the words left her lips, if Parliament would ever give permission. 'Would you like that Henry? Would you like to see your maman?'

'Maman,' the child said and grabbed for a strand of Lucy's hair.

'Oh,' she said with a fake screech to which the child giggled. 'You are a naughty boy. You will pull Lady Carlisle bald.'

'Maman bald,' the child grinned and grabbed another handful.

'If you will let go my hair, we will go to the kitchen and ask Carter for pudding.' The little boy pursed his lips as though considering, then splaying both his hands, he squealed, 'cake.' At least he was learning the courtier's art of negotiating.

A few minutes later, when Carter had scavenged the promised tribute from the diminished cupboard at Syon House, Lucy watched as her two charges divided the sweet tart between them. Henry protested when his sister tried to help, 'I do it,' then crammed a fistful of the sweet into his mouth, smearing the crumbs across his chin.

Elizabeth ate hers in petite bites, tiny wheels always turning in her head, as she quizzed, 'Lady Carlisle, why do you not have any children?' Before Lucy could summon an answer to this impertinent question, the girl followed it up with another. 'Is it because you have no husband? I know this is not your house. It belongs to your brother.'

'You know much about many things, don't you, Princess Elizabeth?' Lucy's tone had just the slightest edge to it. 'But you are right. This is my brother's house. I am called Lady Carlisle because I had a husband once. His name was James, the same as your grandfather, King James, whom he served. Lord Hay, Earl of Carlisle, was a very fine gentleman and a Scots lord, with a grand estate in Ireland that your grandfather bestowed on him,' she said, a bit of wistfulness softening her voice.

'I should not like to live in Ireland. Maman said the Protestants there are savages. Where is your husband now?'

'He died a long time ago.'

'Were you sad when he died? Why did you not have children?'

Lucy felt a forgotten sadness stirring. She looked away on the pretense of wiping Henry's face, unwilling to let the girl read her face as easily as she translated Greek to Latin and Latin to English, and answered. 'I was very sad, but it was a long time ago—stop squirming, Henry. Yes, we had a child. A little boy. He died very young.' She held her breath lest the child ask, *how old was he*, as she pressed her lips against Henry's head.

Words formed himself in her mind. *The age of this child when I last held little Jamie in my arms. I smelled the fever on his hot skin when I cradled him.*

But she did not utter them.

'We had a sister who died,' the girl said, bringing the subject back to herself. 'I never knew her, but Maman cried when she told me about her.'

Lucy had known that long-ago child. She had been particularly fond of baby Anne with her rosy cheeks and bright eyes and remembered well the Queen's tears and the hours she had spent in her chapel, praying for the child who coughed up blood. Lucy had cried with Henrietta when those prayers were not answered. Real tears. Not court tears.

'Will I be allowed to write to Maman at Oxford?'

'You write the letter and I will see that it is delivered. Please go and do it now,' she said, 'while your little brother gets his nap.' She wiped the child's sticky fingers one last time and picked him up, grateful that the girl's curious mind had turned to her mother.

Later, alone—Elizabeth, closeted with the formidable tutor and Henry with his nurse—Lucy went to her own chamber. As she crossed the threshold a glance at the image of the woman passing in front of the glass pulled her up short: a true reflection, without artifice or contrivance, a naked face she seldom saw when she was at her *toilette*.

She thrust out her chin, turning this way and that, and considered herself with an appraising eye. If beauty had been this woman's blessed wealth, then this reflection in the ruthless light of mid-afternoon promised a reversal approaching penury. Her breasts had lost their perkiness and her waist was undeniably thicker. Not a lot thicker. But enough. And those marks at the corners of her mouth, Holy Virgin's tears, when had they gotten so deep? A toss of her head, the practiced courtesan's smile, but the face was still the portrait of a faded beauty. Even her hair looked dull. *What did you expect, Lucy?* her mind muttered to the image in the mirror. *Nothing lasts forever. Beauty fades. Age creeps, first into the skin, then the bones and finally into the heart.*

This bleak recognition and what it implied for her future brought a second shock. Had she squandered her youth carelessly? A fading beauty with children and a husband was one thing. A withered crone, adrift in a hostile world, was something else altogether, a woman to be pitied—or scorned. Had her best prospect for any kind of security died on that scaffold with Thomas Wentworth? She had taken the man's measure in every way a woman could and knew he would have endured. About John she was becoming less sure. Whatever passion she had lit in him now was more ember than flame.

Turning her back on the image in the mirror, she lay across her bed and closed her eyes in concentration, plotting a path forward. *The bloom is not completely off the rose, Lucy, and anyway, you have more than your looks to sustain you. There is still time. If nothing lasts forever, this horrid war will end, too. Everyone around you will have aged—perhaps not as well as you. If Parliament gains the day, John will come back to you. You will still be the brightest star in his firmament. And the five whom you warned of the King's impending arrest, they will lend support and protection. Because of the Percy name, Algernon will not abandon you. He is the Earl of Northumberland.* And then the voice in her head added, *But what if Parliament does not win?*

Dangerous political alliances—*remember, remember the guns of November*—had haunted her girlhood. Where they to hound her into old age? One brother already in exile with the Queen and one who had deserted the King for Parliament. The one who lost would lead to exile, the Tower—or worse. *And what about you, Lucy? Where will you end up? Right back in the Tower where you once bartered your favors for your freedom?*

Worn out from trying to marshal her wits to hold the middle ground, she longed for that lost interlude of youthful happiness and tried to conjure its images. The Stuart court had provided a wonderful refuge from the penalty of Percy intrigue. The music and dancing, the laughter of breathless flirtations, the thrill of riding to the hunt at the Queen's side, the glory of Whitehall festivals and masques: where had it all gone? The future had not mattered then, only expectations and the seeming certainty of an everlasting present.

But try as she might, she could only summon glimpses of those carefree days: stolen kisses in fragrant gardens, great halls with a thousand candles dancing in their mirrors, and young Lucy Hay, the Queen's favorite, holding a court of her own. Shapes in a fog, as ephemeral as youth. All of London was now a dreary, cold wasteland, its streets littered with broken soldiers and fatherless, hungry children whilst the halls of Westminster echoed with endless argument over how to end an endless war.

Unable to make herself get up and do something, anything, she heard Carter tapping at her door to present her with two messages. With trembling hands, she tore into the one whose hand she recognized. It was from John. He said he was sorry to have been so preoccupied the day she came to Parliament to seek him out. He longed for her 'good company' too, but she should not come to Westminster again. It was too dangerous. She crumpled the paper into a ball and threw it across the room, then repenting, retrieved it and smoothed it out. *Dangerous?* Dangerous for him? Or dangerous for her? Was he tired of her or was he just tired?

Sighing, she opened the other missive. It too was written in a hand she knew, though less familiar. It was signed simply E H. She had to read it twice before she caught its message. Edward Hyde was telling her—in cryptic language what everybody in London already knew. His *cousin*, he said, had returned to England and was looking forward to *renewing dear acquaintances, but travelling conditions being made unsafe at this time*, his cousin was relying on him to arrange it. Further news would be forthcoming as to how such arrangements might be facilitated between his *dear cousin and her friends*.

That the children should be allowed to see their mother suddenly became a burning resolve for Lucy. No purchase in waiting for Hyde to persuade Parliament—even that simple negotiation would take weeks and might not bear fruit. Parliament would never consent to any reasonable conditions. Even John—if she could convince him to intercede—would be unable to persuade them. Maybe there was a better way. Neither Parliament nor John need know the children were gone. Weeks went by without his checking on them. Months since he had seen them, just a note through a messenger inquiring if they needed anything. Yes. The more she thought of it, the easier it seemed. With Hyde's help the children could go to Oxford and be back before anybody at Parliament ever missed them. Such an action, if successful, would rekindle her friendship with Henrietta, while not endangering her position in London. Besides, it would make the children very happy.

And what if it is not successful, Lucy? What if John suddenly gets a burning desire to visit Syon House in their absence? But she banished that cautionary voice, confident in her own resourcefulness, especially in the face of that unlikely circumstance. Much later, as twilight descended, and she went to the nursery to bid the children goodnight, she was still running scenarios in her head.

'Have you decided when we can see Maman?' Elizabeth asked, her eyes lit with eagerness.

Glancing at Cosette, who was struggling to coax Henry into his nightdress, Lucy lowered her voice and answered, 'Not for a while. We must first arrange with Parliament and the Queen for their mutual consent.' The nurse had always been loyal to the children and the royal household, but a dropped word in the wrong place . . .

'But, you said—'

'Best get to sleep, now, Princess, as soon as I have heard your prayers,' Lucy said, brusquely, casting around in her mind to divert the girl, who was nothing if not persistent. 'Mistress Makin says that you will begin translating Plutarch's *Lives* tomorrow.'

The girl's eyes widened with pleasure. 'Did she really say that?'

Lucy kissed her on the top of her head. 'She did. She said you were the best student she has had in a great while.'

Elizabeth snuggled down into bed with a smile on her face, apparently the longing for her mother temporarily appeased. What the good Lord had not given the child in physical strength, he had made up for in intellect, Lucy thought as she checked on the already sleeping little brother. Lucy breathed a prayer in her Presbyterian soul that such a gift would not be wasted.

By the time Lucy returned to her own chamber, Carter was lighting her boudoir candles. 'Do you require anything else, my lady?'

'No—well yes, there is one thing. The messenger who brought the letter. Not the one from Westminster. The other one. Do you know how to contact him?'

'Yes, my lady. He is a footman at St. James's Palace.'

'Will you ask him to call on me tomorrow. I wish to reply to the message.'

Carter looked at her as if he might be considering questioning her request.

'Think you not that he can be trusted?'

'Oh yes, my lady. I have known him for a long time. He is an old servant of the royal family.' He paused and then added. 'It is just that, please forgive me, my lady, but I am thinking of your well-being.'

'Ah. I see. You are a good man, Carter. I thank you for your constancy. And if I may say, for your friendship. I shall be careful. I think we can arrange for the children to meet briefly with their mother without bothering the learned gentlemen of Parliament. Do you agree?'

'Indeed, my lady.' He nodded, smiling softly. 'Indeed. I shall send Tom to fetch the footman tomorrow. Will that be all, my lady?'

'Yes. That will be all.' Then as he started to leave, she called him back. 'Carter, tell the footman it might be best if he not wear the St. James' livery.'

Carter nodded in silent confirmation.

But Lucy was not as sanguine as she appeared to Carter. She lay awake during the long night running scenarios in her head. About midnight the wind rose. The sound of its keening unsettled her. A summer storm building, she thought, not surprising since the day had been warm, but a branch, slapping against the windowpane, scratched at her nerves. She got up and checked the window latches, then went back to bed. In the distance, thunder grumbled.

As the storm blew ever closer, lighting the darkness outside, she listened for any sounds coming from the nursery. All was quiet.

Like a cat worrying a mouse, her mind kept returning to its afternoon's preoccupation. In the heart of the night, she felt less sure of herself. If Parliament did find out the children were not at Syon House but had gone to Oxford, what would be the consequences? With what could they charge her? Even in the unlikely event that John was willing to turn her over— out of a sense of betrayal or to deflect blame—he would be loath to admit to a Parliamentary inquiry that he had made the arrangement without seeking permission. Parliament had put the children under Percy family guardianship. Officially, they were Algernon's responsibility. A cover story could be invented easily enough. There would be no real evidence against her—unless she was discovered in the implementation of the plan.

A flash of lightning lit the pier glass between the windows. Lucy's breath caught in her throat. No. She did not see what she thought she saw there. It was a mere figment of her agitated brain. She was not the kind of superstitious woman who trafficked with such foolishness. James Hay's reflection, with its crooked grin and large Roman nose, was *not* illuminated in the mirror. As plain as if he were standing beside her bed. No. It was a trick of the mind's eye. Pulled from the recesses of her mind? Or somewhere else?

Then in the answering rumble of thunder, she heard the sound of his wry laughter.

Nothing much to worry about, little darling. Though I suppose they could charge you with treason. And as you know, Lucy, all too well, they don't have to prove it.

'John would protect me from that,' she whispered into the empty silence.

Quite certain, are ye now, lassie? The devoted Parliamentarian has another mistress whom he serves with greater ardor— despite your many charms. Still the dear, familiar Scottish lilt in the voice that had played so well in the old King's court. *Consorting with the enemy? A dangerous game, Lucy. But, aahh, who is the enemy? That is the question. You will be forced to pick a side, you know.*

She closed her eyes, but the image was burned on her eyelids. *Go away, Jamie, and let me think what to do. You are just a trick, anyway. Just a remnant of a girl's foolish dream and a woman's fears.*

She concentrated on the fierce beating of the rain against the window as her heart answered with a hard rhythm. Real rain in the real now. She'd enough of the illusions of her youth. When she glanced again at the pier glass, mercifully, its surface reflected only the wavering flame of her bedside candle.

The rain had cooled the air. A draft seeped in. Wrapping a shawl around her, she got out of bed and paced. Her mind was made up, despite Jamie's unsolicited advice. Her only worry now was how to best convey the necessary information most discreetly. She lit a candle—was that a tremor in her hand!—and taking up paper and pen sat down at a bedside table but did not write. This required careful thought. If the letter should fall into the wrong hands, it must not be something that could be used against her, so she must answer in the same cryptic syntax Edward Hyde had used.

Pym was inattentive and preoccupied, with any luck at all, the children could be back in her care before he ever found out. And if he did find out—he would be angry but he would protect her, regardless of his devotion to 'that other mistress.' Wouldn't he? Regardless, she had made up her mind and it must be done now, or she would get no sleep. Dipping her pen into the inkwell and pausing only to glance at the pier glass in which no ghostly image emerged, she wrote:

My Dear Sir,
We would all so very much like to see our dear cousin again. I can arrange to meet you in Reading to discuss the possibility of a short visit whereby aging Cousin Eleanor will not have to hazard travelling over rough roads. Please respond to this letter by the same messenger. You name the time and place, since you are privy to Cousin Eleanor's needs. You may also tell her that every care is being given to the safety and well-being of the nieces who have come to live with us during these difficult times.

She paused here, thinking she should give him another clue, some sign that it was indeed an authentic answer from the recipient and not some trap.

> Also, tell her to please convey to her husband our appreciation for his kind acknowledgement of our gift to him last year.
>   Your servant,

She scrawled her initials L. H. in such a smeared fashion that careful scrutiny and some precognition would be necessary to decipher the letters. She did not seal it. That could wait for morning. She would need to fashion a crude seal. The letter must not be traced back to Syon House.

Blowing out the candle, Lucy went back to bed, but she remained awake to see the dawn creep around the window sill. Only the grey light of a shrouded sun was reflected in the pier glass.

Prince Rupert suggested the Queen should ride in the royal carriage with the Countess of Denbigh and Genevieve. Henrietta refused. Rupert's lip twitched into a pout, but he bent his knee for her to mount a horse.

'I do not see the wagons with my personal belongings. I gave instructions they should always be within my sight.'

'They will follow behind the carriage in which your majesty does not wish to ride,' Rupert said with irritation in his voice.

Churlish upstart. She would speak to Charles about his nephew's insolence. 'See that the Captain of the Queen's Guard escorts them personally. I wish to have access as I desire,' then instructing Rupert to keep his mount a length behind hers, she rode astride, her posture bold and proud. Because the heat of the day lingered, the gold cloth of her miniver-trimmed mantle flowed away from her body, spreading out across the horse's flank. A light breeze released the scent of lavender in her hair as it streamed out beneath a golden coronet and covered her shoulders.

She set a deliberate pace—slow, sedate. This was the way she had dreamed it: a bold reentry, forever erasing the image of a frightened young Henrietta's first entry into England all those years ago. This was the way she wanted Charles to see his Queen when they were reunited. Beautiful. Triumphant.

As her entourage arrived at the encampment in Edgehill, two dozen royal guards lined her entry route. Torches lit the deepening twilight and royal banners floated in the early evening breeze. Each cavalier dropped in salute when her horse passed in front.

At the sound of her herald's trumpet, the tent flaps of the royal pavilion opened. Forgetting her careful pose, she leaned forward, craned her neck, her gaze searching the shadows. There he was. Waiting. Royal scepter in hand. A king poised to greet some foreign dignitary. Not the posture of a man welcoming a beloved wife after so long an absence. So rigid in his stance. Detached. Did he not see her?

Sedately, her horse moved forward between lines of soldiers formed on each side. Still, the King made no move. She could see his face clearly now, expression still unchanged, he turned his face away to speak to an attendant. Did he not long for this reunion as much as she? Was he so busy playing the warrior king that he had forgotten he was also Charles, the husband, and she the wife who cherished him, who bore his children, who sacrificed for him? Holy Mother how she had sacrificed for him, bearing insults from his subjects, laboring in exile to raise an army to save his kingdom.

Having lost its auspicious breeze, the warmth of the declining sun was suddenly stifling, the weight of her mantle heavy on her shoulders. Her thoughts scurried, conjuring doubt. In her absence, had Parliament succeeded in turning him against her? Was it possible another woman had gained his favor? Her mind's eye summoned the young woman who had brought the gloves to her. How her face had glowed with passion when she spoke of her loyalty to the King. What man could resist such adoration?

But Charles was no ordinary man. Her husband's devotion could not be so easily turned. Could it? Not the Charles she knew and loved. But in that instant swirl of doubt, she remembered how easily she, a green girl, had lured him away from Buckingham's affections. This acknowledgement of his weakness made her light-headed. Fearing she might swoon in the saddle, she gripped the pommel, reminding herself to breathe.

Suddenly, with a great shout the King handed off his scepter. Ceremony forgotten, he cast off his royal pose, and closing the distance between them, grabbed the reins of her horse, halting it.

'My lord,' she said breathless with relief, nodding her head. She wanted to fall into his arms, but mirroring his own earlier formal stance, she maintained her royal bearing. 'How good it is to see you.'

'A hearty welcome home to England for our beautiful and brave Queen,' he shouted. He laughed, and holding up his arms, encircled her waist and pulled her from her mount. Beneath the cheers that followed, as her feet touched the ground he said softly, 'My Warrior Queen, my Dearest Heart.' Then holding her out at arm's length, said, 'My eyes cannot drink their fill. It has been so long . . .' and he kissed her, his hands still cradling her waist.

Home. At last.

It was she who broke away first, though it took all the royal discipline she could muster. 'Your majesty, the men—' she whispered.

Later, after the men had been dismissed, after the tent flap had been secured, they made love. Twice. First hungrily, like thirsty travelers stumbling in from the desert, then after a brief respite again, more deliberately. As he slept, she lay in his arms, her eyes exploring the dear landscape of his face: the lines around his eyes, etched more deeply, stray gray hairs hidden in his hair, in his eyebrows, the hairs on his chest. Even his complexion was darker, weathered from many battles. The lines, framing the mouth she loved, had deepened. Unable to stop her hands, her fingers traced its outline. He awoke. 'I feared our lovemaking was but a dream,' he said, huskily.

This time, she coaxed him, gently with her hands.

Finally, just as dawn was breaking and they were hungry for something other than each other, he rang for a soldier, who brought them bread and porridge and salt herring. Charles apologized for the food saying he shared a soldier's rations and the costs of the war—but she cut him off telling him she didn't mind, to share any meal with him was a feast. She told him then about the chests of gold that would help feed his soldiers, told him too, with pride in her voice, about the mercenaries that were camped nearby awaiting his command.

'Send for two stout footmen,' she said. 'I will instruct them to bring you my tribute.'

He smiled as if she had said something amusing. 'No footmen, Henrietta. All my footmen serve as foot soldiers now.'

'Only the most trusted soldiers would tend the King's person. Send for them then.'

The two who came had summoned three others. 'Bring the large chests from my wagon, the three marked with the queen's insignia.'

'You said tribute. The love of my queen, my wife, is the only tribute I require.' And he reached for her again, and began nuzzling her neck with kisses. She pushed him away gently.

'But love will not fund a battle royal,' she said. 'Tell me what it is you need most.'

'Where to begin?' he said, his mood darkening as he complained about the depletion of his military, the cost of weapons and provisions, the truculence of Parliament. With each grievance he became more agitated. He was pacing around the royal pavilion, brow furrowed, his voice rasping out a litany of burdens, when she began wondering what was taking so long. They should be coming back by now. When had she last inspected the locks? They could have been sprung crossing the bridge in Newark and the contents discovered and plundered. But just as she was beginning to really worry, thinking that if this delay—or worse—was Rupert's doing, he would be made to pay, the men returned. Staggering beneath the heavy chests, they placed them at the King's feet.

'*Merci*,' she said, with a sigh of dismissal. 'Come, dearest heart. Sit. Calm yourself. Relief is here.' He sank down beside her on the rug, anticipation softening his visage, as with trembling hands she knelt, retrieved a key from a hidden panel on one of the caskets, and unlocked all three. Throwing back the lids, she exhaled pure relief and exclaimed in exultation, '*Voilà, mon cher.*'

Charles stared at the glittering contents with an expression of awe. Henrietta clasped her hands and giggled like a girl. In the cryptic messages that had passed between them she had hinted that she was not coming empty-handed. He knew that she had borrowed against the jewels of course but the three chests: one with gold bars and nuggets from the Dutch, one with gold florins from Italy, and one filled with Scots brooches, Spanish gold plate, and jewelry—with one or two ornate rosaries among them: this was certainly beyond any expectation. He knelt beside the chests and ran his fingers through the gold, weighing it in handfuls. For a moment she was afraid he would scold when he saw the florins and the rosaries, but he just shook his head and laughed, a quiet, mocking laugh as he said, 'Parliament deserves to be defeated with Papist gold. They have earned it.' Then he stood up and grabbed her to him. 'This,' he said, 'Henrietta, this could turn the tide in our favor. You said you brought men, too?'

She smiled and nodded, but in her heart, she was giddy with delight. 'Your nephew is reviewing the troops now. They are accompanied by a wagon load of weapons.' He just looked at her in wonder. 'Many of the men came from good—' she paused not wishing to say *Catholic* families—'families who wish to show their loyalty to an admired sovereign. Some are soldiers of fortune who have been paid to fight, but they too are well chosen.'

He smiled in a way that she had rarely seen her sedate husband smile and kissed her hard, then held her chin and shook his head and kissed her again. And if Rupert had not approached the tent, she was sure they would have made love again. Right there. On the earthen floor of the tent surrounded by all that gold.

But Rupert called for him and he broke abruptly away to answer. Their urgent voices carried through the thin walls. *Roundheads . . . Waller . . . Roundway Down . . . Salisbury . . . Waller . . . Hopton . . . needs relief . . .*

When he re-entered, he started to dress himself in soldier's clothes. His manner had completely changed, and by the time he had donned helmet and breastplate, it was as though all royal vestige had disappeared.

'A common soldier, my lord?'

'The King does not dress for court. He dresses for battle.'

Her heart squeezed twice. One pinch for fear. One pinch for irritation.

'Now? But I have only just returned. Surely you need not go so soon? Cannot Rupert or one of the generals go?'

He kissed her, but lightly this time. A hurried kiss of dismissal. 'Rupert is going to accompany you to Oxford. Queen's College is preparing to entertain you. Hopton is in trouble. We cannot afford to lose the West. I will see you soon, my darling. I promise.'

'But we haven't even talked about the children, Charles. When can I see my children?'

'We will work it out later, I promise. For now, they are safe. The boys will come to you soon and Hyde will arrange for the younger two. You must know that I miss Elizabeth and Henry as much as you do. And I do not wish to leave you so soon any more than you wish me to leave.' And then with one brief embrace he fastened his helmet and said, 'Pray for me, my darling. Pray for us all.'

Henrietta sat down in the middle of all that gold and wept as foreboding crept into the tent with the murky morning. *What if this should be the last time you ever see him?* Foolish thought, her bolder self scolded. Silly women's worries brought on by her fatigue. The tide would turn now in his favor. Now that she had brought him resources and reinforcements. By Christmas they would be back at Whitehall and this miserable war would be a bad dream.

To be continued in Broken Kingdom Volume II.

ACKNOWLEDGEMENTS

A very special thank you to my long-time agent, Harvey Klinger, for his encouragement and persistence. His publishing knowledge and critical skills have been invaluable. He has always been responsive and supportive, witty in his candid but kind criticism, patient, enduring and very persistent on my behalf.

I also wish to express my pleasure in working with all of the fine professionals at Severn House. I am especially grateful to Kate Lyall Grant for believing in this story and to Holly Domney for making it better.

I am most appreciative of the readers of my books, with whom I have collaborated on works of the imagination. It takes both reader and writer to make a story live. It is a shared creation. I hope they will find this story also worthy of their time and attention. Given the history from which this novel was born, I would be remiss not to express gratitude to Dr. Charles Durham in whose engaging seminars in Seventeenth Century Literature, I first became acquainted with the rich literary legacy and history of the age.

I have also enjoyed the love and support of my brother Gary, my sister Julie and the many nephews and nieces who enhance my life—as well as the friendship of my best writer buddy of many years, Meg Waite Clayton. Most of all, for these and all of the good people who have blessed my life and work, I wish to thank my creator and sustainer, the One from whom all blessings flow.